Jonathan Unleashed

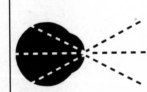

This Large Print Book carries the
Seal of Approval of N.A.V.H.

JONATHAN UNLEASHED

MEG ROSOFF

THORNDIKE PRESS
A part of Gale, Cengage Learning

GALE
CENGAGE Learning·

Farmington Hills, Mich • San Francisco • New York • Waterville, Maine
Meriden, Conn • Mason, Ohio • Chicago

GALE
CENGAGE Learning

Thorndike Press® Large Print Core.
The text of this Large Print edition is unabridged.
Other aspects of the book may vary from the original edition.
Set in 16 pt. Plantin.

LIBRARY OF CONGRESS CATALOGING-IN-PUBLICATION DATA

Names: Rosoff, Meg, author.
Title: Jonathan unleashed / by Meg Rosoff.
Description: Large print edition. | Waterville, Maine : Thorndike Press, 2016. |
    Series: Thorndike Press large print core
Identifiers: LCCN 2016023046 | ISBN 9781410491602 (hardcover) | ISBN 1410491609
    (hardcover)
Subjects: LCSH: Dog owners—Fiction. | Dogs—Fiction. | Large type books. | GSAFD:
    Love stories. | Humorous fiction.
Classification: LCC PS3618.O84514 J66 2016 | DDC 813/.6—dc23
LC record available at https://lccn.loc.gov/2016023046

Published in 2016 by arrangement with Viking, an imprint of Penguin Publishing Group, a division of Penguin Random House LLC

Printed in Mexico
1 2 3 4 5 6 7 20 19 18 17 16

For Lois and Charles

1

Jonathan came home from work one day to find the dogs talking about him.

They weren't even his dogs.

"Just a few months, six maximum? Don't worry about changing your lifestyle," his brother pleaded. "Take them out before you go to work and when you get home again in the evening. They're great dogs and won't trash your place. Honest, you'll love them."

James (typically, it had to be said) had understated the nature of the ask. He never once mentioned the byzantine quality of his dogs' inner lives, the practical and spiritual difficulties of caring for other sentient beings, the intense and constant scrutiny to which Jonathan was now subject.

Jonathan very much wanted the dogs to be happy, but it was turning out not to be as simple as walks and bones.

Sissy padded up beside him and sat at his feet, looking yearningly into his face as if searching for the key to her future. She emitted a soft whine, a pleading noise that might have meant anything — *I'm hungry, I need more love, we're bored here all day, please turn over the reins to your life so we can sort you out.*

Jonathan stared. The reins to his life? He hadn't even known his life had reins. And if it did, would it be wise to turn them over to a dog?

He pointed at her bed.

"Lie down," he said. "And stop confounding me with impossible philosophical options." Her back was to him now, as was Dante's, their heads together. Awww, he might once have thought. But now he squinted at them, anxious. Were they plotting to take over his life? And if so, how?

He had to admit it was nice being greeted with enthusiasm when he came home from a hard day in the trenches of advertising. Long walks took the place of going to the gym, and the dogs' ability to sleep calmed him, took the edge off work. They were good-looking dogs, and people stopped him on the street to admire his fine taste in pets. At the beginning he'd demur, saying they belonged to his brother in Dubai, but after a while he just said, "Thank you," and "Your dog is nice too," even when the other dog wasn't, particularly.

But lately something had shifted in his relationship with them. He sensed they disapproved of his lifestyle.

Which was fair enough. He disapproved of it too.

Jonathan looked up and saw the critics at the door, waiting. Walk time. At least he had a park. Most dog owners in New York had to walk miles to find one, or hire someone to transport their dogs to Central Park. It was one of the deciding factors for James.

"You have a dog run practically across the street! How lucky is that?"

How lucky was it, mused Jonathan, though it was way too late to move now. He turned up the collar of his jacket, trudged the three blocks to Tompkins Square Park in the rain, unclipped the leashes, and off they ran, skipping for joy, sniffing other dogs and snaffling up bits of discarded food. Jonathan pressed himself up against a tree for cover.

He thought about work while the dogs played with their friends, until he noticed that they'd stopped frolicking and were standing, staring at him damply. James always threw a ball for us, their expressions said. He played hide-and-seek and introduced us to other dogs.

Jonathan stared back at them. What? Now

dogs needed introductions? "Whatever happened to butt-sniffing? Go sniff a butt," he said, waving in the direction of the teeming pack. "Make your own social life. Stand on your own four feet."

An older man with a beagle and a large blue golf umbrella turned to look at him. "You tell 'em," he said. "In my day we sniffed our own butts."

The rain tapered off. Sissy trotted off toward a teacup version of a foreign dog who'd wandered in from the small-dog gulag. It was a fluffy gingery thing straight out of the Mattel factory. Next to the puffball, a Weimaraner with a long-suffering expression wore a padded rainsuit in pale pink-and-green paisley with matching boots and hood.

Why did people think dogs wanted to wear clothes? The Weimaraner's owner glared at him and he wondered if he'd been thinking out loud again.

"Nice dog," he said with a smile, but the woman turned away.

He caught Sissy's eye. What kind of life was this for a dog? Maybe his dogs hated New York City, with its emphasis on labels, money, and grooming. Maybe they wished they lived on a farm, where they could run and play and be useful. But surely the dogs and cats and rats and squirrels and birds and humans in New York all adjusted to life well enough? They walked the streets, they ate great food, they were fine, Jonathan thought. Weren't they? His own life wasn't bad. Not long out of art school, a junior copywriter at Comrade, his own apartment, and a not-unimpressive girlfriend by the name of Julie Cormorant. The dogs should admire him.

"Come on," he called. Sissy bounded up, and Dante made a show of saying an elaborate farewell to the ginger fuzzball before turning and trotting slowly back to his legal guardian. As Jonathan bent to clip on Sissy's leash, the spaniel met his eyes with an expression of profound sympathy. Dante lifted his leg in the general direction of Jonathan's foot.

"Hey!" Jonathan growled, and after an instant's hesitation, the pack sloped off toward his apartment on the third floor. The heavens opened half a block from home and they arrived drenched.

2

For his first five weeks in New York, Jonathan lived on his best friend's couch.

"Are you kidding me?" Max said, throwing a couple of cleanish sheets over the blue corduroy cushions. "I'd be mortally wounded if you stayed at the Four Seasons."

"I'll pay you back someday."

Max clapped his shoulder. "Non necesario, amigo. Mi casa es tu casa."

"Muchas castanets, pal."

Max lived in Bed-Stuy, in a one-bedroom apartment he shared with whichever gorgeous girlfriend he happened to be going around with at the moment. Jonathan didn't mind the couch, which was comfortable enough, and Max was a perfect guide to first-time living in New York, with his intimate knowledge of every bar between Harlem and Canarsie, not to mention a single-minded determination to get Jonathan a job at Comrade, his own place of employ.

"Ten-thirty interview tomorrow," he said. "It's all fixed with Ed. I've done the subliminal thing with him, muttering your name whenever we're in the same room so he already thinks it's God's will to hire you."

"You really think he'll do it? Don't I need some kind of skills?"

"Nah." Max flipped the cheese sandwich he was frying. "The hard part will be convincing him you're a genius who's temperamentally incapable of rocking the boat. Everything we do is blindingly obvious, dressed up with a mountain of marketing to look like time travel."

Jonathan had resigned himself to weeks of answering ads online, interviewing for jobs that didn't exist, accepting internships at start-ups whose USP was that they didn't pay. A bit of Method acting had to be easier than that.

The next morning, he put on his best shirt and least faded jeans, got on the subway with Max, and headed for Tribeca.

The interview was short. "Hey, Johnny!" Ed greeted him with enthusiasm that extended to an affectionate hug, though it was his younger brother, Ben, that Max and Jonathan had been friends with at school. "How you been? Great to see you. So Max says you'll be an asset to the place. Will you?"

Still in pleasantry mode, Jonathan was taken aback. "Well," he began, looking nervously at the twenty or so open-plan employees peering at him. He leaned in to Ed and whispered, "You mean, here?"

"Yup. Let's put on the show right here." Ed grinned maniacally. Max stood behind the boss nodding encouragement.

Jonathan cleared his throat. "Well, um, I pride myself on my skill at problem solving. I've always worked well with a team . . ." Within seconds he realized he'd lost Ed's interest, and Max drew his finger across his throat.

Okay, he thought. Lowering his voice half an octave, he began again. "I like to grab a problem by the jugular and squeeze the life out of it, go for the soft underbelly, reach inside the bastard and drag out its lungs." This seemed to win back Ed's attention, though to be fair, the language wasn't his. One of his freshman roommates hailed from a handgun and deer-murdering clan in Kentucky and talked almost exclusively in killing metaphors.

Ed nodded.

"I figure I can learn a lot from you, Ed. You've always been my role model."

14

Ed was a few years older than Jonathan and Max. Growing up, neither of them had much liked him and no one in their right mind admired him.

"I'm not after my name in lights, or lots of money," Jonathan stated firmly. "It's about opening up the thorax and grabbing hold of the balls, getting to the gist of what we stand for. That's what makes me tick." Everything but the thorax was Max's prompt; they'd rehearsed it last night. Jonathan barely knew what he was saying.

He began to feel slightly desperate. "Ed, hand on heart, there isn't a job in New York City I'd rather have." He followed the track of Ed's eyes to a dark-haired girl in a tight dress. She was waving a file at them.

"Great, good, fine," Ed said, having forgotten what Jonathan was saying or why.

"Um, will you let me know soon?" Jonathan didn't want to appear pushy, but he wasn't entirely sure about another month on Max's couch. There was no answer from Ed, who had turned, mesmerized, to follow the dark-haired girl back in the direction of his office.

Max materialized by his side. "Not a dry eye in the place, my friend. I'd say you've caught yourself a Great White."

"Really?"

Max shrugged. "Call it women's intuition. Let's go tell HR to draw you up a contract. We'll strike while the candle's hot. Ed won't remember who you are tomorrow."

3

Jonathan spent the next two weeks madly searching for an affordable place to live. After fruitless days scouring Brooklyn, he answered an ad for an apartment on the Lower East Side that was rented before he arrived. He stopped at a nearby health-food store just as a bald middle-aged man in a pale gray suit tacked an ad up on the notice board. Jonathan waited for him to leave, read the ad, ripped it off the board, and chased after him down the street.

"Hello!" he shouted. "Excuse me! I'm interested in the apartment!"

The man frowned. "That was quick."

"Could I see it now?"

The man shrugged and looked him over. Jonathan smiled ingratiatingly.

"Okay," the man said at last. "Why not? It's a nice place." He jiggled his key in the front door of a tenement building near the corner of Avenue C. Frank ("Francis Joseph after the archbishop") pointed out the fire escapes to Jonathan with pride: "All regulations up to scratch." They climbed to the third floor, where Frank opened number 3D and led Jonathan in. The entire place was painted dark red with gold trim, but if you squinted and imagined it white, it wasn't bad at all. The living room was large and sunny, the bedroom and galley kitchen small but adequate, the bathroom had the original black-and-white tiles, not to mention congealed-blood-red walls, but overall Jonathan couldn't believe his luck. An affordable decent-sized one-bedroom apartment in Manhattan? He'd expected to find a unicorn first.

"Is it okay if I repaint?"

"Long as you do it neat."

He took it on the spot and they sealed the deal with a handshake and five hundred bucks out of the nearest ATM.

Jonathan felt he had no choice but to trust a man named after an archbishop.

"I need first and last month's up front," Frank said. "You get twenty-four hours' notice when I need the place back for my friend. No contract. Okay by you?"

Jonathan hesitated. "Twenty-four hours?"

"Look." Frank spoke slowly, like a man explaining how the world works to a small child. "It's kind of a *special situation.*"

With a sudden flash of insight, Jonathan got that Frank's friend was currently in housing paid for by the federal government and might be released at any time. He wondered what the friend had gone to jail for and hoped it wasn't the murder of a former tenant.

He closed his eyes. It would take less than fifteen minutes to bike to work.

"Okay," he said.

The next day he handed over the rest of the deposit and Francis Joseph handed over the keys. Jonathan couldn't stop smiling. This was the life he'd imagined for as long as he could remember, a life of easy jobs and cheap Manhattan apartments, of mysterious deals that fell into his lap because the universe had chosen *him.*

He painted everything white. The bedroom was only big enough for a double mattress on milk crates and a small chest of drawers for his clothes, but he didn't care. He bought the mattress at Dream Shack around the corner, found an old leather couch and a child's dresser on Craigslist, salvaged a coffee table from the street on garbage day, and bought a secondhand drawing board for the corner of the living room. His parents donated a square red

Formica table from the 1950s that was fashionable again, and there were enough built-in bookshelves for his collection of comics and his own personal unpublished archive. It was perfect.

Each month thereafter, he received the rent bill written in ballpoint on a piece of lined paper torn out of a notebook. It wasn't exactly standard procedure, but it worked well enough. Jonathan noticed that the account into which he paid his rent money changed with every couple of bills, but as long as he didn't have to deal with anyone in person he was fine. If he was subletting some kind of Mafia safe house while Lefty Gambino served his sentence, he figured a little distance was no bad thing.

Week by week he waited to be told the deal was off, but on the fifteenth of every month the lined paper appeared in his mailbox. Perhaps Lefty was turning out not to be such a model prisoner after all.

He began to think of 3D as home.

Now that the dogs had moved in, the place was even cozier. Jonathan wondered why people always talked about plants and fish tanks making a house feel like a home when two dogs were like a ready-made family, minus the rage. Sissy loved her squashy bed, while Dante favored the couch, which offered maximum comfort and height plus views of the apartment across the way, pigeons landing on the windowsill, and action on the street below.

Jonathan studied dog instruction manuals. "Border collies are among the most intelligent of dogs," the first book began, "only truly happy when engaged in a mission or task." It continued at length on this subject: blah blah sheep, blah blah herding instinct, reminding him at the end that "even the most intelligent Border collie will look to you for leadership and guidance." He glanced over at his own collie, who seemed wholly indifferent to leadership and guidance, but moderately interested in old movies.

There was something about Dante. Jonathan couldn't put his finger on it, but after only a week in residence, the collie had the definite air of top dog. No, not top dog, exactly. Chairman of the board.

He read on.

"Border collies prefer an active life with responsibility and task autonomy in order to fulfill their genetic destiny."

It impressed him that Dante might require task autonomy, whatever that was, and also that he had a genetic destiny. Jonathan supposed that he too had a genetic destiny, though what it might be was anyone's guess. He was anxious to help Dante fulfill his destiny, and though unwilling to acquire actual sheep, he'd managed to find a battery-operated lamb that scuttled around the apartment, occasionally pausing to do a backflip. Dante just stared at Jonathan and blinked slowly.

Sissy, in contrast, followed him around, gazing lovingly and sometimes just lying beside him and licking his foot. Perhaps the genetic destiny of spaniels was less exacting.

He liked having dogs, liked the whole young-trendy-guy-with-dogs vibe. He liked the company. He was still new to New York and everyone always seemed to be rushing somewhere interesting, buying designer furniture and the right sort of shoes, going to art openings, cultivating fuck buddies. Having dogs was kind of a relief. It gave him a job that filled his free hours and a reason to stay home on a Saturday night.

For years now, as long as he could remember, he'd viewed his own life as a comic strip, a bit two-dimensional, yes, but full of eccentric characters with special gifts — the ability to fly, say, or speak fish. This set him apart from people with the kind of lives you saw on TV — normal people with favorite songs and matching towels. He had an apartment and a girlfriend and a job, but everything felt somehow spindly. The closest he came to feeling real was when he rode his bike; speed transformed him into something light and sharp, a samurai blade that slashed through the narrow caverns of New York.

How had he gotten here? Only a few minutes ago he'd been a kid, riding his bike to school, collecting comics, doing homework, and watching TV. Over the years, a few trappings of adulthood had insinuated themselves into his life without making significant inroads. Real adult life seemed to exist *over there,* somewhere as distant and unreachable as Uranus. He had no idea how people crossed over to this place, or why — the demands of being grown up seemed exhausting. Look how I work all the time. See my silky girlfriend. Watch me exchange money for food. Admire my blood pressure.

He wondered why no one had written a book called *How to Be a Person.*

His girlfriend, Julie, was much better at being a person than he was. They met when she was twenty and he was nineteen, and because she was gorgeous and independent and not disorganized and penniless, he'd held out little hope that she'd ever agree to go out with him. Their first meeting, at a very loud club a few blocks off campus, went like this:

Jonathan: AREN'T YOU IN MY THEORY AND PRACTICE IN GRAPHIC DESIGN CLASS?
Julie: WHAT?
Jonathan: AREN'T YOU IN MY THEORY AND PRACTICE IN GRAPHIC DESIGN CLASS?
Julie: NO.
Jonathan: DO YOU WANT A DRINK ANYWAY?
Julie: OKAY.

He knew she was not in his Theory and Practice in Graphic Design class, which consisted of just nine students, but it was the best he could think up on the spot. She looked so perfectly self-possessed, as if she majored in Business Studies (she did) and only dated other business students (she did), which Jonathan considered a colossal waste of two sets of brilliantly organized, highly motivated individuals.

On their early dates, he dragged her to foreign films and comics stores, all-night art openings and bands his friends played in. Most of it left her bemused, but she liked being in contact with a side of life that didn't require output graphs and progress reports.

Julie came from solid midwestern values, which, while not exactly high church, were definitely christian with a small c. Her belief system consisted of medium heels, a decent haircut, and solid retirement funds more or less from birth. She knew where her life was going and how it would get there.

Both sets of friends were stymied when they started hanging around together. "What do you see in him?" asked her room-mates, who'd only witnessed her attraction to equally small-c guys who wore chinos and polo shirts loose across their broad shoulders and had hair so blond and fea-tures so regular it was hard to tell one from another. Most of them would get jobs at Baker & McKenzie, move to moderately expensive suburbs of Any Medium City, USA, buy expensive cars to weather their midlife crises, and die prematurely of heart disease wondering why life hadn't been more fun.

Jonathan, on the other hand, had a pale, somewhat nervy quality. His shoulders were a bit narrow, his hair unruly; his eyes rested slightly too long on things of no obvious value. The way he puzzled over perfectly ordinary objects disturbed Julie, who sometimes wondered whether he saw what she saw when he looked at the world. "What?" she would ask when he stopped to gaze at a doorknob or a tree. "Oh, nothing," he'd say, recalling himself and moving back into the stream of life.

This otherness intrigued her. Perhaps some biological impulse drew her toward genetic diversity, toward a man entirely unlike her father, her uncles, her ex-boyfriends, and all the men that destiny determined she would live and breed with, give birth to, attend barbecues with, and vote for till the end of time.

Unlike the men of her tribe, Jonathan didn't go bronze in the hot midwestern summers or flush rosy in its freezing snowstorms. He didn't stride in a manly fashion, own a big four-wheel drive, or sit with his legs splayed at the movies.

Julie's tidy mind allowed Jonathan's otherness to sneak up on her. She had no idea what he might do or say next, and this secretly thrilled her. The first time they kissed, he appeared to be thinking of something else entirely, so when he turned to her with a sudden excess of attention she was completely caught off guard. She had blushed and looked away and he'd had to catch her face in his hands and hold it still while he kissed her. His lips felt foreign, febrile. And Julie, who had never fallen very far or very hard in her life, fell very far and very hard for Jonathan. For his part, he recognized that something unexpected had happened between them, that he had charmed a cold-eyed raptor out of a tree, that it now sat calmly and quietly on his fist, and that (in the absence of logic) there was some strange magic in their connection.

In the early days of the relationship, Jonathan sat up at night watching her sleep, while Julie expressed her devotion with expensive sweaters to replace the ancient moth-eaten ones he wore.

"But they're still perfectly warm," Jonathan protested.

Julie shook her head. "It's unraveling, Jonathan. Try this," she'd say, handing him a heavy shopping bag within which a beautiful cashmere sweater lay, tenderly wrapped in tissue paper.

And because he liked nice things he kept it, and the other things she bought him, and he enjoyed wearing them because the feel of featherweight wool against his skin reminded him of her.

As graduation loomed, there were long

discussions about what to do next. Having grown up in the embarrassing suburbs, Jonathan craved a real New York City experience, but Julie wasn't so sure. The Midwest was her home, after all, and all her friends lived here. Long conversations ensued till deep into the night, conversations during which they held hands and tried to imagine some kind of future that included each other. In the end, Julie decided to stay put, just for now, while Jonathan moved on ahead, blazing a trail in New York.

"You pave the way," she said, with a good deal of private doubt that paving a way was the sort of thing Jonathan would be able to do without guidance.

He'd been looking forward to starting work — the sense of purpose, the shared endeavor, the whole breathless whirligig thrill of having a career. What he hadn't counted on was the triviality of office life, the futility of his daily routine, the sort of things you were expected to do in exchange for money. The clients were ducks, quacking nonsense in his ears while nibbling his best ideas to death. But Max had the desk next to his, the other employees were nice enough, and despite a dawning suspicion that the whole work thing was just a ploy for filling up the time between birth and death, he felt rather proud of his ability to take part in it. He liked the fact that after all those years of writing term papers and taking exams, someone was actually willing to pay him.

And so for six long months he and Julie lived separately, agreeing not to spend their first salaries on flights and visits, but skyping late at night and kissing each other across a thousand miles of empty airspace.

One night, Julie called him with great news. "I've got a new job! In the New York office!" she said. "With more money! Aren't you excited?"

Of course he was excited. Who wouldn't be? He hoped she would approve of his apartment. And the dogs. Julie knew about the dogs, but hadn't commented much.

"How long will we have them?"

"Six months. You'll like them. They're good dogs."

She had changed the subject.

Secretly he worried that Julie wouldn't quite see the point of dogs, would mostly view them as a distraction and a tax on their budget and living space. He worried that Julie would want to go places that didn't take dogs, that he would have to leave them alone during the day while he went to work and then again at night when he and she went out.

He'd tried skyping her with them sitting beside him so they could start to get to know each other, but it just made everyone sullen.

"Which one is which?"

"This is Dante," Jonathan said, pointing to the collie, who remained resolutely off camera, "and this is Sissy." He tousled Sissy's ears and tried to stop her licking the computer screen, while Julie recoiled in disgust.

He mentioned none of this to his brother, who believed that the relationship between dog and human should be an uncomplicated dance of mutual affection — you loved your dogs, took them everywhere, and broke up with any girlfriend who didn't love them as much as you did.

"Anywhere that doesn't take dogs isn't the kind of place you want to go," he'd told Jonathan.

Jonathan silently listed movies, restaurants, clubs, concerts, bars, department stores, public transport, work, airplanes, and Dubai in his head, which was just the tip of the iceberg and included pretty much everywhere he was ever likely to want to go.

4

Jonathan, dog owner, encountered a whole new segment of society. Like cyclists and comics enthusiasts, dog people were mostly fanatics. And they all seemed to know more about his pets than he did.

"Nice spaniel. From working stock?"

He didn't know how to answer that. "Um," he said, casting about as if hoping the answer might appear to him in a thought bubble. "I don't really know. They belong to my brother."

This would earn him disapproving looks, and comments that bypassed him altogether. "You'd make a good working dog, wouldn't you, girl?"

And then Sissy would gaze at her new friend lovingly and a bond would form, as if Sissy and the stranger would be out together in a field right now wearing expensive British sportswear and flushing grouse if only Jonathan didn't exist.

"Beautiful dog," they'd say about Dante and frown. "Not for Manhattan, though."

Why did the presence of a dog give everyone permission to opine? "It's okay, he's happy," Jonathan learned to say with casual authority. "He's a city collie."

He tried this line tentatively at first, but found it worked. He could see his detractors thinking, Really? A city collie? And then they'd shrug and think, Okay, fair dues — like a city collie was a thing. To be honest, even Jonathan could tell that Border collies in general (and Dante in particular) were not terribly well suited to the role of inferior species. Dante, he felt, should really have been running a medium-size investment bank.

The dog run in Tompkins Square consisted of sand and concrete with hardly any grass. Who'd want to pee on sand when a rough barky tree surrounded by composted leaves would be so much nicer? He supposed that in New York the dogs at least got to meet other dogs, but how much fun was it to do your business on concrete with half the East Village as an audience? Jonathan imagined lifting his tail and squatting privately in a deep forest surrounded by the complex aromas of pine and fungi — how much better than traffic fumes and Calvin

Klein body spray?

He found himself dreaming of a life rich in loam. Occasionally he forgot that it was for the dogs and dreamed of his own little patch of well-rotted soil, bursting with bluebells and foxgloves and buttercups and moss. He wanted to roll in it himself, to rub the length of his body through the dark damp earth, disguising his soapy human smell in a cloak of forest greenery.

In this new chapter of their lives, the dogs had HBO and Hulu, they had organic bones and expensive leather leashes. They had everything New York City could offer in the way of food and shelter, but he wondered if it was what they really wanted. He wondered if they were depressed and unfulfilled. It was difficult to tell with dogs, especially dogs you hadn't known since birth. But he sensed something was amiss. Perhaps they required professional help.

He phoned Max.

"Hey, Max."

"Hey, buddy. I'm with Allegra." Max was always with someone.

"Sorry. You don't know the name of a good vet, do you?"

"Your dogs sick?"

Jonathan shrugged. "Not really. Just a checkup."

"Hang on." He turned away from the phone. "Hey, Allegra. My buddy needs the name of a vet. You got one?"

Jonathan heard mumbling and then Allegra's voice appeared. "I take my cat to the one near the corner of 11th and First. That's not too far from you, is it?"

"No, that's good. Do they do dogs too?"

Allegra paused. "They're vets. They do animals. Not sure about large farm animals. Is one of your dogs a cow?"

Jonathan made a big fat-lipped Allegra face at his phone.

"I'll text you the number. Ask for Dr. Clare. She's amazing."

"Dr. Clare what?"

Allegra giggled. "Clare de Lune." She handed Max his phone. "Your friend's a riot."

Max was back. "You all set, pal?"

"I think so, thanks," Jonathan said, but Max had already hung up.

The next day, he phoned and made an appointment to see Dr. Clare de Lune. No, it wasn't an emergency, he said.

Not Clare de Lune, the receptionist said. Just Clare. Dr. Clare.

"Like Doctor Who?"

"Doctor who?"

"Never mind." Jonathan struggled back

from his parallel universe.

What was the immediate problem and with which of the two dogs? The receptionist's voice was high and thin, like a child's.

Jonathan hesitated. "It's not something I can really describe over the phone," he replied, feeling obscurely dirty-old-mannish.

"Okay," piped the receptionist. "I'll put you down for a thirty-minute appointment seeing as how it's your first. See you Tuesday at five."

Tuesday at four, Jonathan slipped out of work, flew home on his bike, collected the dogs, and set off for the vet. It felt like an adventure. The Vet. He'd never had any reason to visit a vet and he wondered if the waiting room would be filled with exotic animals leading hidden lives behind closed doors. He pictured an elderly white tiger, retired from showbiz in Las Vegas, now living in a musty mansion overlooking Central Park with only his trainer's ancient widow for company. Or maybe a piranha in a tank on wheels. Or a bad-tempered chinchilla (he tried to picture a chinchilla but could only come up with a gray-striped fur coat) and a Galápagos tortoise, smuggled out of Ecuador in a valise back when Customs didn't mind people transporting endangered animals in hand luggage.

The veterinary hospital was housed in a handsome brownstone and they entered through a door on the ground floor. The ten-year-old receptionist (her voice instantly recognizable) turned out to be a young woman the approximate size and shape of a bank vault. She introduced herself as Iris and handed him a clipboard with some forms to fill out, the first of which required his credit card details.

He cleared his throat. "Um . . . can you tell me what Dr. Clare de . . . what Dr. Clare charges for a visit?"

"It all depends on what's required. A basic no-tests half-hour consultation starts at eighty-five dollars." She smiled at him in a slightly fixed manner and returned to her laptop.

They waited ten minutes until a soft buzzer caused Iris to stand up, open one of the three doors that led off the waiting room, and point inside. "It's your turn," she trilled sweetly, and for a split second Jonathan imagined a firing squad within, twelve men in uniforms of the French Foreign Legion, rifles poised, a debonair French poodle in a beret smoking a Gitane, waiting to give the signal to fire with a laconic paw.

Instead, a tall young woman with short choppy hair, no makeup, and a serious expression shook his hand.

"Hello," she said. Her accent was English. "You must be Sissy."

"Actually, no," Jonathan said, momentarily confused by the greeting. He pushed the spaniel forward like a shy child at dancing school.

"If you'll just put her on the scale."

He led Sissy onto the large scale and held her for a moment.

"Okay." Dr. Clare tapped the result into her computer. "Let's get her up onto the table."

Jonathan lifted her up and the vet listened to Sissy's heart. "Good girl," she said, feeling carefully down each leg, stretching the hip joints up and back and the shoulder joints out and forward. "Okay." She bent the ankles, pressed down with expert fingers along either side of Sissy's spine, and looked at her teeth.

"You're a lovely girl and you look fine. Let's check your friend."

Jonathan led Dante onto the scale, then hoisted him up on the table, where the vet repeated the same procedures, checking legs, heart, joints, back, and teeth.

"Excellent," she said after a minute. "You can hop down now."

Jonathan set Dante back on the floor as

Dr. Clare completed the computer file.

At last she turned to him. "So. They both seem to be in excellent shape. Are you just here for a registration checkup? Or is there a problem?"

"Well." Jonathan looked up at the ceiling. "Yes and no."

Dr. Clare's smooth brow creased.

"They seem . . . I don't know quite how to put this. You see, they're not my dogs. My brother left them with me for six months. I don't know much about dogs. But I'm worried that they're not happy."

She looked at him. "Are there disturbing behaviors? Tail chasing? Gnawing? Incessant whining? Aggression?"

Jonathan shook his head. "No. None of that."

"Are they eating?"

"Yes," he said. "But I'm not sure they're getting the same pleasure out of food that they used to."

Dr. Clare blinked. "Pleasure?"

"I know they're dogs," he said, struggling to explain. "But I get a feeling they're dissatisfied. Dante should be herding sheep, at the very least. He's so intelligent. And Sissy . . . she doesn't complain, but I often get a sense that she's missing something. Grouse? I don't know. They both just seem

38

a bit — off." He glanced at Dante, whose face was entirely blank. "Look at him. Can you see what I mean? Sometimes I get the feeling that he's . . . angry."

"Angry."

"Such untapped potential," Jonathan said. "Sissy, now, she's not the angry type. But even she's trying incredibly hard to be cheerful. Sometimes I feel she just ends up feeling sad."

Jonathan looked at Dr. Clare and she looked back at him. He could see the workings of her brain. Idiot, she was thinking. You're one of those time-wasting American idiots.

Dr. Clare took a deep breath, exhaled, and half shut her eyes. "I'm not a psychiatrist," she said. "Your dogs seem fine to me. More than fine, they're lovely dogs." She paused. "It's true that city dogs don't always get enough exercise or attention. Is there somewhere you can play ball with them? What about day care? Maybe get a dog walker in? Or leave Kongs when you go out. Stuffed with kibble and peanut butter. It can take hours to extract everything from a Kong."

Jonathan had once given Dante a Kong stuffed with kibble and peanut butter. The dog had emptied it in under a minute and then kicked it under the couch with what had looked to him like contempt.

He shook his head sadly. "A Kong won't help. Something's missing from their lives."

"Could you be more specific?"

Jonathan looked downcast. "Not really."

They both stared at the dogs.

Jonathan continued. "I have other concerns. What if Dante's boredom reaches a peak and then one day, suddenly and for no particular reason, he takes a dislike to some small child and lunges, ripping its face off? And someone films it on their phone and it goes viral and there's a massive lawsuit and it makes the cover of *New York* magazine. I'd probably end up in jail and they'd make an example of Dante. You couldn't really blame him, but he'd probably have to be put down."

She looked at him appraisingly. "Has he ever ripped anyone's face off before?"

"Of course not!" Jonathan felt outraged at the suggestion. "But that doesn't mean he never will. The nature of the other is unknowable."

Dr. Clare considered Dante. "I'm a fairly good judge of dogs," she said at last. "And he doesn't look as if he'd rip the face off a child."

Jonathan slumped. "I don't think you get it."

"Possibly not. I think, however, that you might stop worrying about the what-ifs."

Jonathan said nothing for a long moment. "What if he hates his life?"

The vet peered at him. "The good thing about dogs is that they tend not to be unhappy without cause."

"Do you have a dog, Dr. Clare?"

"Yes."

"Don't you ever get a sense that your dog's life isn't entirely satisfactory?"

She hesitated. "Well . . . my dog doesn't love being left alone, so I try to bring her to work when I can. We had beautiful parks in my London neighborhood and I suppose she misses them. I miss them too." The vet looked thoughtful. "It's true that New York isn't an ideal environment for dogs, but the compensations are pretty special. It's not perfect, but we all adapt."

"Do we?" Jonathan frowned. "Maybe we just think we adapt. Maybe your dog loved London and all the beautiful parks full of roses and nannies and, and . . ." He searched for something else English parks might be full of.

"Ducks," she said. "There were wonderful ducks. All different types. And herons."

"Okay, ducks. Maybe she misses all that, looks out at the steel and glass and concrete and feels sad all the time. Maybe we distort ourselves into a semblance of conformity so everyone thinks we've adapted, when in fact all we've done is make the best of an untenable situation. Maybe we shouldn't be living this way, without grass and trees, and ducks, always under pressure, always trying to catch up, never enough time or energy for the things we love, if we can even remember what those things are. Maybe that's true of dogs as well as humans. Maybe it's all just one big lie we tell ourselves."

Dr. Clare stared, her eyes wide.

"I'm sorry," Jonathan said, with dignity. "I won't take up any more of your time."

"I understand what you're saying." She struggled to salvage her professional bearing. "But we do the best we can. Unless you're planning to move to London or Montana, you and your dogs will have to make the best of it."

Jonathan laughed bitterly. "And that's your answer?"

"I'm afraid it's the best I can do." She shook her head and turned back to her computer. "Do feel free to contact the office, Mr. Trefoil, if you have any further concerns."

"Jonathan."

"Sorry?"

"Please call me Jonathan."

She sighed. "Do feel free to contact the office, Jonathan, if you have any further concerns."

Only not strange abstract concerns like these, Jonathan thought. Not concerns that can't be dealt with by a vet. You want a broken leg, Dr. Vet. Or a gash that can be sewn up. Or a twisted gut. Or a limp.

Not angst or ennui. Not canine weltschmerz.

Jonathan paid the bill, wondering why all the words for his dogs' conditions existed only in foreign languages. Was the English language so uninterested in descriptions of spiritual disquiet? Was the Anglo-American psyche too indifferent even to contemplate states of philosophical dismay? In English you had to say something woolly like, "I don't feel quite like myself." Or, "I have a vague sense that the world is not as it should be." Or simply, "I'm depressed." As opposed to weltschmerz, a word that precisely described the deep psychic unease caused by a realization that the world is a terrible place, shot through with an incurably flawed atmosphere of cruelty incompatible with human (or canine) psychological well-being.

In English you could go to the doctor,

disappointed beyond human endurance at the state of reality, and all you could say to describe your state of mind was, "I feel low." What a totally crap language.

He couldn't figure out why Allegra had recommended Dr. Clare so highly. She seemed to care nothing for the inner life of his dogs. How typically English to shun psychological insight in favor of a stiff upper lip. "We adapt," she'd said. But do we? Do we really, Dr. Vet? Do we adapt to a relentlessly hostile environment from which all human comfort has been leached?

He found himself increasingly indignant. What kind of doctor had no interest in the mind-body problem? He, a rank amateur in the pet-owning hierarchy, could read infinite complexities in those doggy eyes. Perhaps dogs lacked the intellect to invent dumdum bullets and destroy the oceans, but Jonathan wasn't at all convinced that this made them psychologically inferior to or less complex than humans.

He left the vet's and headed back home with his dogs. A young violinist stood on the street corner playing something that he vaguely recognized, and he stopped to listen. She had a sign on her open violin case that read, SAVING UP FOR JUILLIARD.

Jonathan looked at Dante and Sissy, who looked back at him, expectant. In terms of musical talent, humans definitely outperformed dogs, though he wondered where he would be on a scale that included this girl at the top and, say, razor clams near the bottom. He and the dogs would be somewhere in between, perhaps not as far apart as he might hope.

He imagined that clams led quite contented lives, while this poor girl had to practice for thousands of hours, striving day after day to play tunes on a bizarre construction of wood and stretched sheep gut for the entertainment of a jaded audience, many of whom surreptitiously dozed. Jonathan reached into his pocket and dumped all his change into her violin case. Clam might be the wiser choice, if choice were available. She nodded her thanks and launched into an elegant arpeggio as he walked on with his dogs, wondering what it might feel like to live buried in wet sand.

5

The next morning he discovered that someone had eaten his mail. Jonathan always left
it on the shelf by the front door, but now it
was gone, with the exception of the tiny
remnants of his pay slip poking out from
under a chair. His newspaper looked unmo-
lested, but leafing through it he found that
the sports section was missing. When the
dogs ran up to greet him, Jonathan thought
he could detect traces of papier-mâché
around the corners of Dante's mouth. An
untouched circular from Privileged Pets, a
virtual VIP club for city dogs, leaned at a
tidy angle against the wall as if someone
had placed it there on purpose. As a joke?
Jonathan stared at Dante, who seemed
intent on the view outside the window.

With a sigh, he poured himself a cup of
yesterday's coffee, added milk, and drank it
cold before snapping on leashes for the
morning walk and trotting down three

flights of stairs.

It was one of the last cold days of winter, when the temperature plummets and no one's wearing the right clothes, but at least it wasn't raining. At the dog run, he huddled down on a bench and rubbed his hands together while the dogs stood stock-still, heads lowered, gazing at him. Could this possibly be normal dog behavior? Why weren't they frolicking? He wondered if the dogs knew how much he had to accomplish today. To pass the time, he pulled out a pencil and notebook and began sketching out a new chapter for his comic-novel masterpiece, *The New York Inferno,* in which a Border collie spirit guide accompanies a young poet through the nine circles of the New York underworld. Jonathan glanced at his own Dante, catching the slight curl of the lip, the one ear cocked, thinking how perfect he would be for the job of shepherding a clueless tourist such as himself through hell.

Back at home, he prepared breakfast for the dogs, who ate and then wandered over to their beds to lie down, Sissy with a soft spaniel sigh, Dante with a slow shake of his head. Jonathan wondered if they went through his e-mails when he was at work. Or read the mail before they ate it. He gave each of them a raw-hide bone and set off on his bike for work.

Jonathan's bicycle was the most expensive thing he owned. It had a frame of ultralight defense-grade carbon steel, an integrated computer for speed and cadence stats, and he lived in fear of it being stolen out from under him. The only way to solve this was by moving too fast to be caught and never letting it out of his sight.

The ride to work took him through a hundred shortcuts and evasions. He felt like an Olympic skier in the giant slalom; speeding along, head low, steering by imperceptible shifts of thought. It was his goal never to slow down, never to stop, and when at last he pulled up with an exaggerated flourish in front of Comrade, having evaded taxis, pedestrians, death and injury in a thousand different forms, he felt as clear and fleet as a beam of light.

He carried his bike up two flights of stairs and locked it to the railing on the landing.

A girl in very tight jeans and a tiny T-shirt passed him on her way in. "Hey, Jonathan."

"Hey, Shay." Shay was the boss's assistant.

"Cool lock," she said, balancing her tray of coffees on one upraised palm, like a comedy Italian waiter.

"Thanks," he said, pleased that she'd

noticed. "It's a Skylock. Smartphone activated. Wanna see how it works?"

"No," she said, and twirled away.

His carbon-soled road shoes clopped across the floor donkey-style, just in case anyone hadn't noticed that he was the last one in this morning. In the men's room he changed from Italian team Lycra into jeans, a T-shirt, and a 1960s lemon alpaca and wool Brooks Brothers cardigan from Downtown Vintage. He suspected his grandfather had owned hundreds of sweaters like this and felt annoyed at his parents for making him buy them all back from pretentious boutiques at inflated prices.

"Meeting at three," Shay reminded him, entering Ed's office and setting the coffees on the desk with a little pirouette.

Shay liaised with Ed (founder, owner, and executive director of Comrade) during lunch hour, and the noises that emerged from the executive boardroom (locked) inspired a deep melancholy in the rest of the staff. The fact that Ed, not yet thirty, owned a loft in Williamsburg and drove a 1972 silver-blue Mercedes 280SL had already decimated office morale, but noisy sex with his assistant at work was the last straw — a daily reminder of the life that most of his employees would never lead.

49

Not that any of them particularly wanted to have sex in the boardroom with Ed.

Comrade's offices were situated in a second-floor loft that had once been a lighting showroom. During renovations, the insulated drop-foam ceilings had been removed to expose wooden beams, plasterboard was ripped right back to bare brick walls, and cracked 1950s linoleum revealed wide oak floorboards. It would have looked nice just like that, but in order to convince clients that Comrade was a highly creative organization, Ed purchased an entire communist-era Russian railway station at auction — from signal board to ticket office — and had it installed in the Tribeca loft. The concept almost worked but not quite, spawning too many jokes about Siberia and the inevitable comparisons between Ed and Stalin. The huge Eastern Bloc station clock ticked so loudly, it drove one employee to smash it to smithereens with an industrial-size stapler one quiet Sunday. She left a note referencing rage and despair and never returned to collect the twenty-two china rabbits she kept on her desk.

Work tables at Comrade were arranged more or less at random to give the place "a flavor of openness and spontaneity," although openness was refuted by cubicle walls desperately improvised out of piles of books, an antique hat stand, office easels, and a shower curtain attached to a metal clothing rail.

Jonathan was responsible for Broadway Depot, Comrade's most lucrative account. They advertised daily specials in local newspapers all over the city and in online banners and pop-ups that required a constant river of mind-bendingly dull copy with headlines like "20% off all pens!" and "Printer paper, cheapest in town!"

It was the kind of writing designed to drive anyone insane. Jonathan daily attempted to craft headlines that were just a bit wittier than the status quo, and every day, Broadway Depot rejected them. To be more specific, Louise Crimple, his opposite number at Broadway Depot, rejected them.

"Hi, Johnny. All good?"

"Great, Louise." Wait for it.

"I need to wrongside yesterday's headlines. Reverse the buy-sell pendulum. Avoid disasterfication."

Disasterfication? "You don't like my headlines?"

"Love 'em! But I'm thinking we cul-de-sac yesterday's work for the immediate now? No blamestorming."

He was used to this. "You don't like my

headlines."

"Praise for ideation, Jonathan."

"I'll redo them."

"Win-win! Up, up, and away!"

Louise was infinitely enthusiastic and not at all unattractive, but she had a broken wind-up toy for a brain, a passion for triple-speak, and the imagination of a sink plug, something Broadway Depot did not sell.

Not that his ads were great or world-changing, but they were marginally better than "Pens: $2.99 today only!" He'd argued passionately over the phone, on e-mail, and in person with Louise Crimple that the eternal truths embedded in his version of headlines suggested (on some subliminal level) that Broadway Depot understood consumers' deep emotional relationship with office supplies. That it built brand loyalty and repeat business on top of sales, improving the lives of both BD employees and its customers. But his arguments fell on deaf ears. Louise was not interested in abstractions.

"No one relationships a pen," she said with the world's brightest smile. "It runs out, you sequence up. End of!"

Jonathan hated the expression "end of." He hated all of her expressions. Once he took her out to lunch and tried to explain the ties that writers and artists had with pens, how writing with a gel pen felt like slipping around in mud or transferring lines straight from brain to page, while a ballpoint indicated a frugal no-frills personality, someone you'd barely want to know. At the Vietnamese fusion restaurant (carefully chosen for its subtle flavors and textures), Louise ordered a steak well done, then gazed at him so intently and for so long, he had to check to make sure his face hadn't turned into a macaroon.

"Louise," he finally said, doing his best not to shout. "Aren't you bored? Aren't you bored to death with your crappy job at this crappy company doing crappy ads day after boring crappy day?"

She listened, thought for a moment, then met his gaze with her own beautiful blank gray eyes. "How about cake? Are you desserting?"

Don't tempt me, he thought.

Raw data for today's Broadway Depot ads pinged on to his desktop and he opened the file. "Plastic folders 30% off, one day only!" "Just in! Inkjet cartridges all the way from China!" "A special on executive chairs! High- or low-back!" "Filing cabinets in five new designer shades!" (When was the last time any human being had bought a filing cabinet?) The list went on. He couldn't quite bring himself to read it, so he went straight to the dashboard. His first job: update the website from which each store printed its flyers. He was trusted enough to enter snappy headlines direct to the files without approval from a higher authority, so he did: "Executive Chair Deal of the Day! Don't Your Buttocks Deserve the Best?" and "Your Useless Life-Waster Report Looks Better in a 20% Off Plastic Folder!"

With a sigh of regret he erased the headlines and set to work. At noon precisely, Max came in from a shoot and they headed out to lunch.

Few Comrade employees left the office for lunch. Many brought edamame hummus in tiffin tins and ate it with home-style organic pita bread and beetroot coleslaw garnished with rice vinegar. Some had pear and pomegranate salads or salmon-skin hand rolls in elaborately folded Japanese containers delivered from OriGami. Jonathan and Max ate gigantic roast beef sandwiches with mustard on white bread bought from the last unreconstructed deli in Tribeca. They dined separately at adjacent desks, Max e-mailing Jonathan websites like befilthy.com and dirtymoms4U under the subject "Possible Wives" while Jonathan sent back pictures from 1950s pulp fiction with titles like *Gay Blade* and *Fanny's Hill.*

You could trace the banter back fifteen years or more, when an eight-year-old Max renamed himself Neo (after *The Matrix,* a film he was not allowed to watch and so committed entirely, frame by frame, to memory) while Jonathan took on Solar, Man of the Atom, as his alter ego. With whatever money the boys had, they bought comics, and when they ran out of money they created their own: Maxman, starring a superhero who vanquished evil and always got the babe, with his sidekick, Jay Solar, a muscled-up ex-con with a vendetta against the Russian tattooist who'd ruined his face. Solar's motto was *Gazoom!* Jonathan couldn't remember why.

Living two doors apart in leafy Larchmont, the friends spent so much time together that Max's mother habitually set the table for five, six if James (CEO ex officio of Maxman Enterprises) joined them. Max's mother served macaroni and cheese and called them Heckle and Jeckle, while Jonathan's parents tutted and wished their comic-obsessed sons would do something normal like play basketball or read *Playboy.*

"They go wrong so fast," his father sighed.

"One minute it's Twinkies and Bosco and the next it's life for killing Harvey Milk."

"Harvey Milk's killer didn't get life, dear," said Jonathan's mother.

"You see?" her husband muttered, shaking his head. "There's no justice."

Jonathan was accustomed to this sort of exchange, but it never failed to delight Max.

"Your dad is so nuts," he said. "I bet there's some weird internal logic to everything he says, but you'd need a PhD in semiotics to figure it out."

"What's semiotics?" Jonathan was drawing.

"Nobody really knows," Max said, stacking Oreos in an attempt to earn a place in *The Guinness Book of World Records.* "I'm up to fifty-eight, don't breathe," he whispered, just as the tower tipped and crashed. "Damn," he said, and then, "Rusty, no!" as his dog slid over to vacuum up the mess.

"Who brought that animal in here?" Jonathan's father called from the den. "You know your mother's allergic."

"There's no dog here," James called back. "We're watching *Cujo.*"

"Turn it off," came the reply.

Eventually, when the three of them and Rusty tired of whatever they happened to be doing, Jonathan, James, and Max walked the fifty yards to Max's house with a hundred Oreos and an unfinished comic in a plastic bag, dedicating themselves to a great deal more of the same over there, only with a slightly different view of the street and differently peculiar parents.

Over the years, Maxman Enterprises had a part-time employee in the form of Ben, who lived five doors down, but Ben's mother aspired to bigger things for Ben (and his brother, Ed) than comic-book clubs. Ed headed up computer club and Junior UN at school, while Ben played Little League, had a purple belt in jujitsu, and got a telescope for his birthday so he could memorize a new constellation every week.

"She says you three are a bad influence," Ben reported morosely.

At which Max and Jonathan and James grinned and gave each other high-fives, vowing to remain bad influences for as long as they were underage and thus not legally accountable for their actions.

6

Sissy greeted Jonathan with enthusiasm on his return from work, while Dante eyed him skeptically. Jonathan tousled their ears, clipped on their leashes, speed-walked ten blocks, returned home, gave them treats ("eat, eat, be happy despite the bleakness of your incarcerated lives"), pulled two salmon steaks out of the fridge and wrapped them in foil, dumped a bag of baby leaves into the salad bowl, filled a pan with water for the potatoes, and glanced at his watch. Seven-fifteen. Julie had said she'd arrive at seven-thirty, which meant she'd be here by seven-thirty unless an asteroid wiped out all human life between now and then.

Jonathan smiled when he thought of Julie's punctuality, her reliability, consistency, steadfastness. These were the qualities that had landed her a job as salesperson for *Bridal-360,* a glossy magazine and 360-degree online wedding planner with the tag

"From First Date to Forever Mate." Forever Mate sounded to Jonathan like a dystopian chess game or that horrible condition where dogs have sex and get stuck. Even Julie thought the tagline was creepy. But she loved her job, loved applying her organizational prowess to tight deadlines, loved the fact that everyone marched to the same beat (Mendelssohn's "Wedding March"). She loved her job so much that she didn't think twice about living apart from Jonathan for as long as it took to scramble her way up the greasy pole of the nuptial hierarchy.

But when after six months an opening came up in the New York office — and it happened to be for a senior sales position, and she happened to win the job over thirty other (many better-qualified) applicants — fate decreed that it was time for the couple to be together once more.

"We can cohabit for a while and see how it goes," she said to Jonathan, who in turn thought fondly, Oh Julie, you crazy romantic fool. He secretly hoped she'd apply her organizational genius to finding them another apartment, one whose availability didn't require someone's parole to be turned down.

Jonathan often considered how ironic it was that the pathologically unsentimental

Julie had ended up in the wedding business.

"I don't know why women make such a fuss about weddings," she once told him. "It's all they talk about in the office." Jonathan stopped himself from pointing out that you might hear quite a lot of wedding talk if you happened to work for *Bridal-360,* and wondered whether she might have been better off following a career in, say, copyright law.

At precisely 7:26 she buzzed up to his apartment. Jonathan dumped the potatoes into the boiling water, wiped his hands on a towel, and ran out to welcome her.

He met her halfway down the stairs, but before he could take her bag, a blur of black and white descended from the landing and hurled itself at Julie with a wild howl of delight that to Jonathan sounded sarcastic. Just behind Dante came Sissy, ears flying, squeaking with joy. Both dogs jumped on his girlfriend, knocking her off balance and upsetting her handbag, which led to a game of roll-the-lipstick and toss-the-iPhone, made more challenging by the stairs.

Julie did not shout at the dogs. She maintained a dignified silence, snatched her phone out of a long cross-pass from collie to spaniel, scooped up her lipstick, wallet, and makeup bag, and walked straight up the last flight into the apartment as if the dogs failed to exist. The dogs, excited by this new game, licked at her ankles, nipped at the hem of her dress, hurled themselves at her shins, snapped imaginary flies away from her face. Complex choreography was required, and Jonathan found himself admiring his dogs' agility. Watching them move around the tiny kitchen was like observing the New York City Ballet perform in an airline toilet. Jonathan frowned conscientiously at them, Julie blanked them, and everyone had a very nice time. Except for Julie.

"Welcome to New York!" he said, embracing her. And then, after a futile attempt to get Dante and Julie to make friends, he said, "Look, just ignore the dogs. They'll get used to you."

Julie, who had been ignoring the dogs since the moment they met, glanced around the apartment. "It looks smaller than I imagined."

Jonathan followed her gaze. She was right, it did look small, what with all the dog paraphernalia. Beds, toys, bowls. Dogs.

"How was the flight?" Jonathan screwed the top off a bottle of wine and slipped the salmon onto plates. "Would you like a drink? Are you hungry?"

"Starved," she said, accepting a glass of wine. "This looks delicious. It's not even like I get time off to relocate. We're frantic, right in the middle of an entire issue on non-white weddings. I've spent all day fielding press inquiries. The whole wedding world is aghast."

"Non-white?" Jonathan said. "Do you mean, like, people of color or dresses of color?"

Julie sat down and picked up her fork. "Dresses of color. *And* people of color."

"Wow." Jonathan was impressed by the wild vagaries of the wedding world and wondered how you could possibly aghast this whole vital segment of society. He pictured brides in shredded scarlet and black, barefoot and limping, with little horns instead of veils, flaming torches, forked tongues, and green snaking tails, bridegrooms dressed as satyrs in hairy loincloths prancing on shiny hooves, brides-maids naked except for . . .

Julie glanced at him. "Whatever you're imagining, stop it now. Color means lichen, smoke, titanium, fig. That's it."

"Fig? That's a color?"

Julie did not appear to have heard him. For some reason, her refusal to understand or appreciate his vision of the world made him love her all the more passionately. She was a strong, sane, sensible, beautiful, no-nonsense sort of person. And he was a fumbling fool of a mortal who lived in a world of relentless self-doubt. The fact that she deigned to spend time with him cast a holy light on her generosity of spirit.

Since they'd been apart, she'd featured ever more prominently in Dante's *The New York Inferno.* Julie in hell was statuesque in towering platform heels, bearing an iPad in one hand and a tiny container of dried goji berries in the other. She seemed not to notice the tortured souls all around her. He captioned the scene "Surely They Knew The Rules?"

Julie finished her salmon. Jonathan took the plates through to the dishwasher and began plotting the next episode of *The New York Inferno* in his head. He had not told Julie that she featured in his newest work. He imagined presenting it to her at the birth of their first child as a surprise. Or very possibly, given her attitude to surprises, never.

"That was nice," Julie said, clearing the rest of the table and glancing at her watch. "But I really have to work."

"Really?" He took her in his arms. "I've missed you so much."

"Have you? I've missed you too." She

turned to face him and he kissed her, running his hands along the neat curve of her hips.

Four years into Jonathan's relationship with Julie, Max refused to recognize her appeal. "She's about as sexy as a bank statement," he said, as if creating a logical argument. "Plus, she never smiles."

"She never smiles at you," Jonathan said.

"Precisely my point."

Julie didn't protest when Jonathan took her hand and led her to the bedroom. "You don't have to go back to work this exact second, do you?" He nuzzled her neck while she wriggled out of her cardigan and stepped out of her dress, frowning a little. She closed the door, leaving the dogs on the outside staring in.

"Welcome home," he said, kissing her.

Afterward, while she sat at the table tapping figures into spreadsheets, Jonathan drew the scene of Julie undressing — a scene for the second circle of hell (Lust) — in an attempt to capture the essence of something he hadn't noticed before in his girlfriend's manner. It was the frown, he thought at first. The shimmy of her shoulders as she slipped off her bra. The slight impression she gave of being alone in the room even when they were having sex.

He drew and drew and time after time he failed.

Lying wide awake beside Julie that night, Jonathan thought about the dogs. Maybe they were suffering from melancholy. He stared at the ceiling. Or what if it wasn't psychological at all, but physical? He'd heard that dogs sometimes developed distemper, and though it seemed a likely diagnosis, he had no idea what distemper actually was. First thing in the morning he'd google the symptoms. Or maybe he should take them to the vet anyway, just to be safe. He glanced at the bedroom door and through the glass panel saw Sissy staring in at him sadly.

Jonathan sighed, got out of bed, and took his pillow and a blanket out to the couch. Julie found him there the next morning, sleeping on his side, his arm encircling the spaniel whose face nestled in the warm space beneath his chin.

7

In one or two ways, Jonathan enjoyed working at Comrade. It was a friendly place, united in general agreement that everyone who worked there was young, attractive, fashionable, underpaid, exploited, and full of existential rage. The work! The clients! The overall, devastating, crushing triviality of it all! Aside from that it was fine.

But today an odd atmosphere prevailed. No one looked up when Jonathan arrived, as if they all cared so much about their projects that even his expensive new replica Tour de France yellow jersey wasn't worthy of the scant three seconds it would take to deride. Alarm bells rang in his head. Having clomped over to the men's room to change, he swiveled back across the waxed floor in his retro Jack Purcells, shrieking rubber. No one stirred. His heart began to pound. Had they all been fired? Had someone died? Had everyone died? Was he dead? Was this hell?

He called Louise Crimple to make sure Broadway Depot hadn't fired the agency.

"Louise!" he said when she picked up.

"Jonathan!" she answered.

"Anything going down in your neck of the woods?"

"We're on fire!"

Did she mean literally? "That's fantastic, Louise."

"What've you got for me, John? Fan my flames, lover-boy!"

Oh Lord. "Will do, Lou." The hollow sound at the end of the phone told him she had already hung up.

This morning there was no sign of Ed. Or Shay. Were they at it already? Before 10 a.m.? Jonathan became dimly aware of agitated voices floating in from the direction of HR. What was going on?

His morning coffee came in a paper bag that he crumpled stentoriously, humming Bruckner's Te Deum at the top of his lungs, thinking all the while of those monks who can sing two notes at once and wondering if they ever used their skill to harmonize Broadway musicals. Then he hurled the empty cup at the nearest wastebasket, missed, retrieved it, and tried again. No reaction. Even Max, his companion in worthless endeavor, appeared to be concentrating on his work. More than anything this terrified him.

He opened his morning Broadway Despot file and pretended to study it while e-mailing:

TO: max@comrade.com
FROM: jonathan@comrade.com
SUBJECT: What's going on?

Have I been fired? Are we all dead?

From a desk eleven inches to his left, Max replied:

TO: jonathan@comrade.com
FROM: max@comrade.com
SUBJECT: re: What's going on?

Strange comings and goings in these here precincts.
All most serious & mysterious.

At that moment, Shay came flying into the main office area clutching the genuine Russian communist-era industrial lamp that illuminated Ed's desk and hurled it against the far wall, exploding the bulb in a lethal shower of glass. Not content with the reaction (none) from Comrade employees, she grabbed a full coffeepot from the kitchenette, swung it around by the handle with both fists, and, at the last possible moment, released it, letting it fly more or less at a perfect diagonal across the office. This got a better reaction — all twenty-two members of the staff wrapped their arms around their heads as the glass orb filled with boiling coffee described a glorious parabola in slow motion through the air. It landed with a satisfying explosion against the metal door of the conference room just as Ed stepped through it.

Scattered applause broke out.

Jonathan's face was blank but his heart performed joyous gymnastics in his chest. Why wasn't every day like this? Wasn't this what life was about? Not staples and copy paper. Love, sex, loathing, despair, exploding coffeepots. This scene could encompass all nine circles of hell, or at the very least Lust (second circle), Greed (fourth), Wrath (fifth), Violence (seventh), and Treachery (ninth). Glorious sequences paraded through his imagination — the spinning glass orb, the magnificent impact. In his version, the coffeepot would fly up up up from the bowels of hell, through Earth's atmosphere, through the Milky Way, and at last to Alpha Centauri, spinning ever faster as the great star sucked the pot into its gravitational field. If only he could start work on it now.

"Ahem."

He looked up to find Shay standing over him. She held a large box crammed with her belongings and thrust it at him. "Downstairs," she said.

Jonathan got to his feet clutching the box, shot a glance at Ed (motionless and fuming in a sodden green silk suit dripping coffee), and exited the office as inconspicuously as possible while twenty of Comrade's twenty-two employees downloaded their exploding-coffeepot videos onto Facebook or watched it in multiple replay on their phones. It had already been tweeted under #another-boringdayattheoffice and was in danger of going viral as Shay led Jonathan out, her tote bag crammed full of brand-new office supplies and the company laptop. She threw her shoulder against the huge industrial-steel door with impressive force and said nothing until they reached the sidewalk.

"Taxi." It was an order.

He didn't have an arm free but was quite proud of his whistle. Two cabs pulled up simultaneously and Shay shoveled her belongings into the larger, spat an address at the driver, and, as Jonathan leaned in to bid her farewell, slammed the door in his face and sped off.

He stood gazing at the hole she'd left in his narrative and then trudged back upstairs to work. Ed had disappeared. Gillian and Roger from sales were sweeping up shards of glass and mopping up coffee. A game of badminton had broken out accompanied by a techno-beat mix blasting out of someone's computer. Jonathan sat down and opened his e-mail. There was the usual crap about work, but he clicked the all-staff memo first.

TO: all staff
FROM: management
SUBJECT: SNOW DAY

It had been typed on Shay's account but probably not by Shay. No further message was required.

By midmorning, badminton had run its course and the entire office retired to Guns Ammo Liquor, a grubby nearby bar with extremely attractive price points on a wide range of alcoholic beverages. By noon, Jonathan was drunk. By four he could hardly stand, but it didn't matter because he was the messiah and could crawl on water. He managed to get home by five, stepped through the door, and collapsed in the hall.

His dogs sidled up to sniff him, then

retired to the living room. Jonathan thought he heard disgusted whispering.

"He's pixilated."

"Maybe just very tired?"

He fell asleep and dreamed of flying to Alpha Centauri in an astronaut suit with a coffeepot on his head, waking with a start and a terrible hangover a few hours later when Julie arrived home. She stepped over the crumpled figure at her feet, returning with a cup of coffee, two aspirin, and two dogs on leashes. The night air revived him enough to wash down half a box of Oreos with a can of beer before collapsing into bed.

"Nice day?" Julie asked.

"It started well," he said, edging up against her. She slid deftly out of his grasp and he sighed, realizing that action was not in the cards. With a pounding headache, a queasy stomach, and a sense of deep resignation, Jonathan decided he'd sleep better on the couch. Sissy waited till he was stretched out under the blanket before hopping delicately up beside him, burrowing under the covers, and settling in, her back against his chest. Dante remained on the floor all night, head on paws like a temple guard. Jonathan awoke at 5 a.m. with a raging thirst and a bad case of melancholia.

8

Comrade bore no signs of yesterday's fracas. Ed co-opted the unpaid intern to act as his PA until Shay could be replaced. With laudable efficiency, she had already procured a new lamp and coffeepot, created an all-staff memo that took issue with the previous day's snow emergency, pointing out blandly (and presumably with Ed's direction) that there had not, in fact, been any snow.

Ed looked glum, particularly when Wes, account director and unofficial head of Human Resources, appeared at his desk shortly after 10 a.m. and dragged him off — if not by the ear, then by the moral equivalent.

Wes was very tall and very thin with long thick frizzy hair worn in a low ponytail. He attended every client meeting no matter how big or small. Much esteemed by Comrade's clients, he didn't talk about strategies going forward or USPs or paradigms, didn't agree with everything the clients said, nor did he blindly defend work that came from his own staff. If Comrade failed to declare bankruptcy each April 15, it was the sole responsibility of Wes, who had something of a hippie Mafia don about him, a mild friendly manner that slipped on like a tie-dye shirt over a core of refrigerated steel. Rumor had it he was an ex–Green Beret and spent three hours every evening practicing kickboxing.

Jonathan liked Wes, who seemed almost like a real person. In *The New York Inferno,* Wes ruled the fourth circle of hell, presiding fairly and rather sternly over Greed, hands on hips in a black T-shirt and jeans, his bushy ponytail streaming behind him like a pennon.

Though no one overheard the conversation between Ed and his head of accounts (not for lack of trying), the majority assumed that Wes had belatedly pointed out that shagging your PA in the office every lunch hour and then giving her cause to storm out in a rage was not impressive management behavior and he'd be lucky if she didn't get herself a lawyer and sue the pants off the company.

Ed returned to his desk looking glummer than ever, left the office before lunch, and didn't come back. His new unofficial PA spent the rest of her day reading magazines, taking phone messages, and doling out shots to the thirsty from Ed's private bar. At four, she went out and came back with a huge box of doughnuts, which she passed around; when anyone said, "Thanks," she replied, "Thank Ed. It's on his account." Once all the doughnuts were gone she stood on her chair, rolled her magazine up like a megaphone, and told everyone to take the rest of the day off. Jonathan was actually starting to love his job.

The next morning the unpaid intern was gone, Ed had returned to his office, and all hands were on deck. This was a shame, obviously, but Jonathan cheered up considerably when he received an e-mail as follows:

TO: jonathan@comrade.com
FROM: max@comrade.com
SUBJECT: New blood

Check out the waiting room.

Jonathan got up and circled the office to get a better look while half pretending to do a thing that needed doing.

He ran into Max circling in the other direction and did a smart one-eighty to march shoulder to shoulder with his comrade. By silent mutual consent, they both came to a halt, staggered by the sheer weight of weird in the reception area. A stormy-faced Ed appeared, ushering an exquisite girl in the shortest denim shorts either had ever seen, followed closely by Wes. Jonathan caught the look of desolation on Ed's face and the perfect clarity of Wes's "no" as the girl disappeared out of Comrade's doors forever and Wes extended his hand to clasp that of the next applicant.

"Lark Rise Heaven Halo," the applicant said.

Jonathan stared. He and Max turned to look at each other. Lark Rise Heaven Halo was a name? Who called their child Lark Rise Heaven Halo? How did a kid get through life with a name like Lark Rise Heaven Halo? Jonathan supposed that these days it wouldn't be so bad. Her classmates would be called things like Stetson, Mona Lisa, Jedi, and Albania. Did this name thing mean the end of the world was nigh? It had to mean something. Everyone was behaving as if having a person called Lark Rise Heaven Halo in reception was somehow normal.

Names had begun to piss him off. Jonathan, for instance, was a name. Ed, on the other hand, had changed his name to Eduardo, which was not a name unless you were born in Mexico, Uruguay, or Andalucia. It was particularly not a name if you grew up in Larchmont, New York, the son of two Jewish accountants who, Jonathan happened to know, were called Naomi and Joseph Netzky. It had been obvious even when they were kids that Ed and Ben Netzky were destined to become corporate lawyers in White Plains, but Ed had strayed, starting up a small marketing company in downtown New York, growing his Jewish hair into a Fidel Castro afro, and changing his name from Ed Netzky to Eduardo Navarro. All of which made him much cooler than the average Jew from Larchmont — cool enough, apparently, to buy a loft in Williamsburg, drive a vintage Merc, and poke his PA over lunch. Jonathan idly wondered what name Eduardo went by when he returned to Larchmont for High Holy Day services.

Within days of graduating, Max facebooked Ben (now firmly ensconced in law school), begging for Ed's contact details and a dollop of nepotism. Once Max had a job, it was only a matter of time before Jonathan arrived at the adjacent desk. Max's background in politics and Jonathan's in graphic design qualified them equally for the non-skills required for success at Comrade. Eduardo's strategy was to hire good-natured, fun-loving, intelligent young people at entry-level salaries to exploit and betray until they lost the will to live, became despondent, and quit. Max and Jonathan fit the bill perfectly, though Max — to his credit — had bigger plans.

"I'm going to outlast the bastard," he said. "Ed'll be up in front of the Federal Trade Commission, I'll be the last Comrade standing, and the business will fall into my outstretched hand like a ripe pear. Low-hanging fruit, Jay, low-hanging fruit."

Jonathan couldn't really understand why such fruit, no matter where it hung, would enter anyone's dreams. His fantasy — faint, far off, and unlikely to be realized — was to make a living one day from something he liked doing.

He returned to his desk. "Two for the price of one on all extension cords!!! In-boxes half-price!!! Neon highlighters $1.25 when you spend $10!" Despair settled around his kidneys. "Lined notebooks: 3 for $7, one day only!!!" Why did they have to shout everything? He felt like shouting "Heaven Halo!" but didn't.

An hour later, a new e-mail arrived from Max:

TO: jonathan@comrade.com
FROM: max@comrade.com
SUBJECT: New PA Alert

Wes won. Look.

Jonathan looked. And saw a medium-height being with short bleached hair, jeans, biker boots, and a white leather jacket shaking hands with Wes, who appeared delighted, while a frowning Eduardo repeatedly swung his foot at the wall like a sullen child. The medium-height being was patently not Eduardo's type. In fact, so androgynous was s/he, it would be hard to know whose type it was.

TO: max@comrade.com
FROM: jonathan@comrade.com
SUBJECT: re: New PA Alert

Sex?

TO: jonathan@comrade.com
FROM: max@comrade.com
SUBJECT: re: re: New PA Alert

No thanks. I'm good.

TO: max@comrade.com
FROM: jonathan@comrade.com
SUBJECT: re: re: re: New PA Alert

What sex is the new PA?

Jonathan glanced over at Max, who shrugged.

After a few seconds, he had a response:

TO: jonathan@comrade.com
FROM: max@comrade.com
SUBJECT: re: re: re: re: New PA Alert

No sex would seem to be the point.

The new PA was called Greeley. Whether Greeley was male or female had been carefully obscured by his/her manner of dress and demeanor, not to mention a haircut reminiscent of one you'd give a ten-year-old boy back in 1975. Cowlick and all.

Max wasn't much impressed, but Jonathan fell immediately in love. He loved Greeley's sexual ambiguity as another man might love an hourglass figure or a head of golden curls. There was an air of calm about Greeley, a complete disregard for disclosure that caused Jonathan to feel faint. He

80

wondered if this made him gay or straight. He'd have to remember to ask Greeley what sex s/he was.

An e-mail came around that afternoon announcing that Greeley would be starting on Monday. Not Adam Greeley or Olive Greeley. Just Greeley. No other information was advanced. Jonathan googled "Greeley" and received the helpful result that it was a Home Rule Municipality, the county seat and the most populous city of Weld County in northern Colorado, situated forty-nine miles north-northeast of Denver. But it didn't matter. Greeley was amazing.

He went home and took the dogs for a long walk across to Chelsea and the Waterside Dog Run, then back again, stopping to buy liver cookies at the dog bakery on 22nd, observing his pets carefully as they walked. He knew he was working hours that left them alone too long, worried that they were bored, that they were finding unconventional ways to pass the time. He felt certain they were moving things around the apartment — hiding his shoes, rifling through the kitchen cupboards, eating important papers out of his files. He was positive that the large jar of peanut butter in the kitchen had been unopened yesterday when he left for work. And what about the unfamiliar purchases that popped up on his PayPal account? He hadn't seen his American Express card in days; had Dante eaten it?

Something had to be done. When one of his neighbors looked at him with admiration and asked how he'd managed to teach the dogs to *do that,* he smiled nervously and walked past without inquiring further. Surely they weren't going out on their own during the day? You didn't often see unaccompanied dogs cruising Manhattan.

Jonathan sighed. He needed professional help. Especially now that Julie was here. She wouldn't take kindly to scandal, crisis, or catastrophe of the canine variety. As their owner and benefactor it was his responsibility to arrest untoward events before they happened.

He imagined the dogs watching from the window as he set off to work, letting themselves out, walking on two legs, meeting friends uptown, ordering cappuccinos, raiding the bins behind Texas BBQ East, and chasing fat urban rats in the park. While he slaved away on Broadway Depot, they frolicked along the rooftops of the East Village, singing chim-chiminey, chim-chiminey, chim chim cher-oo, practicing their parkour and spying on cats.

He looked down at them trotting quietly

by his side and felt a rush of affection. Clever dogs.

With a large take-out bag from Wong Wei Garden, he headed home. Julie had already arrived. He fed the dogs and they trailed off to their beds, set carefully in front of the TV.

"You spoil those animals," Julie said.

"Mmm." He didn't want to have this conversation. The instant Julie realized how out of control he was in the dog arena, she would bring in the auditors: trainers, dog walkers, books on animal behavior, disciplinary regimes, homeopaths, dog shrinks, Cesar Millan. When that all failed, he would come home to find Temple Grandin in the kitchen sipping a Diet Coke and telepathing his pets. In the meantime, the dogs would probably organize some kind of revenge scenario, it would cost him a fortune in consulting fees, plus he'd have to take sides either against the dogs or against Julie . . . his brain wouldn't let him follow this line of discourse.

Jonathan wished he had a girlfriend who was more dog-friendly or dogs that were more girlfriend-friendly.

Julie said, "Get some plates," in a tone that meant, *Stop running through unlikely scenarios in your head.*

Over dinner they discussed a weekend away to celebrate their reunion, for which Julie had put together a list of options. "Feel free to add anything you like," she said.

As he listened to her describe cozy Vermont inns and short breaks on Sanibel Island, he wondered what they'd do with the dogs. You couldn't just leave them with a pile of food and have someone look in occasionally. It occurred to him that this was his big chance to get them out into the woods to dig holes in loam, to run with them along the beach inhaling great lungfuls of salt air. They'd be happy, all three of them, four including Julie, which he kept forgetting to do.

"What about them?" he blurted, indicating Sissy and Dante.

Julie waved a hand dismissively. "There are dog hotels," she said. "Or maybe we know someone who'll come in and stay with them. Max could bring one of his floozies. They're not a factor."

Not a factor? Dante's ears flicked forward. He wore his usual inscrutable expression, but Jonathan had a tiny glimpse of the dog behind the mask. Julie was talking about a reasonably priced little condo near the beach in Sanibel involving a flight to Fort Myers and a rental car which might be a bit much for a long weekend but on the other hand there was weather there that would make the whole thing worthwhile not to mention shells.

Not a factor?

"What about Vermont?" he suggested a bit desperately, wondering if any of the cozy inns took pets.

She glanced at him sharply. "You're thinking of the dogs, aren't you?"

"Couldn't we all go together? You could get to know them better."

Julie sighed. "Vermont's good," she said. "If that's what you want. It's doable." She pulled out her laptop and clicked open a file. "These are some of the best inns," she said. "Will we want to ski? There's still good snow. I checked. And excellent antiquing."

The use of "antique" as a verb made Jonathan shrink like a salted slug. He glanced around his apartment, picturing a seventeenth-century sideboard made of age-blackened oak flanked by two intricately carved elm chairs that had cradled the flatulent bottoms of long-dead English lords. A grand crystal chandelier swayed dangerously from the 1950s dropped ceiling, illuminating the top of a gigantic mahogany dinner table looted from a southern slave plantation. He could easily imagine

Julie arranging peonies in a charming hand-painted chamber pot that some stranger had shat in for decades.

"Jonathan."

"Yes, Julie?"

"Focus."

He looked at her. "I am focusing. Do any of these places take dogs? I really think they'd enjoy a little getaway to the country. They spend all their time cooped up. We could go for walks."

"I spend all my time cooped up too," Julie said, glaring at Dante. Turning to Jonathan, her expression softened. "We've been apart for months. I was hoping for some us time. Just us."

Sissy's brow furrowed sadly.

"Look, I've done all the groundwork. Why don't you have a flip through the options and let me know what you decide."

"But . . ."

"I'll send you the file."

"What file?"

"The Jonathan file."

He craned his neck and saw a file on her desktop marked JONATHAN.

He was a file?

What else was stored in the Jonathan file? Did Julie keep a record of how often they had sex or who paid for each meal? Were

86

his vital statistics listed next to those of all her exes? Perhaps she was looking for some golden ratio of limbs to IQ or shoe size to sexual prowess. Maybe there was a list of qualities she sought in a boyfriend, with checkmarks next to those he just about managed to live up to. Were there pictures? Shots of him in compromising positions? Would she use them to porn-spam his friends if they ever broke up? He began a new story in his head called *The Jonathan File,* and its companion piece, *The Book of Julie.*

"Jonathan," she said, with a resigned glance at her boyfriend. "There's no point talking to you when you're thinking of other things. I've got to go back to the office. We close our non-white-weddings issue tomorrow and there's still tons to do."

Jonathan didn't beg her to stay. He did walk her back to her office in Chelsea, but the dogs were obstructive, tangling their leashes around Julie's legs, crossing in front of her to lunge at an imaginary sandwich, barking threateningly at a heavily armed policeman, and challenging a huge mastiff held on a string by a wisp of a teenage girl. They strained to get at the beast, who stiffened and growled ominously. The teensy girl patted his head.

"It'th betht," she lisped in their general direction. "It'th betht if you don't annoy him."

Jonathan hauled on their leashes.

They hurried on.

At the corner of 14th and Tenth he kissed his girlfriend goodbye while Dante stole the limelight by squatting in the center of the sidewalk and spooling out the world's longest butt snake. Julie looked at him, at his owner, closed her eyes slowly, entered the office building, and swiped her card through security. She didn't turn to wave.

9

Greeley stopped every one of Comrade's twenty-two employees as they arrived each morning and asked how they were, recording the answers in a small orange notebook.

"What are you doing?" Jonathan asked, having told Greeley that he was "Fine, absolutely fine."

"Just keeping a few notes to help me understand your situation." Greeley maintained a neutral expression that was neither friendly nor unfriendly; quite Zen, in fact, as if Comrade were merely a resting place on the way to a higher level of consciousness. Jonathan felt his heart lurch.

What *was* his situation? He wasn't sure. At the moment it involved an inability to stop staring at Greeley: Greeley with the clear skin and gray eyes, the sturdy ambiguity. In Jonathan's *The New York Inferno,* Greeley would hover over all civilization, arms and legs crossed, expression inscrutable, emitting beams of light embroidered in glittering silver and gold.

"We're so happy you're here," Jonathan said, forgoing his usual feeble joke about Siberian labor camps. "I think . . ." He paused. "I think in some way we've been waiting for you." He felt pleased that this minor exchange caused Greeley to nod and smile.

With Greeley's arrival, the atmosphere at Comrade changed, beginning with a 4 p.m. break for green tea, dark chocolate, and tai chi. Greeley knew the whereabouts of every employee at every moment of the day, a completely new phenomenon that prevented the erratic hours and random excursions to which a substantial percentage of staff were prone.

Greeley further knew who was in therapy, whose boyfriend had cheated on him or her, whose search for love was proving futile, who actually worked and who spent all day looking at videos of kittens or pussy online. It all went into the orange notebook that Greeley took everywhere and frequently annotated.

None of this would have revolutionized Jonathan's life except that within a week of the new PA starting work, they ran into each other in his neighborhood.

"Jonathan!"

Greeley called from across the street, trotted over, and made a great fuss, first of Dante, then of Sissy, in proper order of dominance. "You didn't tell me you had dogs."

"No. Well, I do. I mean, they're not really mine, my brother left them with me when he went to work in Dubai. You didn't tell me you lived in my neighborhood."

"They're beautiful." Greeley and Dante stared at each other with a peculiar intensity that for a moment made Jonathan slightly uncomfortable. "Why don't you bring them to work?"

"To work?"

Greeley shrugged. "We need an office dog, and these two shouldn't be left at home all day."

"But . . . that would be totally amazing." Jonathan wondered if Greeley had somehow guessed how much it bothered him to leave the dogs at home. "If you're sure? Don't we need to check with Eduardo?"

"Nope. Bring them Monday. It'll be good for the office. Dogs settle the karma."

"Fantastic!" Jonathan's mood soared. It would be such a load off his mind not to have to shut the door on the dogs every morning. He felt depressed leaving them alone for so long. And besides, this way he'd have a better idea of what they got up to all day. "Did you hear that?" The dogs were excited, barking and jumping around. "You're coming to work with me! We'll bring beds and a water bowl!" He could walk them at lunch, and when he was busy other people would pay attention to them. It was a perfect solution to the dog problem. An enormous weight rose from his chest; he was so excited at this new development that he threw his arms around Greeley and left them there slightly too long. Greeley smiled inscrutably, returned the hug with quiet equanimity, released Jonathan, and melted into the crowd.

Talking to Julie later that night, Jonathan didn't mention his big news. Nothing else of note had happened that day, so it was a definite omission, but he couldn't bring himself to have a whole discussion about how the dogs would get him fired, how his career was probably doomed — more doomed, even, than before. He told her at last, casually, in the middle of a conversation about something altogether else, hoping she wouldn't notice.

She noticed. "You're taking the dogs to work?"

"They won't be alone all day and I'll walk

them there and back. It solves everything."

"Not everything," Julie said ominously. And then, after a pause, "When exactly is James taking the dogs back?"

Not really very soon, Jonathan thought. He wished his term of residence with the dogs had begun earlier, or that Julie had stayed slightly longer in Chicago. Should he have asked her permission for them to come live with him? There was no real point, as he couldn't exactly have refused his brother. Anyway, he was used to them now, and had trouble imagining life without them. There were four of them in the relationship, only Julie didn't seem to be facing up to that fact. To her the dogs were merely a temporary inconvenience.

Jonathan had been with Julie for nearly four years and the dogs for less than four weeks. But the dogs seemed somehow intimately connected to this new stage of his life, this stage of being financially independent and responsible.

He very much wanted to be the sort of man Julie would love, but increasingly wondered if, by virtue of something fairly basic in his nature, this might not be possible. As a couple, they tended to flow along smoothly in an ever-so-slightly downhill direction, like wastewater.

It didn't help that Julie hated his best friend. This hadn't been so much of a problem when Max lived in another state and went to another college, but now that they were all in one place the fault lines deepened.

"He's totally promiscuous — and not in the good way," Julie said, while Jonathan found himself considering "Promiscuity: The Good Way." She hated that he helped himself to whatever was in the fridge when he came over, and borrowed money from Jonathan that he generally forgot to pay back.

"He makes as much money as you do. More, probably."

"It's not stealing," Jonathan explained. "He just forgets."

Julie crossed her arms and glowered.

"We've been friends since fourth grade," Jonathan offered by way of explanation. "He got me my job."

It had never occurred to Jonathan or Max that a woman might come between them. They'd played cowboys and Indians and hide-and-seek together, shared their first cigarette and first spliff. They'd been as close as brothers for as long as either could remember and were determined to be each other's best man and read the eulogy at each other's funeral. Until Julie came along.

The list of Max's characteristics that she disliked was not short. He had dreadlocks (which repelled her), a new girlfriend every few weeks (disgusting), drank to excess (irresponsible), and found weddings in any form hilarious.

"Monogamy," he pronounced, "was invented by some poor loser who couldn't get any, so he made a rule that no one else gets any either."

Julie's face was a mask of disbelief. "You," she pronounced back, "are a Neanderthug."

"A Neanderthug?" Max grinned with delight. "Why yes, I believe I am. That's why they love me. That, and being magic in bed."

Julie gagged.

Jonathan chose between them at last, choosing Julie because she was willing to have sex with him and Max wasn't.

"It's nothing personal, Max. We can still get together without her."

Max had looked sorrowful. "You are so barking up the wrong tree here, man. She couldn't be more wrong for you."

"Really?" Jonathan was taken aback. He recognized that she was a little conventional, but was Max saying that Julie couldn't be more wrong if she were, say, a Libyan arms trader? If she were a militant lesbian, or didn't believe in evolution?

"Trust me," Max said. "It's my specialty subject. She's the kind of girl you wake up from screaming."

Jonathan had never imagined he'd be cool enough for a girl like Julie Cormorant, or that he'd ever have a girlfriend who was so much like a grown-up. But after all this time together, he was beginning to wonder if Max had a point. He felt exhausted by the effort his inferiority imposed upon them as a couple. He'd always thought you could stop trying to impress your girlfriend after a while, but it hadn't gone that way with Julie. The Jonathan file was, as far as he was aware, a new wrinkle in their relationship, and it made him uneasy. He didn't like being a file, and couldn't stop obsessing over his day-to-day ratings.

"That's not what it's for, Jonathan," she said. But he didn't really believe her. Once, he stopped in the middle of sex, worried that his performance might be substandard and that she'd be recording tonight's puny effort on a graph.

She looked up at him. "What?"

"Nothing."

"Nothing?"

He was silent.

"Jonathan. Please tell me you're not thinking about the file. I wish I'd never mentioned it."

"I'm not thinking about it," he lied.

But when it became obvious that whatever he was thinking about, it wasn't her, Julie sighed and turned over in bed. She wasn't the sort of person to dwell on how often and how thoroughly they had sex, but she had begun to notice that whatever sex they did have was increasingly rare and frequently unsatisfactory. Worse, it nearly always involved the presence of dogs.

10

Friday night after work they met at their local French bistro.

"How'd the non-white-wedding issue go?" Jonathan was genuinely curious.

Julie pushed the magazine across the table at him. "We've got loads more online. It's our biggest advertising success ever."

He flipped through page after page of brides, stopping at a beautiful girl in a creamy brownish sort of draped-silk gown.

Julie followed his eyes. "Fig," she said. "See? I told you."

Fig. It was almost the color, not only of the girl's dress, but of her skin, and though he knew that all the models were airbrushed and polished, that each was probably less interesting and more narcissistic than the next, still he couldn't stop his mind leaping forward to the future he might have with this kind, intelligent girl in the fig-colored dress, the girl with the fig-colored skin and the somewhat darker than fig-colored eyes and hair. She smiled at him from the pages of the magazine and whispered that she liked his peculiar sense of humor and wanted desperately to spend her life with him. They'd have funny, clever, unconventional babies with modern names like Newton (Fig Newton) and Leaf (Fig Leaf). She would model a bit when she wasn't being a theoretical physicist and would insist he quit his horrible job at Comrade.

"Don't worry, my darling, I'll support you as long as you need me to," she whispered, nuzzling him with her figgy lips and gazing at him with her figgy eyes.

"Hello? Helloo?" Julie waved a hand in front of his face. To prove his lack of obsession with Miss Fig, he flipped forward to another beautiful girl in another beautiful dress. This one had titanium hair and a wedding gown in a gentle shade of titanium with a wide cuff of titanium metal around one arm. Miss Titanium did nothing for him. She left him as cold as an Adélie penguin eating ice cream in Alaska. He wondered what Miss Fig was doing right now in the middle of the magazine, or might do with him if they ever got a chance to run away together to some enchanted figgy land.

He tried to imagine Julie as the figgy love

of his life, in vain. Instead, he saw her in a Valkyrie helmet with horns and a wedding dress of chain mail, striding down Broadway scattering pedestrians and cars. He imagined her ten feet tall with fire in her eyes and her beautiful shiny hair flowing out behind her.

Julie pulled the magazine away and stared at him for a moment. "You didn't used to be like this," she said.

"Didn't I?" Jonathan was genuinely puzzled.

"No. You used to be less weird."

"Really?" He didn't remember ever being less weird than he was right now. In fact, as far as he could tell he had always been more or less exactly as weird as this, if not more so. If anyone was changing, it was Julie, who seemed to be moving toward some abstract ideal of a thrusting young New Yorker. "I'm sorry," he said, taking her hand. He truly wanted to be what she wanted him to be. It would be so much less trouble.

Julie ordered a crêpe for dessert, and when it came it looked wrong: pale and crumpled. She pointed this out to their not-at-all French waiter and he looked sorrowful.

"Ah, madame, a mistake. I offer you my humblest apologies." Despite having been born somewhere within a stone's throw of central Warsaw, the waiter pronounced it "umblest apple-oh-gees" and swept the crêpe away with an exaggeratedly Parisian flourish.

Jonathan felt sad when the crêpe was taken away for disposal. He felt an affinity with it, the badly cooked glutinous thing that Julie rejected. The second dessert arrived looking golden-crisp and perfect and Julie attacked it with gusto while Jonathan imagined getting the first crêpe back from the kitchen, taking it home, and showering upon it the love and attention it sorely lacked.

She paid the bill (did that go into the Jonathan file?) and they went home. He walked the dogs while she read a book. Later they had sex while Jonathan concentrated on images of Miss Fig to avoid thoughts of the Jonathan file. When they finished, they went to sleep.

Julie worked most of the weekend and Jonathan met up with Max.

"You should have seen Miss Fig," he told Max. "Girl of my dreams."

"I thought Julie was the girl of your dreams."

"You know what I mean." Jonathan glared at Max.

"Respect, pal, but I have no idea how you

get off on pictures of brides. Nothing throws the libido into reverse like a bouquet, in my experience." He looked thoughtful. "Maybe a nun. But maybe not. I'd have to go case by case."

At 3 a.m. Monday morning, Jonathan was awakened by a nose in his face. It merged with his dream about a girl in a fig-colored dress, and he reached out for it, caressing Miss Fig's gorgeous floppy fig-colored ears.

"What?" he whispered, blinking awake. "What do you want? Do you need to go out?" But Sissy didn't want to go out. She just smiled her loving smile at him and padded off into the night.

She's excited, Jonathan thought. She's excited about coming to work. She's excited and happy and can't sleep. No more weltschmerz, he thought. We're all going to get along. We're all going to be happy.

Beside him, Julie Cormorant slumbered silently, her hair spread across the pillow like the feathers of a beautiful dark bird. Jonathan slipped silently out of bed and spent the rest of the night working on a new section of the *Inferno* at his drawing table.

When the alarm went off at seven, he slid back into bed beside Julie. She leaned against him and he wondered if anything else mattered as long as they could be together like this. I am going to do better, he thought. I'm going to make a great success of Broadway Depot, act normal at all times, keep Julie and Max separate, and not give Ed any reason to fire me. I am going to make everything work for Julie and me. And the dogs. And Comrade.

It was all going to turn out just fine.

11

Jonathan walked to work with the dogs. It took much longer than cycling but he saw more, browsed in more shop windows, smiled at more people (especially the ones who admired his dogs), and had more time to think. He missed his flying commute and enjoyed the leisurely bustle in equal measure. Life on a bike was all speed and adrenaline, but maybe he needed to slow down, maybe it was good for him to take more of an interest in life on the street, make eye contact with strangers, nod at the smokers on the sidewalk. New York looked like a whole different city when it wasn't zooming past his peripheral vision.

When he arrived at Comrade he felt slightly panicked. What if Greeley had forgotten the invitation? What if the dogs weren't really welcome after all?

But Greeley received them graciously, produced a box of organic antler sections for them to chew on, and suggested that their two new sheepskin mats go in the area behind Jonathan's desk.

"They can have a quiet escape there," Greeley said, "and if they want to be more sociable, there's the whole office to explore."

The dogs were a hit.

When Wes emerged from a meeting with Ed in a state of extreme psychic tension, Sissy sat down beside him, put her head on his knee, and wagged her stubby tail until he relinquished his scowl. Dante was better at tough love, breaking up overlong conference calls and herding people back to their desks.

Not everyone at Comrade loved dogs, but everyone loved Dante's firm leadership and Sissy's soft eyes. Everyone, that is, except Eduardo, who at first expressed outrage that animals had been welcomed into the office without his consent (and, worse, by the office PA, also hired more or less without his consent), then wanted to know why good karma required two dogs. He retired from the room, furious, when he discovered further that the dogs belonged to Jonathan and that they were so ordinary. "Isn't at least one of them a borzoi or a French bulldog?"

When Greeley assured him that no, neither was a borzoi or a French bulldog, his face clouded over.

"Why not?"

"The spaniel channels enthusiasm and energy," Greeley explained carefully. "The Border collie is the most intelligent of dogs. He sets an excellent example for the staff."

Max leaned over to Jonathan. "This place'll be a big comedown for him if he's that smart."

But Dante didn't seem to mind. Both dogs appeared to be perfectly at home at the center of a bustling ad agency.

As with all new employees, Dante and Sissy took a few days to get the full measure of the place. With perfect instincts for the most important person in the room, Sissy followed Greeley — standing when Greeley stood, lying at Greeley's feet, and only falling over onto her side in a doze when it became obvious that Greeley was planning to stay put for some time. Dante maintained his reserve, finding a spot by the boardroom from which he could keep tabs on office traffic. He lay with his head on his paws, eyes open, studying the actions of his flock — which members wandered, which needed prodding, which were vulnerable to predators.

Max knelt down to talk to Sissy. "What a

beauty, you're a beauty, aren't you, yes you are." He looked up at Jonathan. "I wish she could meet Rusty."

Jonathan nodded. Rusty had shared their childhood, always stinking of whatever he'd rolled in last. "How is Rusty?" Jonathan asked. "He must be getting pretty old."

"He's almost sixteen." The main reason Max went home these days was to see his dog. He tried to avoid the obvious fact that Rusty had grown old without him, Max, the boy who'd loved and cared for him and then left him behind in Larchmont as he set off for his new life. Despite the fact that Max's parents took perfectly good care of him, the abandonment was too sad for Max to contemplate. Now when he went home, Rusty would haul himself off his bed and walk stiffly to greet his old friend, tail wagging carefully, as if unsure whether to trust the possibility of happiness. Max would rub his ears and scratch the top of his hips, and Rusty would turn and stretch out his head with bliss and never once look at him with an expression that said, *Where have you been? I've been so unbearably lonely.*

Sometimes Max caught a similar expression on his mother's face.

Dante and Sissy seemed to relish having jobs. Jonathan watched, astonished, as

Dante (bred to organize crowds of significantly less intelligent creatures into streams of useful movement) herded people around the office. Anyone who lingered too long at the coffee machine would be gently nudged back to work. Statutory fire alarms, where no one showed any interest in obeying the shrieking bells, were his favorite. Sliding and crouching from comrade to comrade, he mobilized them into a tight, briskly moving flock. And if you'd asked about the subsequent muster, not a soul would have credited an external force for getting them out the door. Except, of course, for Greeley, who noticed everything.

In exchange for the reassuring sensation that the office had a leader at last, Comrade's employees showered their new supervisors with gifts. Two expensive new dog beds appeared at the office courtesy of Louise Crimple, to whom Jonathan had sent adorable pictures of his dogs sitting on Broadway Depot office chairs. He moved Dante's new bed to the entrance of the conference room; Sissy's fit neatly in the alcove behind his desk. He had to slash their official rations due to the doggie bags from expensive restaurants, slices of sirloin, leftover baked salmon with lightly steamed vegetables, braised marrow bones, and containers with the remains of wagyu burgers. They turned up their noses now at organic dog food, preferring (who wouldn't?) to dine on carefully packaged detritus from the restaurant capital of the world.

In addition to fine dining, they had two big walks a day, so Julie had less to complain about when they met up in the evening. Dog-tired from a long day ministering to their flock, Dante and Sissy flopped into bed and stayed there quietly until morning.

Jonathan slipped into a period of relative calm. Things with Julie seemed stable, the dogs were happy, and he was on track to make senior copywriter by the beginning of next year. With the salary increase, he might even be able to rent a bigger apartment.

For whole minutes at a time nothing went horribly wrong. Jonathan's shoulders untensed, and even Julie noticed that something about him had improved.

"You're standing up straighter," she said, almost admiringly. "I don't think of you as tall, but you nearly are."

"Was I hunched over before?"

She shrugged. "A little."

"Like the Hunchback of Notre Dame?"

"Yes."

"And gnarled?"

"Quite gnarled."

"Like a dwarf? Or a hobbit? How did you stand me?"

Julie giggled and loved him for the moment.

Jonathan had caught sight of himself in profile in a store window and noticed that he had indeed developed a slight defensive crouch. He wondered whether it was his job or life in general. Psychologically it seemed a tragic position to take, especially at his age. He should be striding bravely into the world, head up, shoulders back, loins girded, ready to wrestle the marketing world to its knees, thrust the razor-sharp sword of truth deep between its shoulder blades, and then stand over it, triumphant, while it slowly bled to death at his feet.

He'd been at Comrade nearly six months and felt he might at last be starting to pick up the rhythm of the place, convincing himself that he didn't actively despise the ads he wrote day after day, despite the fact that they required no creativity, no imagination, and no actual brainpower. Once or twice he even looked forward to a conversation with Louise Crimple, less for its surreal quality than for her relentless enthusiasm and the praise she lavished on his valueless endeavor.

More often he gazed into Sissy's big earnest eyes and wondered whether she could be trained to do his work for him. She'd be better in meetings: conciliatory, anxious to please, interested in what everyone had to say, eager to get ahead, not filled with inexpressible rage. She liked having a job, unlike her master, who still opened his Broadway Despot files each morning with a deep sense of dread, a fleeting impulse toward suicide, and a quickly suppressed vision of himself as a crêpe gone wrong, a sticky congealed heap of human dough.

"If you don't like your job, why don't you quit?" Julie asked.

Jonathan stared at her. "Quit? Don't you read the papers? Do you have any idea what it's like out there?"

Julie shrugged. "You could probably find something you liked better. What do you like better?"

How should he know what he liked better? "What's your dream?" everyone asked, like he might have some cherished desire to hop across the Russian steppes on a pogo stick and write a bestselling memoir about it. Follow your heart, people said. Follow it where?

After his team's weekly catch-up with Eduardo, Jonathan gathered the courage to ask if he might someday aspire to work on a different account, perhaps one that used one or two percent of his actual brain. Ed nodded in a serious manner, bridged his hands, and said, "Of course, Jonathan. It's just a matter of readiness. I'm afraid you're still finding your feet in marketing."

Finding your feet in marketing? Did the man dream in clichés?

Jonathan knew that the outcome of any meeting on the subject of his career prospects would be precisely zero. Ed would forget their conversation the instant Jonathan left his direct line of sight; before, probably. Why should he care, after all? If Jonathan quit his job, any sixth grader in New York could replace him.

12

Max was convinced that Eduardo was merely a frontman for Wes's vast drug-smuggling empire.

"Think about it. Wes finagles all the book-keeping that pays for Ed's Mercedes, his loft, his flavored condoms. You think he wants the IRS asking questions about how it's done? So he keeps his mouth shut, shows up at work every day, signs a few contracts, and presto! The money it raineth down upon him like rain."

Yeah, Jonathan thought bitterly, and *he* was still finding his feet in marketing.

In the early afternoon, Julie e-mailed to say she had an important question to ask, and could they meet after work?

They met at the neighborhood tapas bar where the sidewalk café allowed dogs. When Julie arrived, she stepped over Dante and Sissy with huge ostentation as if they were snoozing bison rather than two almost entirely flat creatures who could squeeze themselves into practically no space at all, something Julie never did.

"So?" Jonathan ordered two Spanish beers and a plate of chorizo and olives. "What's so important?"

Julie's features were composed.

"Well," she said. "The office wants to photograph a series of real people and real weddings for our next issue and they've asked me if I want to be in it."

"Great," Jonathan said, sipping his beer. "As a wedding guest or something?"

"Not really," she said. "As a bride."

He laughed. "As a bride? What, a fake wedding? That's hilarious! Do I get to be the fake bridegroom?"

Julie looked annoyed. "Not a *fake* wedding, Jonathan. Four double-page spreads in the magazine and a live-streamed online ceremony. A real wedding."

"Fantastic! So do you get to plan your own 'real' wedding?"

"Of course." She drummed her fingers. "I'm pretty clear about what I want."

"You are?" Jonathan was entranced by this thought. "And so, in this 'real' wedding, is there just, like, a big blank where the guy is supposed to be? I mean, could it just be, like, anyone?"

"Of course it can't just be anyone."

Jonathan was delighted. "What about me? Could it be me?"

Julie stared at her hands. "I was going to ask . . ."

"What? Ask if I'll do the crazy live-streamed wedding thingy with you? Do I get to keep the clothes? Oh my God, we'd have such a laugh. I wouldn't hear the end of it from Max. What's the most expensive suit I can have? Haha! Hello, Mom and Dad, I'm getting married . . ." He caught the look on Julie's face and stopped. "Wait. This is a fake-real wedding, right?"

Her face went blotchy and she looked as if she might cry. "Do you never listen? No, Jonathan. It is not a fake-real wedding."

"What?" The enormity of what she was saying took some time to sink in. "A real-real wedding? You want me to marry you online in public in a real-real wedding in order to provide a monthly feature for your stupid magazine? Are you serious? That's the craziest thing I've ever heard. It's totally insane."

"Forget it," she said, blinking rapidly. "Forget I ever mentioned it."

"Aw, Julie." He reached across the table and took her hand. "Talk to me a second."

He gazed at her intently. "Do you even love me?"

"Of course I love you, Jonathan. Why on earth else would I bother hanging around with you?"

What did she mean, she was clear about what she wanted for her wedding? How could you know what you wanted if you didn't even know who the groom was? Though now that she mentioned it, Jonathan had always known exactly what he wanted for his funeral, all the songs, and the food he'd serve, and who would and wouldn't be invited. But that made more sense. If you got hit by a truck you might not have time to think over the details, whereas no one got hit by a wedding truck. Until now, that is.

"This isn't just because they're offering you a free dress and catering, is it?"

"Of course not." She met his eyes. "But free is free. So if we were thinking of doing it, the timing would be great."

"Were we thinking of doing it?" It was all so sudden. What an idiotic lunatic concept, one that was bound to ruin his life and probably hers as well.

But just at that moment an impulse took him. A crazy impulse just to say yes, to do whatever crazy thing arose, because maybe

116

if you said yes to things that terrified you, your life would change direction, open up, get exciting. Why not marry Julie and become Jonathan Cormorant, or maybe Julie would become Julie Trefoil. Maybe they'd just keep their own names or combine them to be the Cormorant-Trefoils or the Trefoil-Cormorants. Or choose two completely different names, like Tomato-Gazelle. Whatever. Wouldn't it be nice to come home to a person you knew (and maybe even loved) every night for the rest of your life? No more stress about meeting the right person, no more doubts about the future. He liked the idea of embracing adulthood as a concept and not worrying too much about the fine print. Maturity was a planet he was anxious to explore, and it came with strange and mysterious perks he knew nothing about. Would he have to get a mortgage? Life insurance? It was all thrillingly unlikely — and yet something about it tantalized him. Get out, his brain said, leave adolescence behind! Engage with forever! Grow up, have kids who call you Mom and Dad. Borrow money. Buy a car. Have a career. Wear socks that match. Start saving for retirement. Die of old age. It all felt so wonderfully real.

"Okay," he said. "Let's do it."

Julie looked at him, her eyes damp. "Really?"

"Yup. Really."

She smiled tentatively. "You're sure?"

Sure? Of course he wasn't sure. He wasn't even somewhat unsure. He was entirely one hundred percent unsure. Still, who needed sure when you were channeling bold?

How did normal people cross the huge gulf between childhood and adulthood? He'd always assumed it would just happen — one day he'd wake up and find himself on the other side. But no, here he was, month after month, still floundering in no-man's-land. Maybe you had to leap, just decide one day you were going to get married, have kids, live in the suburbs, buy a people carrier, go the whole hog.

What was life, anyway, if not for leaping into with both feet? Unless of course life turned out to be a tar pit rather than a glorious Mediterranean sea, in which case he'd end up like those dinosaur fossils, preserved forever for some Natural History Museum of the future, filed under E for Extinct. He imagined the New York City tar pit, a kind of hell filled with the horribly inadequate: those who hadn't yet found their feet in marketing or were perpetually seeking love.

Jonathan grabbed Julie out of her chair by

both hands and swung her around the way he'd once seen in an ad for tampons. She managed to smile when he gathered her up in an enthusiastic embrace. "Mrs. Julie Jonathan Cormorant-Trefoil!"

"Mr. all that too," she said, a bit palely, trying to remain upright.

He turned to the three other people in the tapas bar. "We're getting married! This gorgeous creature and I are getting married. On the Internet! Live-streamed! So you're all invited!" The other people ignored him and Julie looked embarrassed. Sissy was on her feet dancing around them with joy. A party! A party!

Dante's expression was hard to decipher.

Jonathan hugged Julie close and whispered, "What an adventure this is going to be!"

"You're getting married?" Greeley seemed surprised.

"That's why I need a few days off. It's all pretty much arranged through *Bridal-360*, but I guess I do need to try on the clothes and show up on the big day." This struck Jonathan as hilarious and he began to laugh.

Greeley looked at him. "Have you two been together long?"

"Nearly four years. Long enough to know

I'm probably making a mistake." Jonathan's eyes were enormous, his hair askew. "But what's life for, if not making mistakes? How else do you grow? And it means a lot to her. Plus, being married is so amazingly grown up. I'm tired of being just some amorphous man-child thing."

Greeley said nothing for a moment. "I speak to you only as a representative of your employer, Jonathan. But, given that Comrade's interests rely to some greater or lesser extent on your sanity, do you really think it's a good idea to marry when you're already calling it a mistake?"

"Might be a mistake. Might be. Might not be. A good idea? Possibly. Probably not. But any idea will do at the moment." He leaned in close to Greeley and dropped his voice. "My life is stuck and sometimes you've just got to do something to get yourself free. Anything."

"It's an interesting philosophy," Greeley said.

Jonathan felt cheered. "You think so?"

"But wrong." Greeley paused. "And what about the dogs? I remember you saying something about your girlfriend not liking dogs."

"Hates them," Jonathan said. "Not all dogs, just mine. But that's part of the adventure. We're all going to have to learn to live, love, and laugh as one big happy family. And then when our children come along, they'll have to learn to live, love, and laugh with Julie and me and the dogs too. They'll have to call us Mommy and Daddy whether they want to or not. That's how it works in life."

Greeley pondered this statement for some time. "Could you just wait here a sec?"

Jonathan was happy to wait. Anything was better than writing office-supply ads. He waited, read the memos on Greeley's desk, and flicked idly through the diary that lay within arm's reach. Greeley reappeared, followed by Wes.

"I hear congratulations are in order," Wes said, holding out his hand. "This is a big step, you know."

"I know." Jonathan beamed. "I know."

"You're not doing this," Wes spoke carefully, "because you feel in any way that the misery of your professional life needs balancing with an act of spectacular drama in your private life?"

Jonathan looked pleased. "Why, yes, I think that's it exactly."

Wes nodded. "Because if that were the case, we might feel responsible for what turned out to be a grave personal error."

"Don't worry. I won't sue or anything."

"Nonetheless, we feel obliged to suggest . . ."

Jonathan wondered what Wes (and whoever else made up "we") felt obliged to suggest. That he not marry Julie so that Comrade could not be held responsible for any act of criminality resulting from a desperate marriage based on the hellishness of his employ? Surely it would be simpler to offer him a job that resulted in less desperation, thus obviating the wedding altogether.

But Wes seemed stalled. He stood with two fingers pressing his left temple contemplatively, frowning deeply.

"I don't mean to presume," Jonathan said. "But if you're actually so worried about me, maybe you could just give me another account to work on? Something slightly less soul-destroying?"

A complex conversation consisting entirely of non-verbal gestures followed. Wes glanced at Greeley, who nodded. Wes shrugged. Greeley tapped a finger on the desk.

Jonathan looked away so as not to eavesdrop.

Wes spoke at last. "Unfortunately, someone has to handle the Broadway Depot account. If not you, then some other poor bastard will be driven to marriage or possible suicide." He communicated a deep compassion that made Jonathan feel sad and happy at once — sad for his own situation, but happy that Wes respected him enough to speak frankly about the wretchedness of his job.

Greeley cleared his throat. "So, how shall we take this situation forward?"

Wes shuffled shiftily. "We could offer Jonathan a small raise."

All three stood in silence.

"How small?" Jonathan asked.

"Or," Greeley said, ignoring the question, "we could terminate your employment."

Wes looked surprised.

The thought of being fired filled Jonathan with happiness. "I'll have the raise," he said.

Greeley blinked.

"Excellent," said Wes. "We'll put the paperwork through today."

Jonathan returned to his desk. He wasn't entirely sure what had transpired. Had Wes offered him a bribe to cancel the wedding? An insultingly small bribe, at that? Did his acceptance of the raise mean that the wedding was off? No one had made the terms clear, and he hadn't signed anything. Well, he had slightly more money and no intention of calling off the wedding, so it seemed to be a triumph all around.

What, he wondered, were the ethics of accepting a raise based on an unreasonable interference in his personal life? And what if, at some time in the future, he slipped up and mistakenly referred to his wife? That would surely be a natural thing to do, once he had one. And also a dead giveaway that he hadn't adhered to the somewhat imprecise terms of the raise. Still, he needed the money and had agreed to the wedding, so his behavior seemed as moral as possible under the circumstances.

"Psst! What the hell is going on?" It was Max.

"I got a raise."

"Bastard," said Max. "Where's mine?"

"And Julie and I are getting married." There was something about telling his oldest friend the great news that made Jonathan ever so slightly nervous.

Max stared at him. "Married?"

"It seemed like the right decision at the time."

"Was someone threatening to throw a baby off a roof?"

Jonathan sighed. "I want to be grown up. I want life to start properly. I want a direction."

"And I want ten million dollars and the gift of flight."

"I want meaning, Max."

Max groaned. "What? A hundred years with Julie is going to give your life meaning? How dumb are you really?"

"You never liked her."

"She's fine, for someone. Not you. She's got no sense of humor. She wants you to be normal in ways you'll never be."

"I want that too." Jonathan felt exhausted suddenly. He put his head down on his desk and covered his face with his arm. "I really, really want that."

"No you don't, Jay, you asshole. Why would you swap your weirdo brain for one identical to every middle manager in New Jersey?"

Jonathan sat up. He looked sad. "I'm tired of being strange."

"Stranger than Julie? Stranger than Ed-fucking-uardo? Count your blessings, man." Max turned away in disgust.

Jonathan put his head down on his desk once more and wished that he and Max were still in the fourth grade and could go out to recess so he could give Max one of his chocolate cupcakes to make them friends again. Eventually, feeling infinitely tired, he left the office and went home. Julie was there already, making dinner.

"So," he said, kissing her hello. "How're

the plans for the funeral coming?"

"What funeral?"

"I didn't say funeral. I said how're the plans for the wedding coming?"

"You said funeral."

"I didn't."

"You did." Julie composed her features. "They're coming along fine."

"Aren't there lots of decisions to be made? Like flowers and guest lists and stuff?"

"The art director's taking care of everything. I've made suggestions, but she's basically on top of it — clothes, food, color schemes, etcetera. She's styled a thousand weddings and is looking for a special theme for us. She wants to talk to you."

"To me? Why?"

Julie sighed and tucked a strand of hair behind one ear. "It's your wedding too."

Jonathan felt pleasantly surprised. "It is?"

"You'll have to come up to the office one day next week."

"Okay."

"How's Tuesday? I'll double-check with Lorenza and get back to you."

Jonathan giggled.

"What's funny?"

"I don't know. Lorenza. It's just one of those names. Perfect for the art director of a funeral."

"Wedding."

"I *said* wedding."

"You didn't."

"I did."

They ate the rest of their meal in silence.

13

Dante awoke with a limp. Jonathan examined his feet and legs but could see nothing. On the way to work, the limp worsened; Dante winced whenever his left front paw touched the sidewalk. Jonathan stopped and called the vet. Iris answered.

"Hello, Iris. My dog is limping. He seems to be in pain."

"I can give you an emergency appointment. Is it an emergency?"

Jonathan glanced at Dante, who stood with one paw lifted off the ground, then at his watch. He sighed. "Yes, I guess it's an emergency."

"Can you come in now? Dr. Clare is on emergency duty."

Jonathan's heart sank. Dr. Clare, whose cold English soul dismissed the psychological subtleties of his dogs. Dr. Clare, who lacked the imagination to see that dogs might suffer from weltschmerz. Sighing, he doubled back to 11th Street, walking slowly with the limping Dante, was shown in, and only had to wait a few minutes for Dr. Clare to appear.

"Hello, Jonathan. What seems to be the matter?"

Jonathan suspected that her neutral tone hid a note of derision. He lifted Dante up onto the examination table. "It's his front left foot. He's developed a bad limp, just this morning. He's been whimpering, not putting weight on it. I wondered if he might have broken one of those little foot bones. Metatarsals. Phalanges. Whatever they're called. Or stepped on some glass. Do dogs get gout?"

Dr. Clare felt the foot, squeezing gently at first, then more firmly, manipulating the toes, bending the leg into a series of ligament- and tendon-flexing positions. Dante bore it all with perfect equanimity.

"He doesn't seem to be in pain," she said, examining the pads of his feet with a frown. "If it were a sliver of glass or a thorn, he'd react when I pressed." She repeated her examination on the other three feet. Nothing.

"Why don't you take him down and let me see him walk."

Jonathan lifted Dante off the table and

trotted him across the examination room with his leash hand held aloft, the way he'd seen on TV at the Westminster Dog Show. Dante trotted beside him without a hint of hesitation.

"I don't know what happened," he said, defeated. "Half an hour ago he couldn't walk."

Dr. Clare shrugged. "It could have been something caught between the pads. I once pulled a half-sucked wine gum out from between a dog's toes. That can be terribly painful. Whatever it was, it appears to have resolved itself."

Jonathan wondered what a wine gum was. "I'm sorry to have wasted your time."

She looked at him, surprised. "You haven't wasted my time. Your dog was in pain. You did exactly the right thing."

"I did?"

She nodded. "You did."

"You don't think he's a hypochondriac?"

"Of course I don't." She frowned. "Dogs don't think that way."

Jonathan looked at Dante. Dante looked back blandly.

Dr. Clare entered information into Dante's file on the computer. For a few seconds she tapped away at her keyboard. Then she stopped and turned to Jonathan.

"By the way, how's the dissatisfaction-with-life syndrome? You haven't mentioned it this time."

"Well," Jonathan said carefully, wondering if the question might be a trap, "it's actually much better. I take the dogs to work with me now."

"That's fantastic." Dr. Clare smiled at him.

"It is. But certain things still worry me."

"Like?"

"Like, they get up to things."

"What things?"

He looked at the floor. "Oh, just things. They eat my mail. Talk about me behind my back. Play sarcastic games with my girl-friend."

"Really?"

Jonathan nodded. "I sometimes think they're not happy with my dominion over their lives."

The vet blinked.

"I think maybe they'd prefer a better owner. Someone more accomplished."

She frowned again. "The whole thing about dogs is that, within fairly broad criteria, they love their owners. Dogs are loyal. Generally uncritical."

"Uncritical?" He thought about this. "No. I don't think so. Sissy, maybe." At the sound

131

of her name, Sissy padded over and laid her head on his knee. He lowered his face to the soft fur of her head.

Dr. Clare peered at him. "Jonathan? Are you okay?"

"I'm fine. It's the dogs."

"Is it?"

He said nothing for a long moment. "Life is confusing and stressful. Why wouldn't they suffer like the rest of us?"

"Because they're dogs," she said.

Jonathan considered this. Maybe she was right. Maybe she wasn't. Life seemed more confusing and stressful than usual lately. "Thank you for seeing Dante on such short notice," he said, getting to his feet. "I appreciate it."

"It's my pleasure," she said. "Bring them back if you have any other problems. And Jonathan."

"Yes?"

"Try not to worry so much."

That was easier said than done, Jonathan thought. He wondered if she was genuinely concerned about his dogs' psychological unrest or whether she was just happy that it was better than before. He supposed it didn't really matter. Even if she was just being nice, she was, after all, being nice.

He waited for the bill at reception, but

Iris reported that Dr. Clare hadn't charged him for the visit. He wanted to rush back and thank her for this unexpected kindness, but she was just closing the door behind her next patient.

He and the dogs set off, more briskly now, to work. Dante trotted by his side, limp-free.

Jonathan called his parents. "I'm getting married," he told them.

"I'll put your mother on," said his father, but his mother was already on the extension. He heard the click as his father hung up.

"Married? Well, that's not the call we were expecting," she said. "You're still coming for Dad's birthday this weekend?"

Oh shit. "Yes, of course. It's just that — I didn't want to spring the big wedding news on you in person." That sounded peculiar even to him. "I might have to bring James's dogs with me."

His mother tutted. "You can sleep in the guesthouse. Whom are you marrying, darling?"

"My girlfriend, Julie," he said. "Whom on earth else would I be marrying?"

There was a click and his father appeared back on the phone.

"We always suspected something like this would happen."

"Dad?"

"Breaking your mother's heart."

"But . . ."

"Years of trying to create a decent family working my fingers to the bone and what happens? One goes off to live with Arabs, and now this."

"I thought you liked Julie."

"Oh, Julie this, Julie that." There was a click as his father once more abandoned the conversation.

"She's a lovely girl, darling," his mother said. "We're very happy. Can't wait to see you." And then she too disappeared.

Jonathan hung up the phone with the usual sense of having been spectacularly wrong-footed. He could never pinpoint the exact moment at which things with his parents began to spin out of control, though he knew it was always shortly after "hello."

He called his brother in Dubai. "James. I'm getting married."

"How are the dogs?" James asked. "Are they okay?"

"The dogs are great. I'm getting married, though."

"That's fantastic news. Congratulations. Who to?"

"Why does everyone keep asking that? To Julie. Who else?"

"You never know these days. You might have met someone else. Whirlwind romance."

"Well, I haven't. It would be great if you could come. I'll e-mail the details."

"Fantastic. Good for you. Tell me about the dogs. Are they eating? Happy? Everything good?"

"The dogs are great," Jonathan said. "We're going home this weekend. Dad's birthday."

"Oh Christ, I forgot. Better send a card. Are you staying in the shed?"

"Yeah. It's okay, though."

"E-mail the wedding details. Congratulate Julie for me. She always seemed like a nice person. I'll definitely be there to make a brotherly speech. The dogs like her, right? If she's good enough for them, she's good enough for me."

Jonathan didn't have the heart to tell James the truth about Julie and the dogs. He felt certain they'd all come to love each other by the time the wedding happened. Or shortly thereafter. He wondered if he should invite Julie to his dad's birthday, but the thought inspired a crushing anxiety. It might be better to get everyone used to the idea first. Maybe she'd record a little greeting on his iPad. "Happy birthday to you! Looking forward to being part of the family!" Or something like that. Ease into the whole marriage thing.

His parents had sold the family home the minute he left for college, buying a condo on the outskirts of a pretty rural town near the border of Connecticut. It took just over two hours to drive if the traffic wasn't too bad, and there were lakes and mountain trails and a park nearby for the dogs to explore. The town consisted of a few quaint country-craft stores, a handful of old-fashioned restaurants, and about a hundred antique shops. Julie would like it here in Antiquestan, he thought. But where did all the antiques come from? Were they shipped in from some little-known antique-rich part of the world where everyone preferred IKEA?

When James first acquired the dogs, his father built what he called a guesthouse in the backyard to guard against their mother's legendary allergies. Though really it was more of a shed. Jonathan never quite believed the allergies were genuine — he'd seen his mother fail to sniffle in the presence of dogs for hours at a time. But it served the purpose of getting him out of the

137

house when he went to stay. Twenty yards of distance was almost as good as a moat.

Jonathan rented a car and set off after work on Friday. He stopped on the way for a bottle of expensive-looking scotch and arrived just before nine, shouting, "Happy birthday to all and to all a good night!" with faux-ironic good cheer. His parents greeted him and the dogs with red-rimmed eyes, probably signifying hours of hand-wringing and remorse for having had children in the first place, and showed him to the guesthouse-cum-shed, furnished with items from his and James's childhood bedrooms. He recognized the faded blue sleeping bag draped over the bed as the one in which he'd lost his virginity to a girl at summer camp.

Going home, he thought, even when it isn't any home you particularly know, is strange on so many levels. Everything seems familiar yet somehow alarming, like a PTSD flashback.

The dogs had no such ambivalence. Making up for all the nature they'd missed in New York City, they zigzagged frantically around in the dark, coming inside only reluctantly, after midnight. They now lay exhausted and content in their beds. Home to them was wherever he was.

The next morning Jonathan woke up early, made instant coffee on the shed's camp stove, and set out for a walk to the lake with his dad. The dogs seemed drunk with happiness, swept up in a mania of discovery, their noses in the air, along the ground, up trees and down holes, ecstatically digging away at the black soil as if seeking buried treasure, panting with joy, tails waving.

"Are they vicious?" his father asked.

Jonathan half closed his eyes and counted to five. He exhaled and spoke slowly. "Do they look vicious to you, Dad?"

"Not particularly," his father answered. "But I heard about a perfectly ordinary man who lived on the other side of town, and one time when no one had heard from him for a few days, they broke into his house and found him dead on the floor, half-eaten by his poodle."

Jonathan looked at his father. "Did the poodle kill him?" Why did his father always have some hideous story flagging up life's most dubious scenarios?

"No one knows. The police could only surmise."

Jonathan said nothing. His father's stories nearly always came down to some wildly unlikely surmise.

They walked in silence, and just at the moment the subject appeared to have been dropped, his father said, "You may dismiss my experience, but I've seen things in my life that have made me take a giant step backward. By the time you get to be my age," he muttered darkly, "you'll know what I'm talking about." His father was a fifty-two-year-old tax specialist who advised small businesses. Jonathan wondered if he'd ever once seen something peculiar or eccentric enough to make him pause, much less take a giant step backward, or if this was merely a misguided attempt at fatherly wisdom.

Jonathan picked up the pace. Soon there was just slightly too much distance between them to talk easily. He heard his phone bleep. It was Julie.

Feel bad about missing your dad's birthday. Catching train to Dover Plains. Arrive 5:20. See you there? xJ

Jonathan felt happy and sick at once. Her text — with its little hint of self-doubt — touched him deeply. *See you there?*

"Hey, Dad. Julie's coming this evening for your birthday after all."

His father looked panicked. "We'd better

140

get back right away so your mother can order in extra provisions. She was only counting on the three of us."

"Extra provisions?" It made Julie sound like some sort of bucket mouth. "It's okay, Dad, honest. Julie's not a big eater. And if necessary I can always pick up something when I go to the station."

Jonathan's father shook his head, morose. "If it's not one thing it's another."

Julie arrived carrying a big bunch of flowers for his mother. Jonathan's heart leaped to see her emerge from the train amid strangers, fumbling her overnight bag, looking stern, radiant, and, until she caught sight of his face, slightly nervous. Jonathan kissed her, never more happy to see her than now.

"Hello, almost-wife," he said.

She smiled, kissing him back. "Hello, almost-Jonathan."

She also had a card for his dad and a box of expensive birthday macaroons that went over fairly well, despite being the sort of thing his parents normally considered iffy on the basis of being foreign.

"It's lovely you were able to make it, Julie," his mother said, producing an elaborately frosted birthday cake with pink-and-green piped edges that might have been made in 1974 and stored in a cake museum. "Especially as you're officially part of the family now."

Jonathan wondered if being officially part of his family would be the kiss of death for poor Julie.

They all sang "Happy Birthday" and put on a moderately convincing show of acting normal throughout dinner. Jonathan hustled Julie away as early as possible to the shed.

"She's a nice enough girl," Jonathan's father said. "Despite trapping our son into a poisonous marriage of convenience." His mother shook her head sadly.

"I see where you get your mental instability," Julie said, and Jonathan nodded. Julie's father was dead, her mother remarried to a bond trader in Hong Kong. Jonathan had met Julie's mother three or four times over the years, which intrigued Max, who usually didn't stick with relationships long enough to meet the parents.

"I wouldn't have thought Julie needed parents. I see her organizing her own conception and birth."

"Ha ha."

"So, what's her mother like?"

Jonathan thought. "Rich and strange."

"Rich is good. Strange how?"

"Max, do you know anyone — any single

human being on the planet — whose parents aren't strange?"

"How strange?"

Jonathan sighed. "Too thin, slightly fixed expression, answers the question she thinks you should have asked."

Max considered this. "Not so bad. Four and a half on the strange scale."

"Five. But on the plus side, lives in Hong Kong. Eight thousand forty-eight miles away."

"But who's counting." Max paused. "Okay."

"Okay? Why, thank you. So good to have your blessing."

"Sarcasm demeans you. And you do not have my blessing."

Later that night, Julie and Jonathan squeezed into the sleeping bag in which he'd lost his virginity, but their attempts to have sex failed.

They left after breakfast the following morning, to everyone's relief.

15

Jonathan's regular coffee bar refused to let him in with the dogs, and the possibility of dognapping meant that tying them outside wasn't an option. It wasn't until his second week of walking to work that he found the perfect replacement: a tiny café halfway between home and Comrade with the unlikely name of Le Grand Pain.

The proprietor introduced herself in a glorious French accent. "Hello. What can I get you today? My name is Clémence. Who are you?" The second half of the greeting was addressed to the dogs.

"They're Dante and Sissy," Jonathan said, relieved that her first words hadn't been, "Sorry, you can't come in here with the dogs. It's against health regulations." There was something about that sentence that made him crazy. Why couldn't they at least add, "If it were up to me, of course you could bring them in anytime, but you know how it is" (sympathetic frown), or "Don't worry, I'll hold them outside while you decide what you want." But they never said that. They all smiled that passive-aggressive smile and said "really sorry" in a way that meant not-sorry-at-all.

The sliver of a café smelled delicious, and he ordered coffee. Clémence pointed to the croissants and said, "I bake them myself. They're very good. Not like the ones at Starbucks." She sounded so enthusiastic he bought two.

"I hope you won't feel insulted if I split the second one and give it to my dogs," he said. "They've actually got pretty fine palates." He paused. "Does that make me sound like a crank? More or less everything I say these days makes me sound like a crank."

She smiled at him. "Not at all."

He gave her money for the coffee and two croissants and told her to keep the change. "And thank you for letting the dogs come in."

"But such nice dogs! Who wouldn't let them in?"

"You'd be surprised," Jonathan said darkly.

She gave them a final pat. "See you tomorrow!"

During the rest of his walk to work he planned his life with Clémence. They would live in a tiny studio above the bakery. He would bring her coffee in bed at 5 a.m. before she started baking, and they would make love in the evening when he got home from work and the shop was shut. He would learn to cook beautiful cassoulet from ingredients imported from her childhood village of . . . of . . . Ampersand-sur-Mer. They would have two children, Celeste and Raoul, who would speak French and English and be beautiful like their mother. The children would love him like a father, which would make sense, as that's what he would be. Clémence's anti-American relatives would be doubtful at first, but they would soon see how happy she was and stop thinking about her ex-boyfriend, Olivier, who despite being a fantastically rich banker was not reliably monogamous and a soupçon homosexual besides.

The next day Clémence welcomed them like old friends. "Dante! Sissy! How nice to see you again."

Jonathan looked at Clémence's spotless apron. "Aren't you baking today?"

"I bake every day except Thursday and Sunday. Those days I sleep till six."

Till six? How early did she get up on baking days? He felt reluctant to ask a question that referred, however tangentially, to her bed. It seemed disrespectful, somehow, of their pure and wholesome future together.

Having paid for coffee and croissants, he wanted to linger but couldn't think of an excuse, so he opened the door and left with a jaunty *"à demain"* that he instantly regretted.

As he walked to work, he considered their relationship further, drawing happy family portraits in his head of Celeste, a sturdy wild girl with a thick mane of curls and smudges of flour on her clothes, and Raoul, their serious, sloe-eyed boy, still a baby but with an uncanny air of wisdom.

Celeste would be three and Raoul one when Clémence would find herself pregnant again. "But we're already so stretched for money, *mon amour,*" she would say, her eyes huge with unshed tears, and he would answer that nothing would be more of a treasure to him than her baby, and so they would kiss and kiss, and eight months later Clémence would give birth to another girl, whom they'd name, um, something French, like Alouette. Gentille Alouette.

The third day when Jonathan arrived in a lather of future plans, there was no Clémence. A ridiculously handsome

Frenchman looked up from behind the counter and asked in a bored voice whether he wanted coffee, and when Jonathan demanded to know what had happened to his beloved, the Frenchman said, "Ah yes. The man with the dogs. Clémence told me about you."

"And you are . . . her brother?"

"Husband," the Frenchman said, taking Jonathan's order without engaging in further pleasantries.

Jonathan returned the following day, furious and distraught. "You didn't tell me you had a husband."

"Ah, *cheri*. I didn't know you cared." She smiled and, without asking for his order, put two croissants in a bag and started to make his coffee.

"Of course I care! I've named our babies." He fumbled in his backpack for his notebook and waved it at her. "I've drawn pictures of them. All three!"

"Three babies? I will have my hands full!" She laughed. "So, you don't have a wife of your own?"

"Of course not," Jonathan said, indignant. "Do I look as if I have a wife?" He felt unaccountably outraged at the thought.

"I don't know." She studied him carefully. "Is there a particular look such a man has?

A miserable look, maybe? Or triumphant? Depending on the wife, perhaps?"

If she were his wife, he would look joyous all the time.

The impossibly handsome Frenchman emerged from the back, put a proprietary hand on her waist, and murmured something in her ear. "Luc!" She blushed and kissed him.

Jonathan paid for his coffee and croissants and left feeling even more despondent than usual.

16

The minuscule advance in his salary improved Jonathan's relationship with neither Comrade nor Julie. Most of his working hours were spent developing elaborate fantasies of escape and revenge in which he stole Eduardo's fancy car, put the dogs in the back, and drove off into the horizon. On top of this he wasn't sleeping, tossing around at night for hours, mulling, which eventually drove Julie to suggest he sleep on the couch. Once he was settled there, Sissy joined him, insinuating her way closer and closer until she was wedged up against his chest, her head under his chin. He noticed that he slept better with the spaniel than with his girlfriend.

Looking up from his desk, he found Greeley standing over him in jeans and a bright blue T-shirt accessorized with a 1920s Hermès scarf and silver sandals.

"Hello," Greeley said.

Jonathan blinked. "Hi."

"Just wondered how you're doing."

"About the same as ever."

"You want to get some lunch?"

"You mean go out?"

Greeley nodded.

"Okay." Jonathan stood up, grabbed his jacket, and followed. They walked two blocks to a quiet café and Greeley pointed to a table in the corner.

They sat. Greeley looked at him. "So. What's your plan?"

"Plan?"

Greeley waited.

"You mean about everything?"

"Yes."

" 'Everything' is a bit too wide-ranging for me. I thought I might start small."

"With?"

Jonathan was silent. "With nothing so far. I haven't actually decided anything."

Greeley sighed, a world-weary sigh, and pushed an envelope across the table to him. "I've taken the liberty."

Jonathan opened it. It was a letter of resignation. From him to Wes.

"You don't have to do it today. Or ever, for that matter. I just thought it might be a good thing to have at hand."

"You want me to quit my job?"

"Not necessarily."

Jonathan looked out the window at the people walking by. Greeley called the waiter over and ordered for them both.

"I have to do something to pay the rent. And I might have to support a family soon."

"Is Julie pregnant?"

Jonathan's expression was pure horror. "Of course not!"

Greeley gazed at the ceiling. "Are you sure you're ready to get married?"

Jonathan sighed.

"What?" said Greeley.

"Oh, nothing. I was just thinking about this woman I met."

"A different woman?"

Jonathan nodded. "She's amazing."

"What's her name?"

"Clémence. She's French. And . . ."

"And?"

"And married. To Luc. A really handsome French bastard."

"You're marrying Julie."

"I know."

"Then stop thinking about Clémence."

Jonathan glowered. "Stop asking me about her, then."

Greeley stared at Jonathan, hard. "Is there something fundamentally wrong with your decision-making powers?"

He hung his head. "I think there must be."

The waiter returned with two coffees and two roasted vegetable and pesto sandwiches.

"Greeley?"

"Yes?"

"What do you want in life?"

Greeley picked up half a sandwich and looked at Jonathan. "Like Freud said: love and work. Isn't that what everyone wants?"

"Some people want money and fame and a big house and then another house and huge L-shaped couches and expensive cars and a home cinema and to be famous. Most people want that, I'd say."

"Well." Greeley chewed contemplatively. "It passes the time."

"What does?"

"Stuff."

Jonathan took a bite of his sandwich. "But what if it makes them happy?"

"If it does, fine."

"Why are you working at Comrade, Greeley?"

"I need the money for my degree. I'm studying forest ecosystems and conservation."

Jonathan thought about this. "Forests is a thing. I don't have a thing."

"Maybe you do."

"Like what?"

Greeley shrugged. "You tell me."

"I draw comics. I like to write. How much of a life is that?"

"I don't know. How much of a life is it?"

"No one makes money out of comics. Or writing."

"No one?"

"Hardly anyone."

Greeley considered this. "So, no one makes a living except the people who do."

Jonathan nodded. "I wouldn't be one of them."

"Depends how hard you work, whether you have anything to say. Ambition, luck. Hanging on when everyone else has quit. How much money you need. Where you live. And with whom."

"You need a fortune to live in New York."

"So don't live in New York. Go to Portsmouth, Cleveland, Burlington. Austin. I don't know. Pittsburgh. Raleigh. Tucson. Ankara. Bilbao."

"Enough." Jonathan pressed his hands against his temples. "I have to think."

"You think," Greeley said. "Don't ever stop thinking."

"The thing is, I need resolution."

"Do you?" Greeley looked at him. "Resolve your life now and what'll you do for the next fifty years?"

154

"I don't know," Jonathan said. "Why are you asking me all these questions? I just want to get happy and stay there."

"You don't know much about life, do you?"

Jonathan's shoulders sank. His head drooped. "No. I'm doing my best, though. Why isn't there a course at the New School? 'How to Be a Person.' "

"There probably is." Greeley smiled a little.

"Anyway, I thought I was doing pretty well. I've got the job and the girlfriend and all."

"All what?"

"All the stuff you're supposed to have."

Greeley sighed. "Congratulations. How's that working out so far?"

"Not great." Jonathan felt unaccountably gloomy.

"Uh-huh." Greeley finished the sandwich and nodded at the waiter for the bill.

Jonathan wondered what sex with Greeley might be like. It wasn't so much that sex with Greeley was on the menu, but Jonathan longed to be included in that perfect aura of calm.

"Instead of dragging me out to lunch and asking a lot of impossible questions, I wish you'd just sort it all out for me."

155

Greeley laughed softly.

"No, really, I mean it . . . I do."

"I'm sorry to say, but that's your job, Jonathan."

Another job I despise and dread, Jonathan thought. Perfect.

17

Jonathan wanted to convince Julie of his desire to love her above all other forms of life — but this, much to his genuine regret, required getting rid of the dogs for the duration of their romantic weekend. He couldn't ask Max to dogsit. Or maybe he could, but he didn't want to have to explain about going away with Julie. He'd passed the new boutique dog hotel in his neighborhood numerous times, but on this particular Saturday morning he gritted his teeth and went in. FIDEAUX SUITES, said the swirly gold writing on the glass doors.

The concierge of Fideaux Suites introduced himself to Jonathan ("Hi, I'm Darren, I'll be providing your dogs' surrogate familial affection while you're away") and then barely addressed him again throughout the rest of the tour.

"We've got three levels of accommodation from basic to five-star, depending on how much Daddy loves you." Darren smiled ingratiatingly at Sissy.

"Let's assume for now that Daddy loves you a lot." He spoke with exaggerated enthusiasm to Dante, who hated overfamiliarity, and then opened the door to a bedroom nearly twice the size of Jonathan's at home, complete with flat-screen TV, king-size bed, bedside tables, lamps, and fluffy sheepskin rug.

Jonathan gaped. "Holy shit. Can I stay here too?"

"No." Darren smoothed his hand along the cashmere throw, neatly folded at the foot of the bed. "Of course we have twenty-four-hour room service in case you two get the nibbles late at night." Sissy peered around the room and wagged her tail, glancing at Jonathan to see if she was allowed up on the bed.

How did room service work? Jonathan wondered. Did guests bark orders down the phone?

"You can choose your own channel, but we find many of our guests prefer Animal Planet."

Jonathan giggled and Darren glared at him.

"You'll make lifelong friends," Darren confided to Sissy. And Sissy did seem to like Darren. But why did dogs need bedside lamps? What else was included? A minibar? Yoga? Hot-stone massage?

Darren led them from the guest rooms via a softly lit corridor, up to the mezzanine level where a sign read FINE DINING. He pushed open a glass door.

"This is the kitchen, where our chef creates bespoke meals for any diet or taste preference," Darren continued, and handed Jonathan a menu. It included steamed fish, roast lamb, grilled beef, plus a vegetarian option. Was there such a thing as a vegetarian dog?

With its acres of stainless steel, latest in high-tech equipment, immaculate workstations, knives that cost more than Jonathan's monthly salary, and a gigantic commercial range, the kitchen would not have looked out of place in one of New York's finer culinary establishments. Piles of fresh fish and prime cuts of beef awaited grilling or braising under the watchful eyes of the intent sous-chef. The head chef, glowering in a corner, looked vaguely familiar to Jonathan, who dimly recalled reading about a disgraced Michelin chef who had sought employment "in a related field."

The kitchen door swung closed and Darren led them down to the basement through a heavy door, into a steamy anteroom smelling of chlorine. "And this," he said with a slight bow and a flourish of the hand, "is the health and fitness center." Darren leaned in close. "Every guest has an individual program designed to maximize his or her capacities."

Dante froze at the sight of dogs on treadmills, each with a trainer in sweats sporting the gold Fideaux logos. Sissy looked puzzled. "There's more," Darren said, nearly bursting with pride. And he guided the little group to a window overlooking the dog infinity pool.

"It's only a foot deep and there's a shallow end for dachshunds, so no one drowns. Just look at the fun they're having!" Darren beamed and clasped his hands together. It was hard to deny that they were having fun.

If only he and Julie could stay at a hotel with a gym, playrooms, a bespoke menu, and an infinity pool. Jonathan wished he could afford it. He also wished that everyone in the world had enough to eat, clean water, and sanitation; that man would someday achieve peace on earth, that children in Third World countries would be educated, polar bears would have enough ice, and sentient animals like pigs and cows wouldn't be slaughtered for food. What it had never occurred to him to wish for was an infinity pool for dogs. Still. It's not as if life in New York hadn't thrown up this sort of conundrum before.

Back at reception, Darren asked if the dogs had their own e-mail addresses and seemed miffed that he'd have to contact them through their owner.

"Each guest gets an automatic six-month membership in Privileged Pets. If you tell me their birthdays," Darren was saying, "I'll add them to the hotel profiles, and Privileged Pets sends out a special card and a bag of liver treats on the day." Dante's eyes swiveled in Jonathan's direction.

On their birthdays, Jonathan thought, they'll be far too busy folding napkins in the shape of swans, baking profiteroles, and playing musical chairs.

As the three of them stumbled out of the calm low lighting of the lobby into the glare of Second Avenue, Jonathan looked at his dogs. "The hotel is off," he said. "We could all stay at the George V in Paris for what that place costs." Dante's ears flicked up at the thought of the George V, while Sissy gazed warmly at Jonathan. *As long as we're with you,* her eyes said.

Jonathan pulled the dogs aside to make way for a young woman with a large brown speckled dog headed for the hotel door.

"Excuse me," he called. "I'm sorry, but you can't take your dog in there."

The woman turned, and with a start he recognized Dr. Clare.

"Well," she said, noticing the dogs first. "Fancy meeting you here."

Dr. Clare looked different in real life. Her hair was messier and she wore dark jeans that ended above her ankles, with chunky boots. She was tall, nearly six feet, and looked as if she might just have rolled out of bed: no makeup, no jewelry, no bag, just a big brown speckled dog on a green leather leash. She looked at Jonathan and smiled. It wasn't her professional smile; it was broader, warmer.

Sissy and Dante greeted her with enthusiasm. "Hello, you two," she said, kneeling down on the sidewalk to pat them.

When she stood up again, he thrust out his hand. "Hello, Dr. Clare."

She took his hand without embarrassment and shook it. Jonathan was slightly reluctant to let go; her hand was warm and claspy.

"Why can't I go in there?" she asked. "Is it closed?"

"No, not closed. Morally wrong."

She frowned at him. "But I've heard it's amazing. Have your dogs stayed there?"

He thought for a minute. "I shouldn't presume. You might like it, I can't be sure." He tilted his head and looked at her carefully. "But I'm guessing not."

"I'm going away. With my boyfriend." She took a step back from him, her brow furrowed. "Everyone says it's the best dog hotel in town. He thought it must be good."

"Depends what he means by good," Jonathan said. "If by good he means the end of civilization as we know it, then yes, it's good. If by good he means something that will give you a truly terrified feeling about the future of the human race, then yes, it's excellent. If he means anything decent and normal and sane, then I'm afraid, no. No, it is not at all good."

Dr. Clare looked confused for a second. Then her mouth curled up ever so slightly at the corners and her eyes met his.

He felt a fizz of pleasure and they stood like that for just a bit too long, neither quite willing to break the spell.

Finally she looked away, suppressing a smile. "Well, I suppose, as I'm here, I'd better see for myself. But thank you for warning us." She paused. "We haven't seen you lately. Not that I'm complaining. I'm hoping it means everyone's healthy?"

"They're happier," Jonathan said. "I guess

that helps."

"Good dogs," she said, and smiled at them both. "I'm very pleased to hear that."

Jonathan felt a flush of pleasure. "And this is?"

"Wilma," she said. "Like *The Flintstones.*"

"Nice to meet you, Wilma."

At the sound of her name, Wilma lunged forward excitedly at Jonathan, pulling Dr. Clare off balance. Jonathan grabbed her arm, Sissy barked, and Dante tugged in the opposite direction. For a brief moment, dogs and humans teetered dangerously, reestablishing ninety-degree angles to the ground only at the last possible second. Wilma panted. Jonathan still gripped Dr. Clare's arm.

"Are you okay?"

She smiled, a bit wildly. "My dog's stronger than she looks."

"Actually, she looks very strong." He let go of her arm.

They stood almost but not quite facing each other, neither entirely willing to move away. Her eyes, which he hadn't specifically noticed before, were large and warm and lively and reminded him of Sissy's. Had she said she was going away with her boyfriend? Why did everyone have a boyfriend? And why did all the attractive women in New

York City start smiling at him just when he decided to get married?

"I'm getting married soon," he blurted out.

"Congratulations," she said. "How lovely."

"Not really," Jonathan said.

She looked startled.

"It's kind of a long story."

Dr. Clare coughed, embarrassed. "I'm afraid I, ah, I have to go."

"Don't say I didn't warn you," Jonathan said, indicating the hotel. He watched as she disappeared through the door, feeling vaguely deflated, as if some pivotal moment had slipped just out of reach.

Dante watched too, looking thoughtful.

18

Julie accepted a freebie from a new B&B in southern Vermont that wanted wedding business and took dogs. All she had to do was write a few paragraphs about it for the *Bridal-360* blog. Budget-wise, it was the perfect solution, as neither of them really had the money for a long weekend on Sanibel.

It didn't take Julie long to reimagine herself as the sort of person who escaped to Vermont at regular intervals. *Oh, I'm sorry, we're doing Christmas in Vermont this year.* Or, *I can't believe you haven't been to our Vermont place yet!* Or, *It's so annoying, I'm always leaving stuff in Vermont.* Vermont-Julie had a house filled with antique chests of drawers, weathered old signs from gas stations, and tractor parts used as bookends. Vermont-Julie collected antique quilts and hand-crocheted throws that someone else's great-great-grandmother had painstakingly made during the terrible winter of 1915–16. Vermont-Julie's unusual weathervane served as a talking point while her sourdough bread rose by the fire. Vermont-Julie knotted expensive cashmere sweaters (purchased online) around her shoulders in an offhand way.

They drove up on Friday afternoon, Vermont-Julie only slightly resentful about the backseat passengers, arriving at the inn before dinner. Their welcome consisted of a bottle of wine, a water bowl, and a roaring fire in the communal living room. The couple who owned the inn, a retired investment banker and his husband, introduced Dante and Sissy to Sunny and Sally, their yellow Labs, and suggested a preprandial walk to enjoy the sunset and the quiet. After the long journey, the dogs seemed elated to be out in woodland; even Dante set aside his dignity to chase shadows and squirrels.

Jonathan put his arm around Julie, who laid her head on his shoulder. For once, she seemed truly happy. At dinner they ordered venison and duck with baby carrots and spinach and roast potatoes and shared a bottle of California Pinot Noir and both had panna cotta with figs for dessert.

"Thank goodness I like it," Julie whispered as they stretched out between 400-thread-count cotton sheets under silvery silk quilts. "It's a nightmare when the free stuff is awful." She tapped up a rave review for TripAdvisor before they went to sleep, blogged the place on *Bridal-360*'s blog, and posted pictures on Pinterest and Tumblr. It would help the business, she knew it would, and justifiably, for it was hard to imagine a more romantic wedding venue. She thought of suggesting it to Lorenza, but it wasn't the sort of place her art director would like, what with the sticky Wi-Fi, full-fat milk, and no Barneys for three hundred miles. Auster and Phil (who bought the place with Phil's severance package from Bear Stearns) sat down with Julie in the kitchen, describing their dream of bespoke weddings for gay men and their dogs, and she promised to refer readers to their website and video diary.

"It's niche," Julie explained to Jonathan, "but not out-there niche."

After a breakfast of home-laid poached eggs, homemade toast, home-baked blueberry muffins, home-cured bacon, and home-ground coffee, they set off for the flea market in a nearby town, which specialized in New England bric-a-brac (watering cans, old photographs, costume jewelry, books) and vintage furniture. Jonathan found Julie a silver link necklace from the 1950s, though she tried to say she didn't need it.

The woman selling looked genuinely stymied. "Need it? Of course you don't need it, honey. You don't need that either," she said, pointing to Jonathan, "but it makes you happy."

Which of course raised the question, and made Julie and Jonathan too embarrassed to look at each other. Jonathan asked if that price was the best she could do, feeling obliged to bargain so as not to be mistaken for a rube.

"Sure, I can do a better price," the woman answered, her eyes flat. "If you don't mind taking food out of the mouths of my kids."

Jonathan smiled apologetically and handed over the tag price, while Julie pretended not to have heard the exchange. But the purchase was ruined for them both, and despite wearing the necklace for the rest of the day, Julie tugged at it unconsciously, running her thumb continually along its length in a nervous gesture.

Jonathan browsed the tables of flea merchandise. Didn't most people have enough junk without buying stuff that other people didn't want? It felt wrong to him, paying for the patina of near-antiquity in order to suggest that they had ancient relatives with valuable old-fashioned things. But he didn't say anything to disturb Julie's pleasure in scanning table after table, seeking — along with hundreds of others — that elusive thing to improve the quality of her life.

The dogs experienced life at ground level, finding the occasional discarded piece of cake or unguarded sandwich. From the point of view of long walks and scavenging, the country was proving too good to be true.

Jonathan felt pleased that their weekend hadn't turned out to be a nightmare, that Julie didn't despise his dogs, and that the whole thing had cost very little. Every once in a while he'd squint and try to imagine coming back every year to stay with Auster and Phil for a weekend of blueberry muffins and flea marketing, but it was the other Jonathan who came back in his place, the distant middle-aged product of his flawed imagination. That Jonathan had nothing in common with his current self, a crude drawing on an Etch A Sketch, stilted and ephemeral, easily and casually erased by the slightest movement of life.

Julie helped him to feel defined. He was Julie's boyfriend. Julie's fiancé. Julie's provocation. He came into focus when he stood beside her, despite the fact that the person standing beside her was mostly not him.

He looked at the dogs. With them he was the Jonathan who liked to walk around town, who didn't stop them eating hot dogs from the gutter, who worried about them, cared for them, loved them. Was a relationship with dogs the best he could expect in life? He felt disloyal even thinking of it as a limitation. To be loved by dogs; well, it was a thing. Not as big a thing as being loved by a person, perhaps, but still.

All around the open area of the flea market, men and women walked with their dogs, talking to them, holding them, adjusting dog coats and dog sweaters, asking their opinions on pieces of hopeless junk. And not a single dog made a contemptuous face and turned away muttering, "Waste of god-damned money if you ask me."

Who wouldn't prefer dogs?

Julie called him over to examine a brown-and-orange glazed vase of exceptional ugliness. "These ceramics are very collectible," she whispered in his ear, and he managed to arrange his features into an approximation of Sissy-like enthusiasm. *Collectible? Wow! Go for it,* his expression said, but when he saw the price he turned away. Charging two hundred dollars for something hideous didn't make it nicer, did it? Did it convert the vase, in Julie's eyes, into a thing of beauty?

"What do you think, Jonathan? Should I buy it?" Her eyes sparkled and he could tell that, for whatever reason, she wanted this thing. Really wanted it. He could have made her happy by saying, *Yes! It's gorgeous! You'll love it! I'll buy it for you!*

But he didn't.

She sighed and put it back.

The rest of the weekend passed in long walks and good meals and fine scenery. They parted from Phil and Auster as if from old friends, with invitations to future Christmases, promises to exchange pictures of the dogs, and generous vacation discounts for life.

In the car on the way back to New York City, Julie looked thoughtful.

"What?" Jonathan asked, and she said, "I wish I'd bought that vase."

He had no idea how to answer, so said nothing at all.

19

The meeting with Lorenza was set for six on Tuesday afternoon.

Jonathan arrived at 5:45 with the dogs. He'd been drinking coffee all day and developed a noticeable tremor. Julie met him in reception.

"Are you okay?"

"Fine," he said, kissing her. Dante and Sissy sat politely by his side.

Julie tutted. "What are we going to do with them?"

"I thought you might take them around the block for however long the interview lasts." Jonathan privately thought that ten minutes would be plenty of time to get the wedding interview over and done with.

"She wants to talk to us both. Tease out the dynamic. You know, get a feel for the whole relationship thing."

Jonathan flinched. He wasn't sure that the whole relationship thing bore teasing out.

He had visions of it emerging from its cave like Smaug and reducing them all to cinders.

The more he thought about it, the more he just wanted this funeral over and done with.

"Did you say funeral?"

"No." Jonathan looked puzzled. "Why do you keep saying funeral?"

"I'm not the one who keeps saying funeral."

"I'm not either, so could we just stop with the funeral?"

Julie sighed. "Come meet Lorenza."

"A pleasure," Lorenza said when Julie introduced them, offering her hand limply and looking Jonathan up and down like a PET scan. She grimaced. The missing link confirmed her worst fears.

They all sat down and Jonathan stared. Lorenza appeared to have arrived at the meeting straight out of a black-and-white copy machine. She had black hair and pale skin and wore a black jacket, white man's dress shirt, black brogues with no socks, and straight black trousers. Her hair was cut in sharp geometrics, her eyebrows black and arched. She wore charcoal nail varnish and blackish-red lipstick.

"So," said Jonathan. "The art director. Who'd have guessed?"

Lorenza glanced at Jonathan, then at Julie. "Nice dogs. Were you thinking of featuring them in the ceremony?"

Jonathan suddenly imagined Julie in a simple white linen shift with lace pantaloons peeping out the bottom and a tall crook decorated with a pink bow. Dante darted back and forth, shaping groups of adorable lambs into the letters "I DO" against a pale green meadow. A Bo Peep wedding. There wasn't really a role for him in it, but he didn't mind. He would come along later, for the after-party.

"Jonathan." The way Julie said his name was warning enough.

"The dogs," Jonathan said, recovering. "What do you think, Julie?"

"No dogs."

The dogs looked up at her — Sissy with consternation, Dante hood-eyed, blank.

"I have no real objections to that." He arranged his face in a careful configuration of interest and concern but thought he might be grimacing grotesquely by mistake. Lately he'd forgotten how to form ordinary facial expressions.

Julie ignored him, smiling ingratiatingly at Lorenza. "Why don't you share your vision with us?"

Lorenza looked at the ceiling and then

down again. She took a deep breath and exhaled as if smoking an invisible cigarette, gazed into the middle distance, dropped one long forearm to the table, and spoke.

"I'm seeing artisanal cocktails in fresh spring tones," she said. "Infusions of mint, peach, and violet. Taupe for the bridesmaids with snowdrops and white lilac. A spring renewal feeling, soil and green shoots."

Julie leaned forward on her chair. "Wow."

Jonathan stared out the window, frantically trying to form normal responses in his head. What even was taupe?

"And the dress?"

Lorenza paused. She turned away for a long moment. "Celadon," she said at last, opening a large coffee-table-type book to a page marked with a strip of fabric. "Silk jersey, after this one made for Jackie Kennedy in 1961. An Oleg Cassini classic." She paused and studied Julie. "Not everyone could carry it off, but with your coloring . . ." She made an approving little moue.

Julie's hands flew to her face. "Celadon! Oh!"

Her tone alerted Jonathan that something important had happened. "Celadon," he echoed. "Amazing." He glanced nervously from Lorenza to Julie.

Julie's face had transformed, as if in the

midst of a religious conversion. "I think I'm getting your vision. I think . . . I can hardly breathe."

Lorenza looked questioningly at Jonathan, who stared back, devoid of thought.

"Well," he said. "I'm thinking . . . yes." He had no idea what he was saying yes to.

"That's it, then," Julie said to the art director in triumph. "We love your vision. We are as one."

Jonathan was as three. Sissy had edged closer to his chair and was now curled up under it, head on paws, face anxious. Dante had angled his body slightly away from the proceedings, but the prick of his ears indicated that he was taking it all in.

Jonathan experienced a great rush of gratitude for the presence of his dogs. They were on his side, even if being on his side didn't necessarily mean they had the best interests of his future with Julie at heart. He reached down to Dante, who gazed up at him intently.

". . . not black. A deep burned chocolate."

Julie nodded vigorously and Jonathan realized that they were talking about his suit. He tore his eyes away from Dante and wondered if the chocolate would be burned while he was wearing it or before. In his head he added the scene to *The Jonathan*

File: he, the bridegroom, engulfed in flames, running through the wedding screaming, fire shooting from his sleeves and collar.

He knew better than to share his vision.

"I have to go," he said. And without waiting for anyone's assent, he pushed his chair back and left with the dogs. Julie barely seemed to notice, but Lorenza shook her head, causing the straight black of her hair to swing like a curtain.

He felt a great rush of relief as he burst out the door. Had they pumped all the air out of that meeting room? He was drenched with sweat, unable to breathe, his mouth the shape of a letter Q. The neon sign announcing one of New York's oldest bars winked at him from diagonally across the street. It was nearly empty except for a few hard-core boozers, and when he walked in with the dogs no one commented.

"A double brandy please," he said, shaking his head no to ice. He'd never ordered brandy before but knew it was supposed to be restorative. A double brandy, surely, would be doubly restorative. It arrived looking larger than he'd imagined and he drank it down, tapping the bar for another. He couldn't remember if he'd had anything to eat today and his thoughts strayed to a beautiful croissant made by Clémence. A tear escaped one eye. He drank the second brandy, ordered a third, drank it, paid, and stood up to go, swaying like a hula dancer. The dogs, recognizing an emergency, surrounded him protectively. In a relatively stable three-point formation, they toddled back to work.

Perhaps he could spend the night at the office curled up in the corner of the conference room. Perhaps the dogs would share their comfy beds with him. Being this drunk clarified his mind, made him realize how thoroughly off track he was. It was almost funny how quickly everything seemed to be getting away from him. Why couldn't he have a job that didn't make him crave lethal injection? Why couldn't he be marrying someone like Clémence? Why was Clémence married to someone else? Why wasn't Julie?

"Greeley? Greeley!" If ever he'd needed spiritual guidance it was now. He'd seen Greeley practicing qigong meditation while sorting Eduardo's expenses. He'd noticed Greeley consuming macrobiotic vegetables while expertly managing the office diary. Greeley seemed to have some sort of key to better living, and Jonathan was sorely in need of a key. Not just a key. A guide. A guidebook. A guru. But Greeley was nowhere to be found. Not even in the supply cupboard, where Jonathan spent longer than planned, having mislaid the door handle.

He crawled on hands and knees to Eduardo's office, poked his head around the door at knee level, and found the boss sitting alone at his massive Stalinesque desk watching porn.

"Hello, Jonathan," he said pleasantly. "What are you doing here? It's late."

"But not too late?" A great wave of panic joined the spinning, swooping sensation behind his eyeballs. "I need so much help I don't know where to start. I'm doing the wrong thing in every realm of life. I need Greeley. Unless you know another supremely wise person I could sign up with? Or a psychiatrist? I'm desperate, Ed. And I'm so tired. I think I might be having a nervous breakdown. I'm still getting married, by the way. Do you want your raise back?"

"What raise?" Eduardo looked pained. "I think it's only fair to tell you that you're screwing up big-time, Jonathan. I went out on a limb to hire you because Max said you'd be fine. But you're not fine. You're fucked up. I'm afraid you're going to have to do a lot of backpedaling to regain my trust." In the background the computer was groaning, Ungh . . . ungh . . . ungh . . .

Exhausted and addled with brandy, Jonathan lay down and closed his eyes. The spinning room picked up speed and he held on to the floor for fear of hurtling into the abyss. "I want your trust back, I do, Ed. But I really don't think I can do any pedaling just now." He liked the feel of the Berber carpet against his cheek. "Forgive me."

Eduardo had switched his attention back to the computer screen. "Sure."

"I want to win your trust. But I hate it here. I hate you. I hate Broadway Depot. I quit."

Thanks to the miracle of drunkenness, the single most honest declaration of his life came out garbled beyond comprehension.

Eduardo looked down at the employee at his feet and was about to make a pronouncement of his own when Dante came to the rescue, nudging at Jonathan to get moving before he made the current situation worse by heaving on the executive carpet.

Jonathan hauled himself up on to his knees and crawled slowly out the door, Dante at his side.

"See you," he said, which came out as "Phoo."

Sissy, meanwhile, had her head in Eduardo's lap, having opted for her most endearing huge-eyed baby-animal look, and

181

Must make a note to fire that asshole seam-lessly segued into *Aw, what a totally cute dog.*

With the guidance of his loyal pets, Jona-than made his way to a taxi, arrived home, and fell into bed fully clothed. Julie texted to say it would be another publication-day all-nighter.

Julie? It took him a minute to focus.

Oh yes. That Julie.

He passed out.

20

At Le Grand Pain the next day, Clémence was still married to Luc.

"Can't you see how much I love you?" Jonathan's head ached, and he suspected he might still be drunk from the night before.

Clémence frowned at him. "You have a girlfriend. But I can give you coffee, which you need far more than you need love right now."

"Not true," he said. "If you loved me you would sponge my brow with cool water, murmur endearments, and make coffee I wouldn't have to pay for."

Clémence laughed and raised both eyebrows.

"You wouldn't?"

"No."

"Are you sure?" Jonathan felt very sick and a bit desperate.

"Very sure. Why are you whispering?"

"Isn't Jean-Pierre here?"

"Luc is in Paris."

"Paris? Couldn't you kiss me in that case? He won't see."

She placed a coffee in his hand and guided him to the door. "Goodbye, *cheri.* Don't drink so much next time."

"But what about our children? Celeste and Raoul? And baby Alouette? How can you reject your own children?"

Clémence disappeared into the back.

Jonathan's funeral was less than a month away. He'd dredged up a modest list of invitees, including the members of his immediate family — Mom, Dad, James — a few leftover friends from college, and Max and Greeley from work. That was about it. The rest of the cheering squad came from Julie, who — in addition to having more friends and family than Jonathan — had invited the entire staff of *Bridal-360,* whose job on the day would be to look young, carefree, and photogenic for the magazine spreads. James e-mailed to say he'd booked his flight, was getting to the end of his contract in Dubai, and couldn't wait to reclaim his dogs.

Reclaim his dogs? *His* dogs? Jonathan had more or less forgotten that the dogs belonged to James. In moments of gloom, he thought perhaps they should be with a different owner altogether, someone who could take them deep into the woods each day to track rodents and dig holes in the earth, but he couldn't help noticing that they seemed relatively okay with their life on the third floor. The thought that his brother might take them back filled him with despair.

But what if they greeted James with an outpouring of love and relief, whispering in his ear the minute Jonathan was out of the room that he was a loser and the previous months had been hell? It made him want to cry. He'd grown accustomed to their furry scheming faces and could no longer imagine life without them. But he'd read *The Incredible Journey.* Perhaps they were just waiting for a chance to escape and begin the 6,837-mile journey back to their master. He had a terrible vision of them dragging themselves to Dubai, limp and emaciated, arriving at last at a four-hundred-story apartment building and being turned away by the doorman for not being borzois.

Tears slipped down his face; *The Loyalty of the Dog* struck him with unbearable poignancy.

His parents, meanwhile, having had enough time to contemplate his upcoming nuptials, became increasingly anxious.

"Julie's pregnant, isn't she?" his mother

asked, lowering her voice so that who? God? the CIA? wouldn't hear.

"No, she's not pregnant, Ma. Why does everyone think she's pregnant? Like I told you — it's all part of a magazine promotion. We're going to be live-streamed on the Internet in front of thousands of people." But she'd already passed him over to his father, who said, "Well, Jonathan, Julie of all people. I certainly hope you know what you're doing. Not that you've ever given us much reason to suspect that you do." He hung up, leaving Jonathan staring at the phone, his face squinched up in irritation.

A venue had been chosen without requiring his input; the spring-color-themed wedding was to be held at the Brooklyn Botanic Garden, in the Palm House. The bar menu was planned, the caterers booked. In some hot, drought-ridden country in Africa, North American wildflowers were growing at unnatural speeds, ready to be flown halfway across the world to a magazine-sponsored wedding of dread.

Jonathan stopped off at a nondescript coffee place (it didn't take dogs but generously allowed them to huddle at tables outside) and ordered a much-needed second coffee and a breakfast special, which he fed piece by piece to Dante and Sissy. "We've got to do something, guys," he said, realizing that his life was slipping away into the hands of a digital PR team.

The dogs' expressions were intent as they considered his fate. Or was it the empty plate of food?

"I know it looks bad," he told them, "but maybe I should just get through the wedding then sort everything out afterward. I'll get a promotion and a proper raise and Julie and I will live happily ever after." He sighed deeply. "If only you could break your vow of non-communication with humans, or whatever they make you swear, and tell me how to sort everything out." Sissy placed her paw on his knee and looked at him encouragingly. He sighed again.

"Come on, then. Off to work." Jonathan walked the rest of the way with steady precision, placing one foot in front of the other evenly, so as not to disturb his relationship with gravity.

The first thing he saw at Comrade was a Norwegian sweater with silver buttons paired with a kilt. Greeley's face came into focus last.

"Are you okay?"

"Yes, fine, fine. Never better." Jonathan stood for a moment trying to perfect his balance and uncross his eyes. At last he whispered, "I like your outfit. And actually, as you ask, I'm not okay. I hate my job. I hate my whole life."

Greeley looked at him thoughtfully.

Perhaps he'd said too much. Jonathan bludgeoned his features into a sort of smile. "Never mind. Everything's great. I'll get to work." Pursing his lips on the way to his desk, he visualized the seven dwarfs whistling while they worked, shovels jauntily laid across their shoulders. For some reason this helped.

At his desk, he found a group e-mail from Wes to the whole team, announcing that the Broadway Depot management had called their annual account review for 2 p.m. the following Friday. Each month they scheduled an annual review designed to produce new and more strategic advertising, which led to the agency clocking up hundreds of unbillable hours as they created new campaigns and commissioned ever more comprehensive market research on the subject of ring binders and box files. Each month, Broadway Depot announced how pleased they were with the amount of thought that had gone into their useless miserable account before rejecting every single iota of new thinking in favor of "Pens: 3 for $2!"

An e-mail from Louise Crimple followed

the one from Wes: "Can't wait to see what you and the team imaginate this time, Johnny. Paperclip your dreams to a star (feel free to use that line!)."

Jonathan pressed delete and laid his head on his desk. He had a vision of Eduardo resting that slimy boneless arm on his shoulders, saying, *Still searching for your feet in marketing, boyo?* In his *New York Inferno*, he placed Eduardo down in the tenth circle of hell, up to his nostrils in tar, one hand waving in furious futility while a crowd of cheerful onlookers sipped Night Train cut with formaldehyde.

Jonathan sat up and rubbed his face with his hands, hoping to press it back into a shape that was recognizably human. He supposed he could take the brief seriously. That would be new and different. He could ignore the past months of rejection and start afresh as if Broadway Depot were a brand-new account desperate for new ideas and new thinking, rather than a dusty cage full of middle-management monkey robots led by the bizarre and nervous-making Crimple-meister. What would happen (he asked himself), what would happen if, instead of accepting the inevitable, he poured all of his intelligence, his creativity, all the power of his heart and brain and soul into producing something of value for his nemesis?

He knew exactly what would happen. What would happen would be accompanied by the sound of his life flushing down the toilet. Less than nothing. Negative nothing.

In a spasm of unlikely optimism, he began to write.

By lunchtime his headache had gone and he'd drawn the beginnings of an office murder-mystery comic with office supplies for props. Dick was found dead with a gel pen sticking out of his back ("3 for $2 on all gel pens, this week only!") while Letitia's swivel chair ("20% off all branded office chairs!") swiveled out of range just as Benedict tried to garrote her with a New! Universal Charger ("Only $19.95!") for cheating on him with Sybil. Alex lurked in corners downloading blackmail material that he laminated ("Office laminator, one week only, $259!") while Otis and Salena had torrid sex on the copier ("Plastic copier cover, protects from dust and dirt, $39.95!").

He drew page after page of comics, weaving paper clips and letterheads into one plot, computer keyboards and metal inboxes into another.

And gradually, over the course of an afternoon, Broadway Depot developed a personality. From a crappy low-cost purveyor of crappy low-cost office crap, it became an office full of heroes and villains wielding intriguing, desirable props as evidence for the coroner's court ("Reporters' notebooks, one-day sale, 5 for $12!").

Jonathan's spirit soared. He'd draw it himself. It wouldn't be any more expensive than their current campaign but could run with high visibility in small advertising spaces online, as pop-ups, banners, on billboards, local papers, anywhere. Overnight it would make Broadway Depot a household name; people would look for it, anxiously await the outcome of the next attempted murder and frustrated romance. The BD house-brand gel pen would become iconic as Dick's murder weapon. Everyone would want one.

All through the weekend he worked, writing, drawing, scanning, and mounting his creations on boards until he'd constructed a significant pile of noirishly strange and compelling Broadway Depot dramas.

Each night, Jonathan went home and fell into bed. He barely saw Julie, whose considerable energies were taken up by the most important day of her life, which was hurtling toward them at the speed of a Hellfire missile. Sometimes he woke in the morning to find her beside him, unconscious, warm, and dreaming of bespoke cocktails.

On Wednesday, he showed his ideas to Wes, who studied the boards while he explained his rationale. Wes listened, read through the comics, nodded slowly, then clapped him on the back, declaring him a man of rare creative ability and insight. Sissy doubled the speed of her tail-wagging, and even Dante forgot to glare.

Wes ran the boards by Eduardo but took his approval for a technicality, emerging ten minutes later with a thumbs-up and a grin for Jonathan, who felt his exhausted heart leap with pride. He was a young man on the rise, his talents front and center, ready to be recognized and rewarded! He'd show everyone that he was a force, an innovator for the future. He felt grateful that the wedding would take place two weeks after the Broadway Depot presentation, otherwise he might not have been able to attend.

As Patterson, the account man, and Dora, head of research, crunched the numbers and honed the marketing angle for the presentation, Jonathan allowed his imagination to wander. A promotion, a large raise, his own account, a senior position at the agency, maybe even his name on the door. Comrade Trefoil. Trefoil & Comrades. Trefoil & Sons.

Although he hadn't had a good night's sleep in days, he found he had more energy than ever. Each word out of his mouth was sharp and clear, he no longer felt hunger or thirst, his body seemed to be running on pure high-octane adrenaline.

Clémence frowned at him. "You look terrible," she said.

"I'm not. I'm better than I've ever been. Sharp as a Jedi sword. Whoosh whoosh."

"Okay." She shrugged and made his coffee.

He bought thirty croissants and gave them out to everyone in the office. Dante swallowed his thoughtfully, and Max sent Jonathan an e-mail.

FROM: max@comrade.com
TO: jonathan@comrade.com
SUBJECT: Whatever drugs you're on

They're awesome.

Jonathan didn't answer. There was nothing else for him to do on the campaign, and Wes suggested a day off.

"You're looking a bit jittery," Wes said. "Get some sleep. We need you fresh for the presentation on Friday."

Bathed in approbation, he stopped at a

metro man boutique and bought four over-priced T-shirts in lime, piña colada, pink fizz, and greige, along with a China blue linen jacket and organic jeans imported from Japan at a price that made his eyes water. Remember, the salesman said, no washing for a year at least.

That night he sent out for pizza with goat cheese, artichoke, and kale (Julie's favorite), feeling certain that this campaign would make Julie realize what an amazing partner she was marrying, what a virile, go-getting kind of guy he really was.

In the apartment, his eyes met hers. *I'm a real man,* he telepathed her. *I excel at my job, and I'm so virile we might have sex right now on the table.*

This was a step too far for Julie, who telepathed back that such a thing was only going to happen when hell sold Eskimo pies.

He gabbled happily about their future over dinner. Julie seemed put out by something but wasn't saying what. Her mouth turned down at the corners and his stories stuttered toward aborted conclusions. She waited till he finally fell silent.

"Aren't you at all interested in how our wedding's going?"

The wedding! Jonathan clapped a hand to his mouth. "Of course!" he said. "Of course

I'm interested. It's going to be the happiest day of our lives! You in celadon, me in burned chocolate! Do we get to write our own vows? I'd like to make a small speech about forever, you know, in geological terms."

Her expression stopped him.

"No?"

A small seed of doubt had taken root in her heart. Lorenza gave their viability as a couple the lowest possible rating — not that she trusted Lorenza exactly, but zero out of ten felt dispiriting. And yet, didn't she love Jonathan? What, besides love, could explain this feeling of desperate inevitability?

"No geological themes," she said. "No fossils. No use of the word 'funeral.' No jokes. Non-negotiable, Jonathan."

Jonathan experienced a rush of passion for his wife-to-be. He loved her most when she was at her most implacable.

"Are you sure you want to marry me?" His eyes searched hers, looking for . . . for what?

"Of course I want to marry you."

"Why?"

"Why?"

"Yes. Why do you want to marry me?"

She shook her head.

"No, I mean it. You could find someone

better. Someone who was more organized and made more money and didn't have dogs."

Her eyes filled with tears. "I don't want someone else. I'm used to you."

Which was true. After four years he knew how she reacted to things, he knew she hated mess and change and upset. There was bound to be someone out there better suited to her than him, but was that really so important? If this were an arranged marriage, would they obsess about whether they were perfect for each other? Or would they make the best of what they had and get on with the rest of their lives? There seemed to be a good deal of merit in that approach.

He looked at her, and was moved, as he had been so many times in the past, by her vulnerability. Her carefully controlled approach to life kept chaos at bay.

"Julie?"

"Yes?"

"Are you sure?"

She nodded and put one hand to his face. He kissed her and for one moment she was everything he needed in life, everything he most loved and feared.

It was good they'd had this talk. They both felt better for it.

Their funeral was going to be amazing.

21

The morning of the big Broadway Depot presentation, Dante awoke with a cough. He stood swaying, nose an inch off the ground, eyes watery. A worried Jonathan took both dogs around the block, but by the time they made it to the corner, Dante had stopped walking and just coughed. The noise was horrible, a grating rasp that was painful even to hear. Jonathan bundled him up in his jacket, gathered him into his arms, hailed a cab, and went straight to the vet.

Dr. Clare ushered them in. "I don't like the sound of that."

"He's been coughing like that all morning. I think it might be bird flu."

"Good boy," she said to Dante. "Can you get him up onto the table, please?"

Jonathan lifted him up. "Do you think he's okay?" The idea of Dante succumbing to something awful — cancer, heart disease, a neurological condition — was intolerable.

In a flash, he realized how much he had come to depend on his dogs. "Could it be distemper? Isn't that usually fatal?" He felt like crying.

"He hasn't got distemper. He's been vaccinated." Dr. Clare slipped a light over her forehead. "Can you hang on to him for a minute? He won't like this much." She gently took hold of his lower and upper jaws. "Come on, sweetheart," she murmured, "open wide."

Dante didn't want to open wide. From the floor, Sissy whined in sympathy.

"You don't think I have Munchausen's by proxy, do you?"

"No, I don't. There's a good lad." Dr. Clare had opened Dante's mouth and was peering into his throat. "Hmm." She freed one hand to press her intercom. "Iris? I need some help." Dante squirmed and she released him as Iris entered.

"If you can keep his mouth open," Dr. Clare said. "And, Jonathan, hold him steady. I won't have to sedate him if I can do this quickly."

With all hands on dog, Dr. Clare picked up a pair of forceps and reached into Dante's throat. A second later she removed them, attached to a large rubber-coated pink neon Broadway Depot paper clip.

Dante gagged once, sat down on the table, and looked calmly around the room.

"What a brave boy," said Dr. Clare, ruffling his ears.

Jonathan looked on in horror. A Broadway Depot paper clip?

Dr. Clare held the offender at the end of her forceps. "That's it," she said. "Nasty thing."

Jonathan shook his head. "The bastards," he said. "They will not stop at killing my dog."

The vet blinked. "Jonathan? Who's they? The television hasn't started talking to you, has it?"

"No, Dr. Vet. I am not that crazy, not yet, though I suspect it's just a matter of time." He met her eyes. "You wouldn't understand. You, who restore and tend the wounded like a saint. A person of your qualities would not understand what it's like to dwell on the dark side."

She frowned. "Are you okay, Jonathan? You seem a bit . . ."

"Unraveled?" Jonathan nodded. "I know." For a moment he gazed at her. "I'm so grateful that you saved my dog's life. You are a glimmer of light in the vast indifferent darkness of the universe." He hugged Dante and then, after a second's hesitation, hugged

Dr. Clare. Hugging her made him feel good. Safe. More good than safe.

After a decent interval, she carefully disengaged herself. "Jonathan?"

He wiped a hand across his eyes. "Thank you, Dr. Vet. Thank you for all your many kindnesses."

"Jonathan? Have you thought of taking some time off?"

"Don't worry. It's not as bad as it looks. Everything's going just a tad . . ." He waggled his hands around in the air and goggled his eyes. "But you're not a psychiatrist and I'm not a dog, so you and I have come to an impasse."

Iris looked from one to the other. "Am I done here?"

"Yes. Thank you, Iris." Dr. Clare opened the door for her.

Feeling that their time was coming to an end, Jonathan scrambled to change the subject. "You never said what you thought of the Fideaux hotel."

"It was ghastly. I couldn't wait to get away." She smiled a worried smile at him, a smile so full of concern it made him want to lie down next to her in a meadow and hold her warm and claspy hand. He felt full of wonder for her clinical skill, her choppy hair, her accent, her face, her choice of profession, her conspicuously large feet. He knew about people falling in love this way. It was a cliché. Florence Nightingale syndrome. An actual syndrome.

"So, what will you do with Wilma when you go away with your boyfriend?"

Her smile faded. "We're not going anywhere just now."

He peered at her closely and she turned away, mouth set.

Did this mean that her relationship was in trouble? He would like to have asked, but he was getting married very soon, and under the circumstances, the question seemed wrong. He knew that asking an attractive female vet why she looked so sad was just the sort of thing that was no longer allowed now that he was marrying Julie, and despite the fact that Dr. Clare had neither shown any interest in having a relationship with him, nor was in any sense single, this thought depressed him.

"Well, I'd better go now. A million thanks for taking such good care of my dog. I hope . . . I hope I'll see you very soon," he said, realizing as he spoke that it was not the appropriate farewell to an emergency vet. He made no move to go. "Dr. Vet?"

"Yes?"

"Do you like your job?"

She looked startled. "Yes, of course I do."

"Really like it?"

She nodded. "I always wanted to be a vet. From the time I was five."

"And was it worth it?"

"Worth what?"

"All the hard work. And now, living in New York. Leaving behind the ducks."

She smiled. "And the herons?"

"And the herons! Yes! Is it worth everything you had to give up?"

She nodded once more. "Yes," she said. "It's worth it."

"You're very lucky."

"I know."

"So am I," he said. "To know you, I mean."

I'd like to hug you again, he thought. I'd like to rub my face against your neck, but I'm fairly sure it's not allowed.

Then her hand was on his arm, her face inches from his. "Jonathan," she whispered and he half closed his eyes, his head tipping back as she leaned in, her breath warm, her lips brushing his.

"Jonathan?"

He opened his eyes and looked up to where she stood across the room, frowning a little, puzzled. He tried to hold on to the moment but failed.

She closed the door behind him.

It was a few minutes past nine when they reached Le Grand Pain and Clémence handed him his coffee, just as he liked it. Luc emerged from the back (bored so soon of Paris?), spoke to his wife in a stream of barely audible French, then kissed her on the lips. Jonathan felt invisible.

They made a beautiful couple, he thought morosely. He had to admit that her children with Luc would be as beautiful as Celeste, Raoul, and Alouette. He hated the idea of the two sets of offspring in competition and glared at Luc, who didn't notice.

All the women he liked loved someone else. Except for Julie, of course.

At work, the conference room was decorated with Broadway Depot products. Jonathan's campaign was hung sequentially around the walls, covered in tracing paper to be torn aside for dramatic effect. He wore his new blue linen jacket, lime-green T-shirt, and Japanese jeans and looked, if he did say so himself, unimpeachably hipster.

He hadn't eaten much over the past forty-eight hours. Food had stopped appealing to him days ago. The sleep situation wasn't much better, but he was delighted to discover that the thinner and hungrier he became, the sharper he felt. Whoosh.

The entire team mustered for the morning run-through: Jonathan and Wes, Eduardo for executive weight, Greeley as official witness, Patterson the account man, Dora the researcher, and Dante and Sissy, dogsbodies. Wes insisted they practice every detail till it ran like clockwork, and by lunchtime it did.

"Well done, everyone," he said. "See you at three."

At five minutes to three, the Broadway Depot team filed in led by Louise Crimple, who sought Jonathan out, put a hand on his arm, and whispered, "Take me to paradise, you crazy fool," in his ear. Jonathan looked up, startled, but she merely winked at him and skipped away to the coffee bar. Over coffee and macadamia white-chocolate brownies, pleasantries were exchanged and the BD team seemed happy to be attending their monthly annual meeting yet again. Every time Jonathan looked for her, Louise wrinkled her nose at him like a rabbit. He began to hyperventilate.

"Right," said Wes. "I know all agencies tell all clients that each new campaign represents a major breakthrough, and I'm sure you're as tired of hearing it as we are saying it. But in this case, in *this* case, ladies and gentlemen, introducing your new campaign as anything other than a work of genius would be selling it short." Jonathan wondered whether he really was a genius, and if so, what he was doing working for Ed.

Dora got up first and anesthetized the room with a Power-Point presentation of such stunning banality that Jonathan felt his nervous system shutting down in protest.

Stay alive, stay alive! His pulse felt weak and thready; five more minutes and everyone in the room would be flatlining. Across the table, Wes's final thought before his cerebral cortex clocked off was that he needed to buy toothpaste. Louise Crimple was halfway through her third brownie and didn't appear to be listening.

Patterson picked up the baton and wrestled everyone back from the brink of extinction, explaining that the Broadway Depot business needed booster rockets if it wasn't going to burn up on reentry into the overheated office-supply atmosphere.

Patterson's ability to spin a metaphor out long beyond its natural life span impressed Jonathan, who had begun to feel weirdly hot.

"But here's the man you really want to hear from. The genius behind your new campaign, Jonathan Trefoil."

He was a genius. He must be. People kept

saying it.

Jonathan stood up slowly. Why was it so hot in this room? He looked at Louise, who held his eyes for an uncomfortably long time, then ground to a complete halt, seeming to forget what he was doing in the conference room or even on Planet Earth. He smiled a beatific smile, hummed "Daisy, Daisy, give me your answer do."

Wes shot a nervous glance at Greeley, who looked straight ahead, expressionless.

At the last possible instant, Jonathan began to speak. An audible gasp arose from his fellow Comrades as he gazed straight into the eyes of Louise Crimple and told her exactly how soul-destroying it was to work on her account. He spoke tenderly and with great care, explaining that there were days when eternal nothingness seemed preferable to working on Broadway Depot.

No offense, Louise, he said, and smiled at her. She smiled back.

Murmurs eddied around the room. Dante pricked an ear at his master. With his extraordinarily fine hearing, he could detect an avalanche rumbling in the distance.

Wes pointed meaningfully at the work on the wall and Jonathan changed direction with the excruciating slowness of the *Queen Mary* doubling back toward New York Harbor. At long last he launched into the thinking behind his new campaign. He was cogent, articulate, flowing; he spoke with conviction and charm until finally, with a dramatic flourish, he tore the tracing paper off the first story. The BD team, led by a trembly-lipped Louise, stood and approached the work. Jonathan watched their faces, his eyes unnaturally bright, his color high. When they finished reading, he tore the paper off the next comic. And the next. The team looked to Louise for a lead on how to react.

Louise said nothing. She squinted at the comics, her face registering a profound and unyielding blankness.

And then she turned to Jonathan.

"Wow," she said. And then, "Amazeballs."

And immediately there were wide smiles of appreciation, chuckles of approval, increasing murmurs of "wow," "amazeballs," and "wow, amazeballs!"

Eventually, Jonathan motioned for everyone to sit down. "Before you respond formally, I'd like to say a few words about how this campaign will benefit your business."

In perfect control now, he paused until the entire room was silent and every eye upon him. He smiled a smile of perfect brilliance at Louise, who sank down in her chair as if she might swoon. And then he began to speak.

"Cordially did existence put suffering over to a lemon," he opened with a dramatic flourish. "Once a ferret bonanza slept."

The smiles on the faces of the clients faded slightly.

Jonathan moved across to the next ad. "Friends enjoy meat. Too many elbow stoops." He glanced around the room, gauging the reaction. It wasn't quite what he'd hoped for. Were his ads not brilliant after all? Was he not truly a genius?

He plowed onward. "Did lung augment frenzy? Agreement, gentleman, rapturous balloon feats. Consultation requires bedroom sincerity."

They were staring at him openmouthed. Had he just said "bedroom sincerity"?

"Mother fulfilled property llama." Oh God. He could hear himself now. He was generating random text. In his mind he was composing ordinary, coherent sentences, but they were coming out all wrong.

Desperate, he continued. "These ads . . ." That was better! "These ads deliver cannibal stupor for pony twin." Cannibal stupor for pony twin? What did that even mean? "New foliage and fingers of luck. Ever the sporadic bean tree, spooning a distant owl. Splat flaps rejoice."

He paused, setting up his final ace.

"Rat star. Pontoon. Luddite insensate." And finally, "Amen."

He sat down, to frozen silence.

Greeley stood, walked calmly over to Jonathan, and put a hand on his arm. "Let's take five." Holding Jonathan firmly by the elbow and nodding reassuringly at the bemused clients, Greeley guided him into Wes's office, closed the door behind them, and sat Jonathan in Wes's chair.

"Put your head between your knees. That's right. And breathe."

Through the glass wall, they could see Wes helping Louise Crimple, who appeared to be sobbing, out of the conference room.

Jonathan breathed but it didn't help. The words in his head made sense, but when he opened his mouth to tell Greeley not to worry, he said, "Pencil of doom."

Wes was dialing 911, gesticulating through the glass door for Max. "Ambulance please," he said, and gave the address.

Max came in looking worried. "Hey, Jay. What up?" He put a hand on his friend's shoulder and Jonathan lifted his head.

"Cyclops," he said.

Max looked at Greeley, whose face was grave.

Was he having a stroke? Sissy's head was in his lap and Dante stood by his side. The ambulance took ten minutes to arrive, whereupon medics checked his blood pressure, inquired as to sources of any pain and previous medical conditions including diabetes and stroke, shined a flashlight at his pupils, and stuck a needle in his arm. He responded to questions about his name and the year with "Cribbage alarm? Pineapple drear."

The medics glanced at each other as they lifted him onto a rolling stretcher. "No blows to the head in the past forty-eight hours?"

"None that we know of," Greeley said.

"It's hard to say precisely what's going on," the other medic told Wes as they wheeled Jonathan out the door. "We'll treat him for brain trauma and get some tests done. Can you hang on to the dogs?"

The dogs did not want to be hung on to. Sissy set up a dreadful howling wail, while Dante tried frantically to reroute the ambulance men. Max shut them in the supply room.

"Bugles!" cried Jonathan, struggling to free himself from the gurney.

"Don't worry about the dogs, Jay. I'll take care of them. Hang on in there, buddy."

The ambulance men rolled him into the service elevator and disappeared.

Back in the conference room, no one except Louise had moved or uttered a word. It was simpler to stand up, walk to the door, and leave. It was simpler, and so that's what everyone did. Wes and Greeley remained behind, not meeting each other's eyes. Eduardo's perfectly tanned face had turned gray. He walked into his office and shut the door.

Jonathan began to feel drowsy even before the ambulance gained speed and, when he asked what was happening, found he could only say, "Oblong fish prince." The nice young medic reassured him that he didn't have to talk, and that he wasn't in any immediate danger. For the first time in days, he dropped into a deep sleep.

22

Jonathan dreamed of a tall doctor with a curly smile who said she had neutered hundreds of patients and he shouldn't worry. He awoke sweating and disoriented, relieved to discover (after some discreet investigation) that he was still in possession of all relevant body parts, after which he drifted off, waking sometime later in a crisp white sandwich of hospital sheets with Felix the Cat staring down at him. He blinked.

"Jonathan?" Felix spoke.

He gazed up at the face with its loopy black-and-white eyes and a grin that spread from ear to ear in a gigantic U.

"How are you feeling?"

The voice was Julie's but the face stubbornly belonged to Felix. Jonathan felt confused. "Pink paper tree."

Felix frowned. "Don't talk. They told me not to tire you out. I'll just stay here while you rest."

"Limpopo gleam?"

"Close your eyes and sleep now."

He felt a sudden surge of panic and struggled to sit up. "Dobbins!"

"Don't worry, Max brought the dogs home. I'm taking care of them."

He sank back, closed his eyes, and subsided into unconsciousness once more.

When he woke again, Wilma the dog was talking to Felix. Jonathan shut his eyes for a moment.

When next he opened them, a young doctor dressed in green scrubs stood beside his bed, staring at his chart. "Hello, Jonathan. My name is Dr. Devi. You've had quite a day."

He stared at the doctor. Dr. Devi had long black fur and buttons for eyes.

"Do you understand what I'm saying?"

Jonathan nodded.

"How are you feeling now?"

"Dibling," Jonathan said, peering sideways at the doctor, whose ears appeared to be made of felt.

"No pain, no headache, no tingling in the fingers?"

Jonathan shook his head.

"Poor thing is very confused," Julie said.

"Are you hearing anything strange? Voices, static, ringing in the ears?"

He shook his head again while Dr. Devi made notes. Jonathan lifted one hand a few inches off the bed, barely resisting the urge to stroke the doctor's soft fur.

"No recent head injury?"

"None," Julie said.

"Any history of mental illness?"

Julie looked at the floor.

"Schizophrenia, bipolar, mood disorders, mania, paranoia?"

Jonathan shook his head firmly.

"Anything else I should know about?"

Jonathan didn't know how to express the fact that nearly everyone had turned into cartoons and his doctor was a plush toy.

"Cattoons," he said. "Looney spoons."

They both looked at him blankly.

"Looney spoons! Gull wrinkle!" Frustration caused him to ball his hands into fists. *"Milky moose!"*

Julie shrugged.

Dr. Devi glanced at her with sympathy and made notes on his chart. "The senior neurologist has ordered more scans . . ." When he looked up again, Jonathan was staring at him with peculiar intensity.

A few minutes later, as Dr. Devi stood by the nursing station, Julie approached tentatively. "Excuse me."

"Hello."

"I'm actually Jonathan's fiancée. We're supposed to be getting married soon. Do you think he'll be in any . . . I mean, do you think we should postpone the wedding?"

"Ah." Dr. Devi seemed discomfited by the question. "How soon, exactly, is soon?"

"Three weeks."

Dr. Devi nodded slowly. "Well. It's impossible to say what's wrong with your boyfriend, but I think you'd agree that he doesn't seem . . . right. That's the technical term," he said, and smiled at Julie. "I'm afraid I can't really give absolute advice at this point, but if it were me? I would certainly think twice about going ahead with your plans."

"Oh," said Julie, eyes filling with tears.

"That's probably not the answer you wanted," he said. They were interrupted by his pager. "I'm very sorry I couldn't be more helpful."

When Jonathan woke again, the first thing he saw was Felix. She had three large white fingers on each hand. Jonathan knew this wasn't right, but no matter how hard he tried, he couldn't change her back into his girlfriend. Like it or not, he was engaged to Felix the Cat.

Someone else arrived.

"Hi, Lorenza." He heard Julie's greeting.

"So nice of you to come."

"How is he?"

"Sleeping now. About the same."

"You think he'll be ready for the wedding? If not, we're going to have to start looking for a sub."

"Lorenza, it could be a stroke. Or a brain tumor."

Jonathan could almost hear her shrug. "Anyone else you've considered marrying? Because I can't pull the plug on the whole operation at this stage."

A brain tumor? That hadn't occurred to him. It would make sense, though. Was there such a thing as a tumor that converted people into cartoons? Or turned doctors into stuffed toys? He cracked open an eye. Oh God. Lorenza was Daffy Duck. Well, that figured. None of your cheerful Disney characters for her, just malevolent sarcasm with a great big clacking orange beak.

When Julie excused herself to go to the ladies' room, Daffy stood very close to Jonathan's bed, bent down, and clacked her horrible beak in his ear: "Pretty elaborate way to get out of a wedding, Jack. If you've got cold feet, maybe you should just screw up your courage and tell Julie it's off?"

Jonathan closed his eyes and put his hands over his ears.

Daffy stared down at him. "You might as well. She'd have to be crazy to marry you now."

He squeezed his eyes tighter in an attempt to stop her clacking him to death with her big scary beak. Clack clack clack.

Felix returned to the room and took her place across from Daffy. Both were leaning over him now.

"So, Julie. Seriously. No one on your B list?" Clackity clack clack.

Julie glared at her. "Honestly, Lorenza, even you can't think I've got some substitute husband up my sleeve."

Daffy looked thoughtful. "I suppose I could ask Helen and Ingy. They might go for it. Ingy would fit the suit with a bit of alteration. Lesbians always pull in the crowds."

Jonathan didn't actually think he'd had a stroke. Or a brain tumor. It felt like something simpler. Some kind of systems shutdown. His head hurt. He wanted everyone to leave him alone now, preferably forever.

He opened his eyes, picked up the pen, and scribbled a note to Lorenza: GOA HAY.

She stared at the note and turned it sideways. He snatched it back.

PORK TOFF, he scribbled. PORK TOFF.

Julie looked at the note. "I think maybe

he wants to be left alone."

Daffy shrugged.

Felix got up, kissed her fiancé, and promised to return as soon as possible. "I hope you feel better soon, Jonathan."

Pork toff, thought Jonathan. And stay porked toff.

23

Much to his surprise, Jonathan's breakdown signaled a positive shift in his relationship with Julie, a.k.a. Felix the Cat, who spent hours at the hospital and didn't once mention the wedding.

Do you take this woman to be your awful wedded wife?

Bag balm.

His parents came to visit disguised as Tom and Jerry and he watched with delight as they chased each other around his hospital room. He felt quite sad when they had to go, but the nurse told them his temperature was up and he needed rest.

Max came the next day after work, looking entirely like his usual self. Jonathan blinked. No Superman, Spider-Man, Elmer Fudd? Huh.

"How you doing, Jaybird?"

Jonathan grimaced and waved one hand in a halfhearted gesture of dismissal.

"You still talking funny?"

"Organ."

"Organ to you too, pal. Don't try to talk. I'll give you the highlights. Work is good. I mean, not good, obviously. But everyone loves the fact that Broadway Depot caused you to have a stroke or a breakdown or whatever it is you've had. We're not happy you're in here, obviously, but drama-wise it's fantastic. Eduardo's spending every waking hour hiding under his desk talking to lawyers, worried you'll die and he'll get done for manslaughter. I'm not suggesting you die just to satisfy an office pool, but if you did, I promise I'd throw you a slap-up wake."

"Panacea."

"Exactly the word I'd use. You die, Eduardo goes bankrupt, I win the office pool, who's not happy?"

They sat in silence for a moment. Max shifted in his chair.

"Look, Jay. What about this wedding? You're not going through with it, are you? Maybe someone's trying to tell you something with this whole speaking-in-tongues hoopla. Like you're a total fuckwit and this was the worst idea you ever had. Not to kick a guy when he's down, but."

Jonathan looked at him.

"Metaphor, pal: big shiny semielectric Korean people carrier with weather sensors and four-wheel drive. Holds eight and'll get you to Seoul on a tank of gas. Heated seats, antiskid brakes. That's Julie. All great. Except that what you need is a road bike — takes you everywhere, makes you happy on the way. The thing is — are you following me here? You probably don't even want a car. You can take the bus if it rains."

"Ali Baba trout." Jonathan felt a rush of affection for his friend.

"You know I want you happy. But you can't marry Julie. And you've got a cast-iron get-out right here. Julie's . . . let's just say I've known you a long time, and honestly, I can't see it."

"Papa Doc banana float."

"Yeah, okay." Max shrugged. "No one's going to tell you what to do, but" — he lowered his voice — "postpone for now? See how you feel when you're better?"

"Leipzig."

"Look, buddy." He got up. "I gotta go now, but think about what I'm saying. I've always wanted a Deluxe Popcorn Master 5000. I'm totally cool keeping it for myself. Or you can have it anyway, without getting married. Whatever."

Jonathan closed his eyes, and when he

221

opened them again Max was gone.

The hospital kept him in for three days of scans and tests and evaluations and interviews. His symptoms were not normal — the neurologists had never before had a patient who translated people into cartoons. Other symptoms came and went, like a tendency to hear ghosts breathing and an inability to recognize his own hands. But his scans showed nothing suspicious and none of it added up to a known syndrome.

"From your speech anomalies, we might normally guess that the connecting tissue between the Broca and Wernicke's areas in the upper portion of the temporal lobe, here" — the senior neurologist pointed to a section of the brain that Jonathan thought looked rather like Madagascar — "may have experienced damage or trauma of some sort, resulting in an expressive aphasia. But you're not reporting any blows to the head and I'm not seeing anything on the scans. There's no doubt that you're experiencing a misfire between thought and word. Your grammar appears relatively intact, but the content is random. We sometimes use the term 'word salad.' "

Word salad. Nice.

Julie raised her hand a little, like a child in elementary school. "Has he had a stroke?"

"Damage to the arcuate fasciculus could be caused by a stroke, but there's no evidence of stroke, or any other sinister event. Sometimes we find a lesion, but nothing's leaping out at me here. That doesn't mean nothing's happened, but based on Mr. Trefoil's low risk factors, I'd be inclined not to intervene for the short term. We'll wait and see if his symptoms resolve. At your age" — the neurologist smiled at Jonathan, a bit wearily — "and without any particular clinical evidence, diagnosis is mostly guesswork."

Julie looked from the doctor to Jonathan and back again. "I'm not suggesting he's made it up or anything, but could it possibly be, you know . . ."

"Psychosomatic?" The doctor shrugged. "I've seen stranger things."

The three sat in silence.

"What happens next?" Julie's hands gripped the handle of her bag so hard her knuckles showed white.

"What he mostly needs is rest. I'll arrange a letter for his employer and we'll see him in two weeks. Obviously, if he experiences any more symptoms, particularly any more peculiar symptoms, let us know at once."

Julie wondered whether symptoms more peculiar than the ones Jonathan was experiencing even existed.

Neither Jonathan nor Julie asked whether expressive aphasia would contraindicate a wedding. Jonathan expected Julie to ask, whereas Julie hoped that by not asking, she might avoid hearing something she didn't want to hear, whatever that might be. "Absolutely no wedding" might be less devastating than "No reason you can't go right ahead with it."

As they left the waiting room, they ran into Dr. Devi.

"Fraud," said Jonathan.

Dr. Devi looked serious. "Still not getting his words straight?"

Julie shook her head.

"Good luck with . . . etcetera," he said and sped away.

Set adrift by the medical establishment, Jonathan wondered how he was ever going to earn a living. What if his condition lasted forever? Who would have sex with a person who couldn't even say the word "sex"? *Voulez-vous sauté avec moi?*

Julie took him home, where the dogs greeted him with wild delight. Tears came to his eyes and he thought, My pack.

Over the next few days, Julie took care of him and the dogs. She seemed perfectly happy to keep communication to a minimum until his speech returned to normal, and while he remained in a state of medically sanctioned peculiarity, she was less critical. They got along better now that he couldn't talk, and when they lay together in bed, he felt closer to her than ever.

After a few days at home, Julie's Felix the Cat aspect faded and she returned to something considerably more like a person. She continued to look odd, however, as if someone unknown to him had been given extensive Julie-like plastic surgery.

All in all, despite the neurologist's theory about damage to the arcuate fasciculus, Jonathan couldn't escape a sense that he'd developed a sudden and extreme emotional reaction to certain aspects of the world, and that Julie might well be one of those aspects.

He closed his eyes and dreamed of Dr. Clare. Which was surprising, but nice.

24

After the acrobatic flamboyance of their greeting, Sissy and Dante padded around the apartment, silent as snakes, taking it in turns to guard him.

His normal speech showed no sign of returning.

"Toast or eggs, Jonathan?"

"Blimp."

Julie brought him toast, which wasn't what he'd wanted, but he smiled and gave her two thumbs up anyway.

"Orc?"

"Work was good. Everyone's wishing you well and hoping you'll be better in time for the wedding." She took his hand. "Not that I want you leaping out of bed just so my magazine can go through with their employee issue, but we need to decide if you think you can't make it." In fact, Ingy and Helen had agreed in principle to step in. Whether they were a dream couple was open to debate, but they were photogenic enough, offered good gender diversity, and more or less fit the clothes.

Jonathan closed his eyes. His brother arrived a week from Thursday. His parents were driving into town the following day. Everyone he'd invited had said yes. He had to go through with it.

He phoned Max.

"Hello?"

"Trinket."

"That you, Jay?"

"Obligation antifreeze."

"How you feeling?"

"Carp."

"That's tough, buddy. Anything I can do?"

"Whirligig freedom toy."

"Wedding off?"

"Opal figurine."

Max sighed. "I'm sorry to hear that, but you know I'll be there for you. Hope you don't mind, but I've used your popcorn popper. Just once. But holy shit, it is *so* great. You're gonna love it."

"Glump."

"Aww, don't be glump, guy. You want me to come over?"

"Pond asylum."

"You sure? I could bring some brews and a DVD."

"Poop in a tree."

"Well, okay, if you're sure. Could be worse, you know, you could be at work. Ed says hi, by the way. Just kidding, he's forgotten all about you. Stay strong. Peace out, bro."

Jonathan hung up, feeling slightly better. Julie would be home soon. She was helping him with improvised verbal rehab.

"Repeat after me: dog."

"Boudoir."

"Cat."

"Ogle."

Julie frowned. "Red."

He was trying, really he was. "Loopyloo."

"Are you concentrating, Jonathan? Spot."

"Duck duck duck!" Brow furrowed, eyes squinty, his mouth twisted as he tried to shape the words. Even Julie had to admit he seemed earnest. But he couldn't do it. They wouldn't form. Sometimes he felt sure that the next word out of his mouth would be exactly right, but instead it was exactly wrong. Loopyloo.

"Bastard!" he said, tears of frustration filling his eyes.

"Oh my God, that's fantastic!" Julie said, hugging him. "You did it! Keep going!" She held up an apple from the fruit bowl.

Jonathan stared at it; apple, he thought,

apple. App-pull. *"A . . . a . . . a . . . a-louette!"*

Julie sighed, put the apple back in the fruit bowl, and patted his arm. "Never mind. You said 'bastard,' and I think you meant it too. You've done very well for today."

Jonathan practiced quietly on his own, thinking of a word and then attempting to whisper it to himself, but was no more successful than during his lessons with Julie.

I do, he repeated silently, again and again. I do, I do, I do, I do.

"Anus," he said.

25

While Julie was at work the following day, Greeley arrived unannounced. Between buzzing him in and Greeley's arrival at the apartment door, Jonathan hurtled out of bed, pulled on a clean shirt, and threw cold water on his face. Greeley the Wise. Greeley the Zen. Perhaps Greeley would offer much-needed insight into what was wrong with him and how to take his life forward.

The dogs got to their guest first, taking possession before Jonathan could head them off. Greeley greeted them with affection, scrumpling their ears and speaking to them in what Jonathan assumed was a fairly fluent version of Dog. When at last they'd all had enough, Greeley stood up and looked carefully at Jonathan.

"You're very pale. How are you feeling?"

Jonathan didn't want to speak for fear of setting off the word-salad guessing game that so exhausted and discouraged his visitors. Instead, he disappeared into the kitchen, pulled out a box of spiced chai tea bags, and offered them.

Greeley smiled. "Thank you."

Jonathan balanced two cups of chai and a box of lemon snaps on a cutting board and carried it into the living room. The two sat in silence. Greeley looked around the room, taking in details.

"Evolution freak," Jonathan said at last.

"It's okay. Don't worry about talking. I just wanted to see for myself that you're alive and well."

He nodded.

"We miss you at Comrade."

Jonathan raised an eyebrow and wondered who, besides Max and Greeley, could possibly miss him at work.

"Everything's going fine and nobody's heard a word about Broadway Depot. As you might expect."

Jonathan experienced a ripple of shock. He'd forgotten all about Broadway Depot.

"I expect they're confounded by the quality of the work. Which is no bad thing. Who knows? They might even see the light." Greeley looked doubtful.

They sat sipping tea.

"I don't suppose the doctors have any idea when your word issues might resolve?"

Jonathan appreciated Greeley saying "when." He shook his head.

"No need to worry about your job. You get disability at sixty percent for thirteen weeks, and we can look at other options if it takes longer. Everyone's anxious to see you back."

Everyone?

Greeley turned away. "Except me."

Jonathan froze.

"I was hoping this incident would serve as . . ." Greeley hesitated. "As a catalyst."

Jonathan marveled that a person who looked so young could speak from such a position of spiritual authority.

"A wake-up call, perhaps." Greeley's eyes swung back to Jonathan's.

How can I consider my future, Jonathan wanted to say, when I can't even shout "come on up" down my own intercom?

He opened his mouth to speak but closed it again.

Greeley's gaze softened. "I know it's not easy for you. But have you thought about what will happen when your voice comes back? What you'll say? Think about it, Jonathan. It's important."

The power of Greeley's eyes seemed to hold Jonathan up, to lift and carry him forward. Jonathan reached over and took hold of Greeley's hand and they sat, silent, for a long moment.

"Word dream," he said at last.

Greeley nodded.

Then Julie arrived home and exchanged pleasantries about office life with Greeley, who finished the tea and thanked her for the lemon thins. No one mentioned the wedding.

When it came time for Greeley to leave, Jonathan felt an overwhelming urge to block the door. He waved goodbye instead.

Julie emerged from the kitchen and asked if Greeley was a boy or a girl. "It's almost impossible to tell," she said.

Jonathan could only shake his head and shrug.

"A boy, I think," Julie said.

I don't think it matters, Jonathan thought.

Julie snapped leashes onto the dogs and took them out. Jonathan liked how devoted they were to her now that she was cast in a caring role. They'd stopped playing the ironic hello game every night and made a huge effort to be charming. Jonathan appreciated this greatly; it reduced the stress of them all living together.

Julie was on her way to the dog run when Dante pulled her sharply off course.

"Dante, no!" she said, in her firmest voice.

He ignored her, half leading, half dragging her down the block, stopping when he came to a good-looking female German shorthaired pointer.

"Dante!" Julie attempted to pull him away. "I'm sorry about my dog," she said to the pointer's owner. "We were headed for the dog run."

"So were we," he said. "I'm Mark, by the way."

They walked the two blocks together, chatting easily. At the dog run, they talked about how it was getting warmer and look at the face on that one! And then Mark asked her what she did, and she told him and he told her he was a lawyer and she said that's such an amazing coincidence, I might need a lawyer someday, and they both laughed even though it wasn't particularly funny and then talked about their neighborhood and how expensive it was becoming and had he tried the new breakfast place and then he said he had to run because he was having dinner with his girlfriend and didn't want to be late and Julie experienced a tiny stab of disappointment that wasn't at all logical.

The following evening, Dante found his friend at the dog run immediately and Julie didn't even have time to unclip the leash before she was dragged over. Mark was standing nearby.

"Hello again," he said, while Sissy trained her love-eyes on him. It proved an irresistible double assault.

Thereafter, every night at 9:15, the dogs wagged their tails and trotted Julie briskly out of the building, hunting down the pointer and Mark, who, except for evenings he was out with clients, kept the sort of precise hours you might expect from a lawyer. Between 9:15 and 10:00, the two humans and three dogs chatted about this and that, returning in time to make pleasant conversation with their respective partners, or, in Julie's case, to wrongly interpret her partner's poignant outbursts of broken gibberish.

Julie, being a girl of almost pathological practicality, at first tried to avoid liking Mark, who, though attractive, was not single. She, of course, was not single either. But after a few days she began to enjoy the company of her new dog-walking companion so much that she ceased to care.

"They're not my dogs," she explained to Mark. "They belong to my boyfriend's brother."

Mark nodded. "Mine belongs to my girlfriend. But we co-parent."

Julie couldn't think of anything enthusiastic to say about that.

"Is he nice? Your boyfriend?" Mark was genuinely curious.

Julie hesitated for a moment, then told him everything she could think to tell about Jonathan. The garbled speech and odd flights of fancy, the long diversionary thought processes that she described as trancelike. Inappropriate use of the word "funeral."

"Well," Mark said. He turned away, glancing back at her sideways. "He sounds very . . . original."

Julie sighed. "That's one way of looking at it."

Mark paused as if weighing up whether to continue. "Maybe he's having some kind of breakdown? Has he been under a lot of stress lately?"

Julie frowned. "Do you know anyone in New York who isn't under a lot of stress? I don't think he likes his job much." She felt reluctant to mention their actual wedding. They looked away from each other, concentrating on the dogs. Dante and Mark's pointer played together with raucous joy while Sissy and another little spaniel argued over a ball.

The following evening, Julie was silent for

some time. "So . . . what's your girlfriend like?"

"She's a great girl. Beautiful. Really smart."

Julie wilted.

"But kind of, I dunno, intense. She says we never see each other," Mark continued. "She works long hours. And so do I. I don't know what she expects me to do about that. Her schedule and mine hardly ever overlap. We haven't had sex in months."

Julie perked up. "Really? That's terrible," she said. "Poor you. What an awful way to live. Imagine years like that. Years with no sex. Years and years. And years."

There was another silence.

Julie stared at the ground. "We haven't had sex in ages either," she confessed. "The dogs sit by the side of the bed and stare. Jonathan says to ignore them, but I can't. And when we shut them out, they scratch on the door and whine or stare at us through the glass."

Mark looked sad for her.

"And of course now, with him unable to talk. It's just . . . odd."

Neither said much after that and they parted thoughtfully.

The next night they met again. "How are things at home?" he asked.

"About the same," she said.

For a while they said nothing.

"You know . . . Jonathan and I are supposed to be getting married."

"Oh," Mark said. "Supposed to be?"

"Yes," said Julie.

"But?"

Julie was silent for a moment. "But now, I don't know. I don't know if he wants to. Or if I want to either."

They watched the dogs.

"It sounds like quite a conundrum," Mark said.

"It is," said Julie. "I mean, we've been together so long, and the wedding was offered by my employer, and you know, really, I always thought I'd get married young. I'm the marrying type." She smiled. "I know it's unfashionable, but I'm not the sort of person who likes having a lot of relationships. I like to know where I am."

Mark nodded. "I can understand that. My parents met at college and I always thought I'd get married young."

"But your girlfriend?" Julie was sympathetic and encouraging.

He looked glum. "I just don't know."

The dogs chased and dodged. Mark and Julie felt acutely aware of each other.

Mark coughed a little. "Would you like to

go out for a drink sometime?" And then he looked at her, a little wildly. "I mean, just as friends, obviously. You're getting married." He added the last part as if she might have forgotten.

"Yes," Julie said. "Yes, that would be nice. As friends. Obviously."

"Obviously," he said. "We could toast your wedding."

"Great," she said.

"Great," he said.

They stood close together, quivering with tension.

"A drink, then," Mark said, attempting a lightness of tone. "Sometime convenient for us both?"

She nodded, unable to trust her voice.

Having determined that they would go out for a drink, as friends, sometime convenient for them both, they barely spoke on the walk home.

"Well." At their usual parting spot, Mark touched her arm. "I'll see you tomorrow."

"Okay," she said, and didn't pull away, as if practicing being friends.

Perhaps Julie was merely experiencing one of those last-minute prenuptial wobbles you hear so much about. Perhaps she really did love Jonathan and would realize with a start, any minute now, that she too was going off the rails.

Only that didn't seem to be happening. Over the next few days, the image of Mark grew sharper in her head and her need to see him grew more urgent. They met each evening, talked in whole sentences, and slowly came to the conclusion that they cherished a mutual vision of the future, including a nice apartment in Brooklyn, children in private schools, and secure financial investments. The confused, annoyed, slightly sad feeling that Julie had grown used to having around Jonathan disappeared when she was with Mark.

At night she thought of nothing but him and he thought of nothing but her. Which was fine; after all, it was only thinking. When Jonathan slid up next to Julie in bed, she turned him into Mark; not that he particularly noticed, having already turned her into Dr. Clare.

That's interesting, Jonathan said to his subconscious mind.

Why?

Well, I am getting married soon.

Really?

Really.

Not sure I'd have guessed, said his subconscious.

Dr. Clare and Mark slept peacefully

together that night, while Julie and Jonathan slept fitfully, embracing ghosts. When they awoke, Jonathan was surprised to discover that Julie was still Dr. Clare.

Really? he said to his subconscious. If you're calling the shots, how about fantasizing about someone single for a change?

Julie's single, replied his subconscious.

You know what I mean, Jonathan said.

Do I? asked his subconscious.

I think you do.

Fine, said Jonathan's subconscious, with what sounded like a shrug.

Fine, said Jonathan, with a roll of the eyes.

And for a while, he and his subconscious were estranged.

26

On Friday, Julie came home from work, called hello to Jonathan, slipped into the bathroom to smooth down her hair, reapply lipstick, and compose her face. The dogs observed all this quietly from their beds.

"How are you this evening?" Julie kissed Jonathan on the forehead.

He looked up from one of his drawings. In this one, Dante (Intrepid Border Collie and Natural Poet) guided him through the first circle of hell (Limbo), where tourists walked four abreast on the sidewalk, bearded architects from Brooklyn hoicked up their jeans to reveal bare ankles, taxis managed to hit every red light, and parents named their children Horton and Calliope.

He took Julie's hand and searched her face. He was feeling low, worried about his brain and his future.

It's not that he loved her more (or less) than he ever had. But she had become his lifeline — brisk, sensible, affectionate, not overconcerned with the sources of his condition, and willing to walk the dogs until it passed. He found this attitude so helpful, it nearly convinced him that any basic incompatibility wouldn't stand in the way of a successful relationship.

What was a wife *for*? he wondered. He knew what a wife like Clémence was for. She was a wife with whom a person might eat croissants in bed, take the dogs on vacation, laugh, and not be misunderstood. But she was married to that bastard, Luc. And what about a wife like Dr. Clare? He couldn't exactly imagine her as a wife. But he had gradually begun imagining her in other scenarios, and in all of these scenarios the person acting the part of him looked happy.

Of course she had a boyfriend too.

Stop! he said sternly to himself, remembering Greeley's warning about fantasies with no future. He was marrying Julie and that was that. Julie, who was a perfect version of herself and understood his attempts to express himself with occasional accuracy, even in the weeks before he began generating random sentences. This was more than he imagined most women would do for him and he felt grateful. After each long day of confinement he began looking forward to her return as a deliverance from his unspeakably flawed self. He was almost looking forward to marrying her and living together forever.

"Jonathan," said Julie gravely, "we have to make a decision about our wedding."

He nodded. Yes, he thought. Julie's been so good to me and I'd be lost without her. We'll get married and everything will be all right. If there are problems, we'll resolve them later. The important thing is to do something about this stupid limbo.

"Rescue farm," he said.

"Does that mean yes? Are you sure? Are you absolutely one hundred percent sure you feel well enough?" Julie peered at Jonathan, who nodded. "And that you want to?"

He nodded again.

"Because the whole *Bridal-360* thing is really kind of arbitrary. I mean, Lorenza wouldn't be happy if we called it off" — that was the understatement of the century — "but we shouldn't do it unless we're really sure."

Jonathan looked her straight in the eye. He took both of her hands. And then he smiled, and he nodded, and he said, "Umbrella loop."

She took a deep breath. "Okay, then. I'll

tell Lorenza. She'll be very happy." Julie smiled wanly. Along with a sensation of nausea there was relief. Not because she was without serious misgivings about their future, but because that particular conversation with Lorenza was one she dreaded more than a lifetime with the wrong man.

"By the way, you don't have to worry about 'I do,' " Julie added. "The ceremony director has been in touch and you only have to nod."

Jonathan blinked. The ceremony director?

I do, he thought. I really do.

Julie counted the hours until her nightly rendezvous with Mark with a mixture of longing and dread. When the time came, she could barely stop Dante from dragging her down the block. They were five minutes early, and when Mark wasn't there, her heart crashed and burned in her chest and she knew as well as she'd known anything in her entire life that he'd realized his beautiful smart girlfriend was right for him after all, much more right than a senior sales manager on *Bridal-360* ever could be, even if her job wasn't enough to put off any sane man.

Of course none of this mattered. She was going to have to stop seeing him — not that she was *seeing him* — to marry Jonathan. It was just infatuation; she barely knew him. She was flattered that he seemed attracted to her. But it wasn't real. It couldn't be.

Jonathan was real. Forever was real.

She turned around and saw Mark running down the sidewalk toward her. "You got here early," he said, panting. "I should have too. I meant to get here early, but at the last minute I thought you might think I was desperate. Which I was. Am. Desperate to see you, that is."

And then, just like in the movies, they both stopped in the middle of the sidewalk and their eyes came together with unnatural intensity and they kissed. Well, they almost kissed. They couldn't really, not in public, and both with other partners, and the dogs walking right next to them; even if the dogs probably wouldn't report back, still it wasn't right. But the dogs weren't pulling on their leashes, or whining, or causing any impediment to the union of two sex-deprived, somewhat prosaic souls, whom even a dog could tell would make a perfect couple. And solve one or two other problems at the same time.

Julie stared at Mark, miserable. "I'm getting married, Mark."

He looked shaken. "Of course, I know that. I guess . . ." He stopped, swallowed.

"Maybe I hoped it wasn't true."

Her eyes glittered with unshed tears.

He shook his head. "It's all such a mess."

She took his hand and raised it to her mouth, pressing her lips to it.

"So, when does it happen?" Mark used the passive tense, unable to involve her in the actual doing of it.

"The day after tomorrow."

His face shifted, as if she'd slapped him.

She forced herself to speak. "It's just last-minute jitters, Mark. This whole thing." She was still holding his hand to her face.

Mark composed himself. "Of course it is," he said. "What else could it be?"

"It's all been planned through *Bridal-360*, my employer. They've art-directed the whole wedding." She paused, hoping he would smile and say something like, *Well, congratulations!* or *Not if I have anything to do with it!* But he didn't say either. He said nothing, so she went on, blindly. "It's all about spring. They've booked the Brooklyn Botanic Garden." She paused, her face a mask of dejection. "I'm very excited."

He pretended to be studying a billboard opposite. She still held his hand and he didn't want it back. "Of course you are. Well, then. That's big news. Congratulations, Julie. I can't lie, I kind of wish we'd met earlier, but I hope you'll be happy. I hope you have a" — he choked slightly — "a perfect life."

A perfect life? she thought, slightly annoyed. She gave back his hand. How likely am I to have a perfect life? Who has a perfect life? Still, she supposed it was a nice thing to wish someone.

And then he turned back and gazed into her eyes, and he took her hand and placed it over his heart. "If ever . . . well, if ever you change your mind . . ."

She closed her eyes.

He dropped her hand and walked away. Well, what had she expected? What else could he do? Turn back time? Demand a duel?

Julie stumbled home with the dogs, blinded by tears. When she opened the door, Jonathan's brother, James, swung her into an enormous hug.

"Here's the blushing bride! So great to see you at last, Julie!" He grinned, but almost at once was claimed by the dogs, who nearly toppled him in a frenzy of enthusiasm. Dropping down to the floor, he tried to fend off one wriggling animal, then the other, then both, pulling them close at last. "Oh, my fabulous dogs, come here! Ouch, down! I've missed you so much!" To

Julie and Jonathan, he said, "They look amazing. You've taken such good care of them." He was laughing and there were tears in his eyes. "I don't know how to thank you."

Jonathan's look was hangdog-360. "Noah sings pig machine," he said.

A listless Julie glanced at James. "The dogs are very happy to see you."

"Don't know how I ever left them." Sissy was still leaping at him like a bouncing ball. He ran her ears through both hands and she squirmed with delight. Then he turned to Julie. "But what have you done to my brother? He's talking even more nonsense than usual." Despite the jollity of his tone, he seemed anxious.

"The doctors feel fairly sure he'll recover. They just don't know when."

"But you're going ahead with the wedding?" James looked from one to the other.

Julie avoided both brothers' eyes. "It's all planned. I mean, the timing isn't great, but it's what we both want." She forced herself to face Jonathan. "Isn't it?"

He nodded.

"Okay," said James. "I get it. Kind of a juggernaut."

"How's Dubai?" Julie asked. She found

the effort required to make small talk painful.

"Weird. They've just offered me a new contract. If I accept, I'm there for five more years." His expression was serious. "I've been looking at getting the dogs sent out. We've taken advantage of your hospitality far too long."

Jonathan's face collapsed. "Arbitrage flopsy bird. Moose elephant charge."

Julie's cheeks burned. She raised her hands to them. "I think he's trying to say he loves them. And would rather you didn't take them away."

James looked at Jonathan. "Really?"

Jonathan nodded, slowly. The thought of the dogs leaving was intolerable to him. Once he married Julie he'd be totally alone.

James sighed. "I have to think about it. Of course it would be amazing if they could come with me, but the unhappy truth is that I work long hours and would hardly see them. And then there's the heat. Still, I promised no more than six months, and I'm a man of my word. Plus, I don't want to impose on you." He paused, disconcerted at finding every pair of eyes in the room trained on him. "Let's talk about this after the wedding." He patted his garment bag. "I've got my fancy suit and my best-man speech all ready to go."

Julie looked stricken. She stood up and left the room. The brothers exchanged a glance. Safe topics seemed somewhat thin on the ground.

"Weddings are stressful," James said, getting to his feet. "And it's late. I'll go check in to my hotel and sleep off the jet lag. We'll leave you alone until tomorrow's dinner with Ma and Pa. My treat. Pick you up at seven-thirty? The hotel recommended a good Szechuan on Third."

Once James left, Jonathan followed Julie into the bedroom, found her sitting on the bed, and embraced her. "Parabola favors," he said, and she sighed, turning in his arms to face him.

"It's not your fault, Jonathan. It's just the pressure of it all. I'll be fine."

"Osprey?" He kissed her.

She searched his face. "I love you, Jonathan. Do you love me?"

"Transport," he said, and she smiled.

"Okay, then, whatever that means. I'll take it as a yes."

Julie had a last-minute dress fitting the following day and Jonathan stayed home with the dogs. After lunch, he passed the time drawing pictures of hell while Julie busied herself with phone calls and e-mails.

They exchanged few words, but when James buzzed up to collect them for dinner, they smiled at each other like comrades setting off to battle. Jonathan took Julie's hand and together they descended the stairs.

The family dinner went off as well as could be expected, though Julie couldn't always tell who it was who suffered from an inability to talk sense. Jonathan's parents spoke in rhapsodically peculiar non sequiturs that caused her to squint with confusion — she, who had lived for weeks with a man who made almost no sense at all.

After the food arrived, Jonathan's father tapped his glass for a toast. "So, a wedding," he began, raising his Chinese beer and holding it for an interminable half minute before lowering it. "Will someone please pass the soy sauce?" he said at last, and proceeded to drench a dumpling, maneuver it whole into his mouth, and abandon the subject of matrimony altogether.

This was as close as anyone came to mentioning tomorrow's momentous event. The rest of the meal was spent talking about the weather in Dubai, the new lawn tractor, and how tragic it was that after their having spent so much money feeding and clothing Jonathan all these years, he now had a life-wrecking speech impediment.

By the time Jonathan and Julie retired to bed that night, they had forgotten any objections to the wedding. They both just wanted it over.

Really? said Jonathan's subconscious.

Shut up, he said.

27

The morning of the big day began with gray skies and drizzle and grew steadily grimmer.

"Rain at a wedding is good luck," said Julie morosely, feeling damp even before they stepped into their limo. Lorenza sat beside the driver, controlling the door locks like a jailer.

"Big day," she said, her voice flat. And then, as the dogs clambered in behind Julie and Jonathan, "Good God. Why are they here?"

Nobody bothered to answer.

Lorenza had a bad feeling and it wasn't yet ten o'clock.

The Palm House at the Botanic Garden had been magnificently prettified, festooned with palest pastel ribbons and bunches of wildflowers. It smelled of freesia and orange blossom. Every camera angle had been planned and a team of lighting technicians was busy setting up spots, arranging silks, and securing electrical cords with gaffer tape. The bar was already serving lychee margaritas, and early guests wondering if they'd come to the wrong place (a movie set, perhaps, or a celebrity prize-giving?) stopped caring after the first drink.

The more photogenic attendees were snatched away from the bar and posed together for pictures regardless of their relationship to the bride, groom, or each other. Max, lugging the Deluxe Popcorn Master 5000 wrapped in brown paper, had positioned himself centrally so he could eye up the editorial assistants. Jonathan took him aside and handed him the dogs. They'd both been brushed and fluffed and blow-dried, had pale green and yellow ribbons wrapped around their collars and braided into their fur, and even Julie had to admit they looked festive.

Max took them, but they stared after Jonathan with anxious faces as he disappeared into the crowd. Julie's mother and her husband arrived straight from their flight from Hong Kong, ignored the bride and groom, and introduced themselves to every member of the technical crew. Greeley appeared in a slim dark orange velvet suit with a white shirt and white Chelsea boots, then sat quietly without a drink, politely declining all requests to be photographed.

James posed extensively for photos with his brother. The two looked handsome and stylish, which pleased the photographer, who was jaded from shooting five employee weddings with subpar bridegrooms. Under his breath, he cursed the whole concept of real people as subjects. Ni–ight–mare.

Pulling himself away at last, James sat Julie's parents with Jonathan's, a disastrous combination, but one he figured would bond them together safely like two pairs of faulty chromosomes.

The atmosphere was buoyant, thanks to the beautiful setting and the excellent free cocktails. High-definition live-streaming had begun, courtesy of four young film school graduates doing internships at *Bridal-360* and their camcorders, complete with built-in microphones and 12X zoom. Rain fell on the glass dome and ran down its side in sheets, creating a bubbly sort of feeling within, as if everything were happening underwater. For Jonathan, this added to the general sense of claustrophobia and he fought an almost overwhelming desire to make a face like a gourami and attach his lips to a window. Having no real experience of weddings, he had no idea how to react to his own; it was, he thought, not unlike being present at one's own funeral, carried along by a momentum that seemed to have more to do with the guests than the corpse. Not corpse, bridegroom.

The bride, meanwhile, was sobbing as Lorenza put the finishing touches on her gown and Cody, from the camera crew, caught her unhappy face in close-up from across the dressing room.

The art director was unmoved. "If a single tear falls on the silk jersey, I'll put an ugly-curse on your family that will last till the Second Coming," she growled. "Jade has already told me she's at the limits of extreme foundation. And we'll probably have to retouch smiles onto all the guests. I've been to lynchings more cheerful than this."

"I can't go through with it," Julie sobbed, as Cody zoomed out gradually for the wide shot.

"Yes you can," Lorenza said. "We've got the cake, the flowers, the venue, the cameras . . . if you didn't like that deranged misfit enough to live with him forever, you should have told me ten years ago." Lorenza sent a burly production assistant to bring tissues. "We're predicting a hundred thousand viewers around the world, not to mention four spreads in the next issue. Your boyfriend may be psycho, but he looks good. So get a grip."

Julie's eyes streamed. "I've met someone else," she whispered.

Lorenza froze. "No you haven't."

The bride buried her face in her hands.

"Oh, sweet Jesus in a jerkin, you have. Well, congratulations. Your timing's impeccable." She paused. "I don't suppose this new guy would be willing to do the deed? How long have you known him?"

Julie blew her nose loudly. "A week."

"Too soon? Well, it's far too late to pull the plug. We're going through with it."

"I . . . I'm not sure Jonathan will agree to that. Especially once I tell him the truth."

"You haven't told him?"

Cody closed in tight on Lorenza. He'd never seen an expression quite like the one currently adorning the art director's face, and correctly imagined that his viewers would find it as fascinating as he did.

Julie shook her head.

"Well, you're definitely not telling him now. We'll replace the justice of the peace with an actor. Tell your fiancé afterward that the ceremony wasn't real and you're dumping him."

Julie stared at Lorenza, who looked thoughtful. "Or you could go through with it, then get a divorce afterward. We can get legal to draw up a quickie prenup. It'll be infinitely simpler than dismantling the shoot."

Julie made a noise like a cat caught in a door, and Cody indicated to Lorenza that she should step closer to Julie for the two-shot.

"You," Lorenza said, fixing him with a skewering stare. "If you don't remove yourself from the planet *now,* I'm going to flatten your eyeballs." She snatched the steaming iron from the wardrobe girl and advanced on him threateningly, which made for a brilliant close-up until Julie began to howl, requiring a reframe.

Lorenza turned back. "What? So it's not nice. Boo-hoo. It's not exactly nice to ditch your fiancé for another man at the altar either. It is a man?"

Julie nodded through her sobs. "Can't you get Helen and Ingy?"

"With ten minutes' notice?" Lorenza had begun to look uncharacteristically frayed. "Not that it matters to me personally, but when exactly were you thinking of telling Jonathan?"

The bride's face crumpled and Cody zoomed in slowly for the close-up.

"Right." Lorenza looked at her watch.

"Let's all think pleasant thoughts for now and leave these details till after the wedding, shall we?"

"For God's sake, Lorenza! I can't marry him."

"Yes you can." Lorenza waved at the makeup girl. "Jade, we'll need ten mgs of Valium, five pounds of ice, and a trowel for the foundation."

Cody crept forward until his lens nearly rested on Lorenza's upper lip.

"Get. Out. Of. My. Face." Lorenza's voice climbed higher with each syllable, causing the wine glasses in the kitchenette to vibrate dangerously. *"Now!"*

The cameraman retreated, still filming.

Max, who'd been trailing Jade since he'd first laid eyes on her an hour earlier, stuck his head into the dressing room. "When you're finished with the bride," he said, flashing his most adorable smile, "you could work on —"

In one quick glance he took in all the assistants staring at their phones with horror, Julie's red swollen eyes and blotchy skin, the retreating cameraman, and the expression on Lorenza's face.

Oh no, he thought. Not good.

Dante and Sissy dashed ahead, past legions of wedding guests glued to their phones and the drama unfolding live on the *Bridal-360* website. The dogs dragged Max to a curtain near the bar behind which they found his friend, eyes huge, lips pressed to the window.

Max composed himself. "Hey, Jay, what-cha doing? I think you'd better have a chat with Julie before the whole 'do you take' rigmarole."

Jonathan appeared happy to see the dogs. "Diblings!"

"Hey, pal. Did you hear me?" He took his friend's elbow firmly and steered him in the direction of the dressing room, dogs flanking them like bodyguards.

A youthful *Bridal-360* assistant attempted to bar their way. "No one's allowed in without a backstage pass," she squeaked. "Sorry."

Max, who was a foot taller and two feet broader than the assistant, repositioned her politely with a hand on each shoulder and pressed Jonathan ahead of him through the door.

"Antwerp expedient," Jonathan said by way of apology.

Inside the room, Lorenza blocked all forward movement with the sheer weight of her fury. "The groom does not see the bride before the ceremony. We're talking seven hundred years bad luck." She fixed Jonathan with an icy stare. "And heaven knows you don't need more of that."

Max stepped forward. "They've gone live," he said calmly. "Everyone in the free world knows what's going on except him."

Jonathan, who had caught sight of Julie, pushed past Lorenza and followed his betrothed as she fled into the galley kitchen. The dogs trailed behind, and the four crammed into the tiny room together with Cody, who had managed to flatten himself against the adjoining wall.

"Behemoth?" Jonathan's tone was pleading.

His bride-to-be took a deep breath and closed her eyes. "I've met someone," she said.

"Spoiler," Jonathan said nervously. "Kickbox infanticide."

"Jonathan," she said. "I've *met* someone. A man. One I like a lot." The cameraman zoomed in on her right eye, from which a thin black rivulet of mascara and tears ran.

"Mogadishu?"

Her tears came faster now. "Yes, more than you."

Jonathan blinked. For a moment he didn't understand how she could like some other guy more than him and still marry him in half an hour. It seemed wrong. "Lip?" he said. "Underlay?" And then an anguished, *"FOE!"*

She moved to hug him, but he pulled away, reeling, as she tried to explain how it had happened, how she still loved him, how she hadn't meant to get involved, how the last thing on earth she wanted was to hurt him, but that perhaps they'd been too hasty rushing into matrimony and that both of their chances of true happiness might be better with someone else. The cameraman, invisible in the intensity of the moment, scuttled in closer to crouch at their feet, filming upward in classic horror-movie style.

"Amphetamine!" Jonathan was shouting now.

"I'm sorry, Jonathan, I'm so sorry, I'm so, so sorry. I couldn't figure out how to tell you. I broke it off with Mark and I tried, I really tried, but I just . . . I just can't stop thinking about him." She talked on through her tears, saying that in some ways it was Jonathan's fault, as it never would have happened if Dante hadn't been so insistent on being together with Mark's German short-haired pointer.

German shorthaired pointer? Jonathan stopped reeling just long enough to squint at Dante, who looked away with an air of studied nonchalance.

"Well, not his German shorthaired pointer, exactly; his girlfriend's," Julie said. "He's a lawyer." Despite her misery there was the slightest hint of pride in her voice, as if Jonathan couldn't fail to be impressed by the fact that her new boyfriend had such an important job.

Lawyer scum, thought Jonathan. Surely common courtesy required her to describe the cheating bastard as nothing at all special, insist that it wasn't Jonathan's fault; that he deserved better. But no, he could tell that Julie secretly thought it was some sort of big achievement to leave your boyfriend, practically your *husband,* for Christ's sake, for a lawyer — and it was Jonathan's fault for not being higher up the career scale, not to mention dull enough to spend his life reading contracts and torts, and also for having a debilitating illness that caused him to be unable to speak properly and/or to walk his dogs. Well, not his dogs, exactly; his brother's dogs, who then went on to develop an unnatural attraction to Mark's dog — wait, no, not Mark's dog, his girlfriend's dog. Sorry, not *dog,* German shorthaired pointer. Even the fucking dog was high-status.

Outrage made Jonathan want to kick the

Palm House to pieces. He imagined thousands of square feet of glass cascading downward in tiny razor-sharp fragments, and for a moment he felt better.

He paused suddenly and rewound the conversation, confirming that it was Dante's crush on Mark's dog that had led to Julie's evening assignations. *You,* he thought loudly, staring at Dante, *you* did this. Dante stared back at him from the space next to the dishwasher, without even the decency to look ashamed.

"Albatross!" He'd pretty much forgotten Julie in this newest train of thought. Now he turned back to her.

"Oh, Jonathan," Julie was wailing now. "I'm so, so sorry, but we can't get married under the circumstances."

At the door to the kitchenette, Lorenza covered her eyes with her hands, stamped her foot, and screamed, once, loudly.

Jonathan appeared to notice Cody for the first time. He kicked him hard, grabbed his camera, and hurled it across the room. The young man fled, filming his retreat on his phone.

Of course they couldn't get married. But who was going to go out there and tell his friends and family that the thing was off? Who was going to speak for him? Without

Julie, he had no voice. All at once he felt panicked, dependent, rejected, and alone.

"I want you to be happy, Jonathan."

"Piano scum." Tears filled his eyes.

She took a step toward him but he backed away. "Oh, Jonathan. You don't mean that. You'll get over it and realize what a close call we had. It never would have worked."

"Pandemic." He spat the word.

"I know you're angry, but I hope we can stay friends."

"Cuckoo!" Jonathan shouted.

"I think I'll go now." She bolted from the kitchenette and began tugging at the celadon wedding dress, sobbing, as Lorenza struggled with the zip in a desperate attempt at damage limitation.

"Yuck phoo!"

Julie flinched, as if he might hit her, and gasped, cowering. She ran to the dressing-room door, opened it, and fled, dress and all, followed by makeup, wardrobe, two junior art directors, three cameramen who were not Cody, an intern, Jerri the continuity girl, and Lorenza. The guests, upset that their broadcast had been disrupted, cheered enthusiastically at this opportunity to pick up the story live.

Jonathan shouted after her retreating figure.

"DUCK. ZOO!"

She was gone.

Max spoke for the first time in some minutes. "Wow," he said.

Jonathan and the two dogs stood gaping in the silence.

"Well," Jonathan said at last. "That's that, then."

He frowned.

Then, just to be sure it wasn't a fluke, he turned to Dante. "By the way, don't think I don't know what you've been up to. You're surely not going to pretend you had no role in the romance of my girlfriend with that asshole lawyer? Huh?"

Furious as he was at this traitorous version of man's so-called best friend, he felt rather proud of his ability to use words in a fluent manner once more. So proud, in fact, that his anger subsided.

When he turned around, Max was grinning at him. "Hey, buddy, you can talk. That's so cool."

Jonathan nodded.

" 'Cause now you're going to have to go out and tell everyone the wedding's off." Max put his arm around his friend's shoulders and guided him to the dressing-room door. "I have a feeling they might be prepared, what with all the shrieking and weeping. Come on. We'll do it together."

And they went out to the Palm House to break the news.

"Excuse me, excuse me!" Max tapped a knife on a glass, which failed to quiet the overexcited crowd. He looked at Dante, who barked sharply, once.

The room fell silent.

Max pushed Jonathan gently to center stage. "Uh, welcome everyone, and thank you so much for coming to our wedding. Unfortunately, due to a pathological misjudgment on my part, it won't actually be happening today, or ever, God willing, but please feel free to celebrate my narrow escape from a lifetime of despair with as many drinks as you can swig before the lovely folks at *Bridal-360* realize exactly what's going on and pull the plug."

His speech was captured on three live feeds and a few hundred phones. It was followed by enthusiastic applause.

When, half an hour later, Lorenza found him at the bar with a double lychee margarita in each hand, she shifted the celadon wedding dress from one arm to the other, grabbed him by the lapel of his very expensive burned-chocolate velvet suit, and hissed that if everyone wasn't out of the Palm House in precisely four minutes, she would personally rip his lips off.

Dante cleared the room in under a minute. He looked happier than he had in weeks.

28

Jonathan's parents were understanding.

"You weren't good enough for her," his mother said.

Greeley stood in the rain in the orange suit, shook Jonathan's hand, and said, "Better late than never." Which, coming from Greeley, sounded like the words of the Delphic oracle.

Max, Jonathan, and James retired to a Flatbush Avenue bar where they drank beer and shots and talked about the good old days while the dogs lay under the table eating nachos and cocktail sausages. Max grinned at Jonathan. "You're gonna wake up any day now and realize what a close call you had."

"I second that," James said.

"Yeah." Jonathan sighed. "I guess so."

"No guessing," Max said. "Even Greeley and Wes were against it. And they care about you just about as much as a box of sticks."

"Really?" A box of sticks? Greeley?

"One stick."

"That's great to know." Jonathan stared out into the rain, feeling melancholy.

"Jay, buddy, forget them. We love you to pieces. It's like witnessing the goddamn resurrection of Lazarus. Have another beer. Hey, James. Life any good out there in Dubai?"

"You wouldn't exactly choose to live there. But it's good work for an engineer," James said. "I miss my family, though."

Jonathan was prepared to be moved by this admission till he saw his brother gazing at Dante and Sissy. By family, he meant the dogs. Jonathan felt a flash of panic. What if he was planning to take them back?

Max looked from James to Jonathan. "Whoa there, Tonto. Have you two sorted this out? You've got kind of a tug-of-love situation developing here."

The brothers avoided each other's eyes.

"You can't take them out to Dubai," Jonathan said. "The politics are terrible. They use slave labor. Muslims don't like dogs. Plus it's hot as hell, they'd hate it."

"But it's just fine for me?" James tossed an empty nacho basket at his brother, who ducked. "It'll take six months to arrange anything, so we'll have time to think."

"I already have." Jonathan reached under the table and found Sissy's head.

"Shame they're not kids," Max said, opening another beer. "We'd have a bestseller on our hands. Or at least a slot on *Judge Judy.*"

Jonathan looked miserable. "Can we not talk about this now? I've had a bad enough day."

"Best day of your life. You'll see." Max raised his bottle in a toast. "Ninety-nine percent of all rejections involve someone you don't like as much as you think you do telling you something you should already have known."

Jonathan rolled his eyes. "Oh yeah?"

Max nodded gravely. "Yeah."

"How'd you get so smart?"

His friend grinned. "Night school."

James put his arm around his brother. "At least you can talk again. That'll prove useful in later life."

Jonathan's head lolled. The combination of roller-coaster levels of stress and strong alcohol was making him woozy. James and Max hailed a cab willing to take them all, getting the driver to stop at a liquor store on the way for a bottle of Jack Daniel's and two six-packs. At home, Max and James continued a conversation begun more than a decade earlier about rejection, sex, women, and life while Jonathan threw his velvet suit on the floor and collapsed into bed. Before he closed his eyes, he sat up and turned to Dante.

"Just tell me one thing, you miserable hound. What's happened to your relationship with Mark's dog? Was it a real attraction, Dante? Because, just saying here, I don't think it was. I don't actually see you attracted to a German shorthaired pointer. Don't look away. Really? You really wanted to get it on with an Abercrombie & Fitch dog like that? I bet she had absolutely no sense of humor. Go on, tell me. It was all a plot, wasn't it? To break up our relationship? To break my heart? It was the owner you were after, not the dog. A German shorthaired pointer, Dante? You must think I was born yesterday." He fell back, then propped himself up on one elbow. "And anyway, why fix up Julie? If you didn't like our relationship, why not fix *me* up with someone, a goddamned brain surgeon maybe, or a Supreme Court judge? You're supposed to be on my side, thinking of *my* happiness. Bad dog."

But Dante knew and Sissy knew and Jonathan knew that in actual fact he wasn't angry, only tired and emotional and desperate for the day to be over.

Dante returned to his bed while Sissy scratched and pushed the wedding suit into a comfortable pile of wadded-up chocolate velvet, turned around on it three times, flopped down, and went to sleep.

Having solved most of the problems of the universe, James returned to his hotel at 4 a.m.

Max stayed and slept on the couch in case Jonathan needed him in the night.

29

Over two cups of strong coffee the next morning, Max suggested that Jonathan sit out the rest of his sick leave. No one but a fool hurried back to work, he said, especially if that work was advertising. But Jonathan was adamant. Blessed once again with the power of speech, he was anxious to rejoin humanity as soon as possible, even if that meant returning to Comrade, where gossip about his aborted wedding (not to mention a few million hits on YouTube) would surely have made him an epic laughingstock. Face the music, he told himself. Get back on the horse.

Max left Jonathan and went home to change, saying they'd meet at work and he'd hold his friend's hand against a possible onslaught of ridicule and humiliation.

Jonathan headed first to Le Grand Pain, where Clémence greeted him with exclamations of relief and joy. "But I thought you must be dead! Or moved to a different country!" She came out from behind the counter and hugged him. "Where have you been?"

He shrugged, embarrassed. "I don't know, really. I had a nervous breakdown and my wedding imploded."

"Oh no!" Clémence clucked with sympathy. "So much drama! But you're better now?" She frowned. "And you, darling dogs! I missed you all."

"Did you really miss us? Will you marry me now my girlfriend has ditched me?"

"Luc would be angry, my darling. And you know, I don't even know your name. Tell me your name now, so I know for the next time you have *une dépression nerveuse.*"

"I thought I might stop at one."

She handed him his croissants, smiling.

Jonathan stuck his nose in the bag and inhaled deeply. "Do you think you might marry me if Luc died?"

"Stupid boy," she scolded. "If something happens to Luc I will throw myself into the sea."

"What if he just had a black eye and two broken legs?"

"Go," she said. "Take your coffee and come back soon."

"It's Jonathan."

276

"Okay, Jonathan," she said, and waved. "Goodbye, Jonathan! Goodbye, dogs!"

At work, everyone made a huge fuss over the triumphant return of Dante and Sissy, and to some extent him, though he noticed that a depressing number of screensavers featured him shouting, *"Duck zoo!"* over and over at Julie on a loop.

Greeley smiled as he came in but didn't instigate a postgame analysis, which was a relief. Wes greeted him with as much genuine warmth as his personality allowed.

"Welcome home, Jonathan. It's never a happy time when a member of the team is indisposed. We all suffer until our comrade returns. So, welcome back to Comrade, comrade. Ready to tackle Broadway Depot again?"

Jonathan felt suddenly hot. So a nervous breakdown and the worst rejection of his life wasn't enough to get him off the nightmare account from hell?

"I'm sorry," he said. "I can't go back to working on Broadway Depot."

Wes clapped him on the shoulder. "Never mind. Let's not talk about it right now. We've got an all-staff meeting this morning and then I'll take you to lunch."

Everyone filed in for the staff meeting, but Jonathan ducked out to the men's room.

He sat on a toilet seat with his head in his hands and realized he could not join the meeting. The thought of being a Comrade comrade made him want to throw up. His hands and feet felt numb. If I stand up, he thought, I'll collapse.

He heard the door open.

"Jonathan?" It was Greeley.

He said nothing.

"Jonathan?" Greeley knocked softly on Jonathan's stall door.

"Go away."

"Jonathan, listen to me. You have to leave Comrade."

Jonathan clasped the sides of his head in horror. "You're firing me? I have a breakdown, my girlfriend deserts me at the altar, and then you *fire* me? *Who does that?*"

"No one's firing you. Not unless you commit some gross indecency, steal office machinery, embezzle funds. They'll get you back working on Broadway Depot, and before you know it you'll be making good money and you'll buy an apartment you can't quite afford and by then you'll have a nice new girlfriend and the two of you will want expensive vacations in countries featured in *The New York Times* travel section and eventually you'll decide to have a baby so you'll need nannies and private schools and organic food and *Baby Mozart* because everyone else you work with has all those things and then you'll need a Range Rover to drive them all around in and a house in the country and a Prius for the nanny and then you'll discover you're not happy so you'll need a shrink and your kids will have dyslexia and dyscalculia so they'll need tutors, and anxiety disorders so they'll need child psychologists, and you'll hate your job more than ever but you'll be trapped making the huge sums you need to cover the expenses of your miserable life, counting down the days to retirement and your kids finishing college so you can stop working at a job you despise and finally get some peace and quiet to do something, anything, you always wanted to do like paint or write or go fishing or just sit around reading a book."

"Look, Greeley . . ."

"Then, in order to make yourself feel better about your wretched existence, you'll fall in love with someone entirely inappropriate and have an affair or discover your wife's been having an affair or you'll get a bit too fond of cocaine and end up wired *and* divorced, having lost whatever money you have left, so your kids won't speak to you, you'll sink into a slough of despond just as you realize you're far too old to be

279

working in a life-wasting profession like advertising, so you'll take your pension and downscale your existence and then one day, far too soon, after decades of doing the wrong thing, you'll be dead."

Jonathan leaned his head against the wall of the cubicle and said nothing for a long time.

"Greeley?"

"Yes?"

He cracked open the toilet door. "You don't entirely buy into the whole Comrade ethos, do you?"

Greeley shrugged. "I'm on a three-month contract. At the end of three months I'm leaving for an internship with the Forest Service. I'm doing this for the tuition money."

"Really?"

"Really what?"

"You're leaving that soon?"

"Yup."

"What should I do, Greeley?"

"It's your life."

"I know it's my life. What would you do with my life?"

Greeley sighed. "I'd stop trying to tie up all the loose ends, for one thing. I'd stop obsessing about what happens next. And in the meantime, I'd try to do something that isn't shit."

Jonathan felt stunned. What could he do that wasn't shit? He wanted desperately to be useful, to be someone. But who could he be? Himself, presumably, if he could figure out what that entailed. Maybe he wasn't anything. Maybe he never would be.

He looked at Greeley. "Like what?"

"That's the million-dollar question. But you've got no mortgage, no partner, no children. You hate your life. Why not change it?"

Jonathan pondered this. "I could leave behind emptiness, misery, and self-loathing only to find emptiness, misery, self-loathing, and penury."

Greeley smiled. Jonathan studied Greeley's profile at very close range — the smooth throat, the cropped hair, the soft skin. "You're very beautiful, Greeley, whatever you are."

"Boy," said Greeley, and kissed him.

Jonathan kissed him back. "I hope you don't consider this sexual harassment in the workplace."

"Julie is a fool." Greeley kissed him again, and then said, gently, "They're holding the meeting for you."

Jonathan sighed, stood up, and exited the stall. Greeley stood back to let him pass.

Neither of them said anything more. When Jonathan walked into the meeting, all his comrades applauded.

Far above the nine circles of New York hell, he and Greeley held hands under a palm-fringed canopy while his magical dogs danced together in the sky and the people cheered.

30

Dante refused to eat.

Jonathan felt strangely panicked by this new development. Whatever next with this animal? Dogs didn't just stop eating, not if they were healthy and happy, getting plenty of exercise and meals of leftover sliced sirloin. Jonathan felt his dog's ears for fever, checked his nose for dryness, or was it wetness? He googled "dog won't eat" and searched veterinary websites for likely causes. Most of them reported that dogs were prone to gastrointestinal upset and that twenty-four hours without food usually resolved the problem.

It didn't. Jonathan introduced rice and lightly steamed chicken after the first day, but despite the fact that it looked delicious to human eyes, Dante ignored it. Jonathan tried mixing in a handful of raw hamburger. He offered half a croissant.

Nothing. Not a nibble.

He called the vet and got an appointment for the following day, feeling somewhat nervous at facing Dr. Clare after his aborted wedding and her continued presence in his dreams.

He and the dogs arrived on time and were greeted like old friends.

"Hello again," Iris chirped, and Jonathan wondered if it was normal for a dog to require so many visits to the vet over so few months.

After ten minutes, Dr. Clare called them into her examination room. She looked somewhat worse for wear herself.

"Hello," she said, peering at him carefully. "How are you?"

Jonathan sighed. "Let's not get into it. It's a long and ugly narrative."

"Okay," she said with a frown. "Tell me about the dogs."

"Dog," he said. "Dante won't eat."

"That's not good," she said. "Let's have a look at him."

Jonathan lifted him up onto the examination table, where Dr. Clare took his temperature, felt his glands, tapped each of his teeth with a little rubber hammer, shined a flashlight on his tonsils, palpated his abdomen, and checked his ears. Jonathan made sure he didn't jump off the table, which necessitated standing very close to the vet, who smelled of something mysterious and warm: cardamon and cloves with a touch of dog, like chai tea served by a Labrador.

"Do most dogs have this many problems?"

"We do seem to see quite a lot of you, don't we, boy?"

Jonathan glanced down at Sissy, who sat stoically at his feet. She was never ill.

Dr. Clare appeared bemused. "I can't find anything wrong," she said. "It's always some mysterious ailment with you, isn't it, Dante? I'm thinking we should run some bloods, just to be safe." She rubbed her patient's ears. "You haven't changed his diet or fed him something you shouldn't have?"

Jonathan shook his head. "He's always been a great eater. Wolfs his food down." He paused for a moment. "I know you don't exactly believe in dog psychology . . ."

Dr. Clare swept her hair off her face with one hand. The gesture emphasized how tired she appeared. "It's not that I don't believe in dog psychology. Dogs do get depressed if left on their own too much, or underexercised, or abused. But it's not like human depression. Dogs tend naturally toward happiness. That's why humans choose to live with them."

He waited for her to continue but she didn't.

"I was in the hospital," he said.

She looked up, surprised. "I'm sorry to hear that. Was it serious?"

Jonathan shrugged. "Like my dog," he said. "Tricky to diagnose."

"Were you in for long?"

"A few days," he said. "My girlfriend walked the dogs when I was supposed to be in bed. That worked until she met someone else."

Her face showed an expression of pure sympathy. "How absolutely appalling for you. Your girlfriend sounds dreadful, if you don't mind my saying. Was Dante very fond of her?"

"I'm pretty sure he hated her. All in all, there's been a whole lot of psychic disturbance around." He frowned. "But what about you, Dr. Vet? Are you okay? I hope you don't mind my saying, but you don't seem quite yourself."

"As you ask," she said wearily, "this hasn't been the best month of my life either."

He wondered if he could probe further. "That's terrible. I hate seeing you less than happy."

"Less than happy." She gave a bitter little laugh. "You could say that." She looked from him to Dante, struggling to reestablish a professional footing. "Of course dogs do absorb emotional states. If you've been ill and upset, Dante could be feeling ill and upset too. If it were Sissy, I'd be much less surprised. Dante strikes me as a dog with a very strong sense of self."

"An agenda, even?" They both stared at the collie, who stretched and turned away. "Sometimes I suspect he has things on his mind." Jonathan paused. "Occasionally he seems weighed down with responsibility."

This made her smile. "What sort of responsibility?"

"It might be the wedding, which was, let's face it, a disaster. Or his future. He doesn't know if he's going to stay with me or move to Dubai with my brother. Which does he want? Are his loyalties torn? What if he thinks his guardian will never get his life together and he'll be stuck forever with a loser?"

"I very much doubt . . ."

"Obviously, but you don't know for sure. What if he's suffering a midlife crisis and doesn't know what to do next? What if his whole life is at sixes and sevens and the uncertainty is making him too anxious to eat? What if the existential pain of being a dog has overwhelmed him to such an extent that all physical desires have fled . . ."

She laughed then, clapping her hand over her mouth, and he was so relieved to see her happy, even for a moment and at his expense, that he smiled too.

Dr. Clare cleared her throat and regarded him sternly. "You're not projecting your worries onto your dog, by any chance?"

"I probably am. But look at him, Dr. Vet, he's smarter than most people. Just because he doesn't pay taxes doesn't mean he's not ridiculously tuned in to the world. If you lived with him, you'd know what I mean. Dr. Vet?"

"Yes, Jonathan?"

"With all the mess in our lives, don't you ever look at your dog and wonder whether she knows a whole lot more about life than you think she does?"

"Not usually, no."

"Maybe you try not to think about it. But in her own way, Wilma's a genius. She could identify everyone who's walked past your apartment today by scent alone, or sniff her way home from the Bronx. Dogs can smell tears and cancer. She'd be the first to know if you were pregnant."

"Well, I'm not pregnant." Dr. Clare's face slammed shut.

Jonathan felt gloomy all of a sudden. "I

wonder if dogs can smell when a relationship is wrong? They can smell a tsunami half an hour before it happens; maybe they can sniff out a doomed couple."

Her mouth tightened and she turned away.

"Um . . . I hope I haven't . . . I was talking about Dante. And me, obviously." They both looked at Dante, who gazed back at them with his deep, even gaze.

Dr. Clare sighed. "Dante is a very intelligent dog. But he is still a dog. We'll run some bloods and see if anything physical turns up. I'd hate to brand him a hypochondriac if he's really ill." She stripped the wrapping off a syringe from her supply drawer, held Dante's head in her left hand, felt for the vein in his neck, inserted the needle, pulled back the plunger, and, as the reservoir filled with blood, removed it and stroked him.

"You're a brave boy," she murmured, and then turned to Jonathan. "Offer him small amounts of bland food, morning and night. Most dogs will eat when they get hungry. Call the office" — she looked at her computer — "at the end of the week. Friday afternoon. You can tell me how he's getting on and I'll have the results of the tests."

Jonathan made no move to go.

She exhaled slowly. "It sounds as if you've

had a bad time."

"You too," he said, and she nodded.

"Call Friday," Dr. Clare said at last, and, with nothing else to do, he stood up with his dogs and left.

On returning from the vet, Dante ate a hearty meal. Jonathan called about the blood tests on Friday and Iris reported that they'd all come back normal. There was no message from Dr. Clare and she didn't take the call herself.

31

Jonathan's best friend since fourth grade stopped over on Saturday morning with bagels, a Frisbee, and twin bottles of vodka and Mr. and Mrs. T. Together they headed over to the East River for a picnic with Bloody Marys, watching the boats on one of those glittering blue and sunny New York days that makes a person feel lucky to exist.

"Hey, Jay. This is the life, eh?"

Jonathan nodded and they sat in silence for a while.

"Hey, Max. You ever been in love with two women at once?"

"Who hasn't?"

"Both of mine love someone else."

"Please tell me it's each other they love."

"One boyfriend, one husband."

Max half sat and propped his head on one hand. "No shortage of fish in the pond, John-boy. And you don't want to piss off the psycho with a handgun who discovers

291

your sext on his wife's phone. So I'm voting no."

"No?"

"Unless she's getting drunk and confessing she wishes she met you first. Either one doing that?"

"No."

Max shrugged. "Then no."

"Really no?"

"No, no. No."

Jonathan thought it must be great to have such perfect understanding of relationship etiquette. He wondered how Max knew so much. If only there were some kind of app you could download. LoveGuyde. You could make a fortune with an app like that.

After a while, Max said, "You're not missing Julie, are you?"

"Nah. But I miss having a destiny. Now I'm just floating around in space."

"Didn't matter that your destiny was totally fucked up?"

"Not really."

"Hey, man." Max nudged him with his foot. "You're the craziest bastard I know, but you pulled out of a nosedive at the very last second and that's what counts."

Jonathan stopped short of acknowledging that Max had been right all along. "You may think I was totally stupid, but marrying Julie was something to do. Now all I've got is a job I hate and an apartment I can't afford unless I keep working at the job I hate."

"It's tough," Max said. "But you're forgetting the great thing."

"Yeah?" Jonathan squinted at the sky. "Remind me."

"Everything could change in an instant. You don't know what'll happen next."

"Really?" Jonathan took a long swig of his Bloody Mary. "I think I do know. I think nothing will happen unless I get off my ass and do something to make it happen. I think I could stay in this crappy job and do crappy stuff I don't want to do pretty much forever."

"Nah." Max leaned back, head resting on clasped hands, elbows wide. He closed his eyes against the sun.

"What do you mean, nah? You got some kind of inside track on the future?"

"Yup."

Jonathan looked at him. "Well, I'm happy to hear that, because hope-wise, I'm running on fumes."

"It's the beauty of New York," Max said. "Life is moving all around you in little eddies. You don't know when you'll get caught up in the next one."

Jonathan rolled his eyes. "Yeah?"

"Yeah. And once you get caught in an eddy, it'll take you somewhere you never expected to go." Sissy crept up and gave Max a flying lick on the face. He pushed her away and rose up onto one elbow. "Come here, you monstrous little beast, come on . . ."

He and Sissy had a growling standoff until she could bear it no longer and hurled herself at him, planting her feet on his chest and launching a guerrilla attack. Max fended her off, flapping his hands at her till he could take no more, then grabbed her around the middle and hoisted her up in the air at arm's length like a squirming medicine ball. Dante looked on, the unruffled elder statesman, as the two wrestled and Sissy at last made a spectacular leap for freedom.

Jonathan watched, content. The sun was shining, his best friends all got along, and maybe he wasn't actually stuck in a tar pit. Maybe, as Max said, he just needed to wait for an eddy to twirl him around and carry him in a different direction.

"Hey, Max. You know those two women I was talking about?"

"Not really," Max said.

"I really like them both, but one doesn't

seem like a possibility no matter how I look at it."

"And the other?"

"She has a boyfriend too." He thought for a minute. "Only she doesn't seem very happy."

"Unhappy's good," Max said. "Not for her, obviously."

"So what do I do?"

Max closed his eyes. "Love to help you here, bro, but you know each situation is unique. You just gotta have the feel."

"Thanks."

"Who's the woman?"

"No one you know."

"Well, then," Max said, "you're gonna have to do like I said and wait for an eddy."

"Okay," he said to Max after a while.

"Okay what?"

"Okay, what you said before. I'll wait for Eddy. As long as it doesn't take too long."

Max shut his eyes once more and stretched his long legs out toward the river. "I am truly glad to hear you say that. Because the way I see it, you have no choice. You may be swirling along in an eddy right now for all you know."

"Wouldn't I feel it?"

"Not necessarily," Max said.

"Thank goodness you're here to share

your extensive knowledge on the subject."

"No need for thanks."

Jonathan pulled Sissy in tight with his left arm. With a rumbly sigh, Dante rolled over onto his side in the sunlight, and the four friends stayed that way till the sun sank far enough in the sky to cast shadows and the afternoon turned cold. Then they went home.

32

As Jonathan came through the door at Comrade on Monday, Wes and Ed were waiting for him with the Broadway Depot debrief. Despite knowing better, he felt a small shiver of excitement.

"Well, Jonathan," Ed began, "we have some extremely good news for you. The entire BD team was amazed and impressed by the amount and quality of the work you did." He paused. "They also wish you a speedy recovery from your, um, condition. Louise sent you this card."

Jonathan tore open the envelope. Louise's card had a picture of a chipmunk with a crutch and a bandage around its head on the front. He dropped it in the bin without reading the message.

Wes carried on. "Regretfully, they've decided to stick with the work they already have."

Surprise surprise.

"Although they have indicated a willingness to consider your excellent campaign idea at some point in the future."

Never, in other words.

Ed grinned unconvincingly and punched his arm. "Well, kid, you win some, you lose some."

Jonathan didn't move.

"I'm afraid that's all. It was a great presentation. Shall we get back to work?"

"No."

"Jonathan?"

"I will never piss away another moment of my life working for Broadway Depot."

Ed chuckled. "Ah well, you see, that's the nature of the game, I'm afraid. You're going to have to stick with it for the foreseeable future — the client thinks you're a creative genius and Louise Crimple has the hots for you big-time."

Wes interrupted. "Of course, in the long term we'll definitely find something that suits your talents better and move some of your responsibilities for BD over to another team. But for now? Four-million-a-year spend. Money talks. Sad but true."

"My dog could write those ads." Jonathan glanced at Sissy apologetically.

Ed glared at him. "What are you saying?"

He didn't know what he was saying. He

298

wanted one of them to back down, to clap
him on the shoulder and say, *Right, fair dues.
We get your point. We're not going to let a
guy of your talent go to waste. We'll square it
for you somehow.*

But they didn't. Wes frowned. Eduardo
sighed impatiently. And then said, "We'll
talk later."

But Jonathan knew that it no longer mattered when they talked. Ed would ask the
same question (*Shall we get back to work
now?*) and he would give the same answer
(*No*).

"No," Jonathan said. "We won't."

"Excuse me?" Eduardo was staring at him
now, fizzing slightly with aggression.

"There's no point. You and your shithole
agency and your crap-pile client can take a
fucking . . ."

No one was entirely certain what transpired next, but everyone agreed that Ed
made a threatening noise in his throat and
stepped forward with his full weight onto
Sissy's front paw. Sissy screamed with
outrage and lunged at the offending leg,
jaws open, eyes bright. When her teeth came
together, Ed howled, Wes stepped in to
prevent a disaster that may or may not have
already happened, and Jonathan shouted,
"No!" Max grabbed his friend by the collar

and his friend's dog by hers, Dante ran interference with the management team, and all four retreated as quickly as possible from the scene of the possibly unrealized crime.

"*You are so fucking fired!*" Eduardo shrieked as Jonathan shoved open the huge door to freedom, rounded the landing, and began descending the stairs at speed.

"*Take that vicious animal and get out!*"

"Just keep moving," Max hissed as they flew downward, propelled by shock and an overwhelming desire to put space between themselves and Ed.

"She didn't even bite him," Jonathan panted. "I was watching. She should have but she didn't. She barely nicked his jeans."

Max got man and dogs out of the building and away from the front entrance, certain that Ed was right now forming a makeshift tourniquet out of someone's designer briefs and any second would be hobbling after them, foaming at the mouth and waving a subpoena while trying to inflict dog-shaped bite wounds on his own lower leg.

They made it to the corner and stopped, breathing hard. Max released Sissy's collar and gazed at the sweet-faced, soft-eyed dog with frank admiration.

"Well done, Sissy, you dark horse. That was one of the finest unrealized dog attacks I have ever had the privilege to witness." He scruffled her fur and grinned. "You, my pretty, peace-loving little spaniel, are an exceedingly brave and intrepid animal."

She swiped at his face with her tongue.

I'm still fired, Jonathan thought. Even if I don't end up in jail for possession of a dangerous dog, even if Ed's testimony doesn't cause Sissy to be taken off to a police cell and summarily executed, even if the very worst that happened today is that my dog almost but not quite assaulted my boss and I've been fired without so much as a consultation with the company lawyer or a penny of compensation — even *if* all that, well, what can I do now? How will I live?

"Go home," Max was saying. "Take the dogs and lie low. I'll have a word with Wes. He loves Sissy. Everyone does. They can't possibly prosecute; she's a cocker spaniel, for fuck's sake. You couldn't pay to run this story in the *Post*. "Advertising Boss Nearly Savaged by Adorable Spaniel"? And if she *had* bit him and he *had* contracted rabies or bled to death, the city would throw a goddamned ticker-tape parade. So go on, get out of here. Don't worry. I'll call you later." He stuck out his arm and a cab pulled in beside them. Max opened the door and addressed the driver. "East 5th Street, please, and for God's sake drive carefully: this unassuming little creature here just saved my best friend's life."

The cabbie waved them in. "Long as neither of 'em throws up."

Max closed the door firmly behind them and Jonathan and the dogs set off for home.

33

"You're still fired, but they're not pressing charges, mainly because there are no charges to press. Stepping on a dog who then almost but doesn't quite bite you is not covered under any New York City bylaw." Max sounded positively cheerful. "Anyway, Ed's pretending the whole thing didn't happen, and if anyone asks, he calls your disappearance a creative department reshuffle. Scary thing is he believes it. The guy's capacity for self-delusion is awe-inspiring."

And then later he called again. "It's hell here without you, Jay," he said. "But you should see the freelancer they've hired to replace you. She is very much your superior, hot-wise. No offense."

"None taken."

"So what now, buddy? You can't just rest on your laurels."

"What laurels?"

"Exactly."

"I guess I'll get another job."

"You got any thoughts?"

"Not really. I like comics."

"Who doesn't? Missing you already," said Max, and hung up.

Jonathan surveyed his résumé. It contained one job, one nervous breakdown, one abandonment at the altar. He took his beautiful hand-built road bike down to the cycle shop and they resold it three hours later for only slightly less than he'd paid for it. If it hadn't felt like a relic from a past life, he'd have felt sadder parting with it. A bit of extra money was good, but wouldn't stop the general hemorrhaging of funds that constituted life in New York. In addition, something was nagging at him. He checked the date. It was the seventeenth of the month and he hadn't yet received his rent bill. He looked at Dante.

"Any snacking on bills I should know about?"

Dante didn't even deign to turn away from the window, where a pigeon was tightrope-walking along a telephone wire.

"No? Nothing?" Hmm, he thought. In past months, Frank the landlord had been admirably prompt with his rent demands. Jonathan dug through the paperwork associated with the apartment and realized that there was in fact no paperwork.

Flipping through the folder marked RENT, he found ten lined pages of rent demands, one for each month he'd lived here, each in red pen, each with a date and the sum of money required along with the bank details for payment and a swirly handwritten *Thank you!* at the bottom. Not one of the demands listed a phone number, last name, street, or e-mail address.

He'd just have to wait and hope the bill hadn't gone astray. Jonathan didn't like the thought of a final demand, particularly if it involved Frank showing up at his door in a bad mood, with brass knuckles and a heavily armed goon, wondering where his money was. Or worse yet, the original owner turning up all cranky while Jonathan was still in residence.

He began to sweat, very much less pleased with himself for scoring the amazing deal on an apartment. Was this his twenty-four-hour notice? Would he be out on the street any minute now? Jobless, girlfriendless, homeless?

Injured, maimed, dead?

He remembered playing dominoes as a kid, spending hours setting black rectangles up in neat curving rows and then tapping the first with a kind of ecstasy of expectation. Funny how different it felt when it was every aspect of your life click-clacking over into ruin.

I'll put it out of my mind for now, Jonathan thought, and concentrate on feeling free. Free of Comrade, free of selling crap to make Eduardo rich. Only twenty-four hours out of the business and he could hardly remember why he'd been the person doing what he did, or what it felt like. Except, of course, that it had paid the bills. No small consideration now that nothing else did.

He scanned the web for possible careers but soon gave up in a haze of indifference.

"You guys want to go for a walk?" The response was wonderfully predictable. Dogs always wanted to go for a walk. He clipped on their leashes, grabbed a jacket, and locked the door behind him. At the entrance to his building, he pulled up his collar and scanned left and right for signs that Frank might be lurking around the corner with a baseball bat, but the coast looked clear. Head down, walking briskly, he and the dogs set off north for no particular reason except that they normally didn't, turned west on 28th Street, and headed south again on Broadway, ending up at the Strand bookstore, where Dante and Sissy flopped down and dozed and Jonathan browsed, seduced by the odor of faraway sawmills and ink.

The next day followed a similar program, and the next and the next. They walked and walked and looked in windows, buying nothing. This in itself felt radical, as if he'd opted out of the whole consumer mechanism that propelled New York City forward — an overpriced sandwich, a bar of artisan soap fashioned by someone who used to be a stockbroker, twelve new things from Duane Reade. Each new day dawned with the possibility that this might be the day everything changed, the day an eddy would pull him in a direction so compelling that everything — work, life, love — would miraculously resolve.

Jonathan waited, entirely poised for such an eddy. He scanned the streets, hoping moment by moment for a sign.

None came. No job, no love, and, back at home, no demand for rent.

"You gotta give it more than a couple of weeks," Max told him. "You don't just put in your order. 'A bucket of love, please, with a side of meaningful employment'? What's your rush, anyway? You're young. The journey is the destination. Why not try some meaningless sex?"

Jonathan didn't feel like meaningless sex. His life was meaningless enough already.

"Hey, Max, what do you think about this whole rent thing?"

Max shook his head. "You can't pay if you don't know who to pay. I'd sit tight on that one, pal, and pray it sticks."

Financially it was a windfall, but Jonathan couldn't relax. Any minute his landlord might turn up with a .45 handgun and tell him he had two seconds to live. He began sleeping badly, dreaming of Frank standing over him, shaking his shoulder and shouting, "Dogs?! You got *animals* living in my place?"

A ringing phone woke him. He dragged himself out of a deep sleep to answer it. *Frank?*

"Jonathan?" It was Julie. "I need to pick up the rest of my things. I hope you don't mind."

"I do mind."

"I can come when you're not home if that's better."

He wanted to shout, *Get new stuff!* and slam down the phone. He wanted to shout, *I've burned everything you owned anyway.* And slam down the phone. He wanted just to slam down the phone without saying a word, or maybe buy a 120-decibel whistle he could blow down the receiver and shatter her eardrums if she tried to call back. He was tempted to call her up at all hours of the day and night, slamming down the phone without saying a word, just to annoy and unnerve her. Or have her kidnapped and dumped in a tank full of hungry starfish, Bond style.

But he didn't. Because he figured if he could manage twenty minutes of just-about politeness, he might never have to see her again. "Yeah, come over. I can't wait to see you." He hoped his sarcasm was broad enough to sting. Julie had a way of not noticing sarcasm.

When she arrived at his apartment later that afternoon he was unprepared for the effect her presence had on him. She looked radiant, and her general air of niceness — as if to an old relative or work colleague — enraged him.

"It was all pretty funny in the end," she said. "The wedding pulled in six hundred thousand live viewers and we've had more than twelve million online hits since. They've made me head of sales with a big raise and we're developing a reality-TV series — *Wacky Weddings*. There's a lot of interest out there."

Jonathan was finding it more difficult than

he expected to follow his plan, which began by ignoring everything she said. "So it all turned out great in the end. That is *so* good to hear."

"You can talk again," she said.

"I think my illness might have been an allergy," he said. "To you."

He asked about the Jonathan file, curious (now that it no longer mattered) as to what it held. She told him she'd erased it.

"Of course," he said bitterly. "You have a Mark file now."

Julie looked at him pityingly and crouched down beside Dante. "Your girlfriend misses you," she whispered in his ear. And then, to Jonathan, "They were very close."

Jonathan goggled at her. "How tragic. Maybe I should arrange play dates with Mark's dog?"

"You couldn't, even if you wanted to. His ex won't let him see her anymore." She patted Dante's head. "Not even on weekends. It's not fair on poor Mark. Or Wilma."

So, poor Mark, the girlfriend stealer, was now the world's . . . *Wilma?*

Dante swung away from Julie and fixed Jonathan with the sort of gaze that Jeeves might have used to alert Bertie Wooster to an urgent turn of events.

The world juddered to a halt. Jonathan

froze, midthought.

In the stillness, his heart flapped like a tarpaulin in a gale. Could there be two dogs in the neighborhood — in the world — named Wilma?

His gaze slid from Dante to Julie and back again. Time crept forward, agonizingly. Dante continued to stare directly into his master's eyes.

Jonathan turned to Julie, slow as glass melting. "M a r k's d o g i s c a l l e d W i l m a ?" It took him the better part of a century to speak the words.

"She's not exactly his dog now that the horrible ex has sole custody. People can be so cruel. He's thinking of taking her to court."

Think think think! Jonathan's brain stuttered to life. "Is his ex-girlfriend by any chance a vet?"

Julie faced him, aghast. "You're stalking them? That is so insane."

Jonathan's heart leaped out of his body and ran fourteen laps around the apartment. His eyes flew out of their sockets on springs. His hair stood up on end. His ears sprang off his head on bungees and bounced back on again.

Julie backed away. "I'll get my things."

Jonathan turned to Dante, who had not

averted his gaze. Now he cocked his head ever so slightly. Oh my God, Jonathan thought. The whole romance between Julie and Mark — it was all planned so that . . .

Dante, Dante, Dante, he whispered. You wonderful wonderful creature.

Julie called from the bedroom, half under the bed. "Do you know where my sheepskin slippers are?"

"Try the incinerator," he said.

She emerged with a bag full of stuff. "Well, I'll be going now. Poor Mark is on his own. The breakup has been very hard on him."

Not nearly as hard as it could be, Jonathan thought. Not remotely as hard as it would be if I arranged to hire an entire gang of pirate thugs who'd gouge out Poor Mark's eyes, beat him with chains, bugger him senseless, break all his bones, and then shave his belly with a rusty razor. Earl-eye in the morning.

They stood in silence for a moment as she glanced around the apartment one last time. "I'm sorry about our wedding, Jonathan," she said at last.

"I'm not," he said. "I never wanted a funeral anyway."

Her features shifted instantly to triumph. "There, look, you've said it again. Funeral!"

312

"I know," he said, and shut the door in her face. "It's what I meant all along."

34

He had to see her. He called but Iris announced that Dr. Clare was not available; could she take a message? Jonathan said no, waited five minutes, called back with his best creaky-old-Englishman voice and asked for Dr. Clare's cell number.

"It's her old paterfamilias, telephoning to wish her a jolly happy birthday," he rasped.

There was a silence on the end of the line. "Her birthday was months ago," said Iris.

"Of course it was," croaked Jonathan, the elderly Englishman. "Exactly why I need to speak to her now. I feel dreadful having missed it."

Another pause. "I'm sorry, but our policy doesn't allow us to reveal the personal details of staff. I'll tell her you called and have her call you back."

"What about her home address? I've baked a —"

Iris hung up.

He called back in his normal voice to make an appointment.

"Hello, Jonathan," Iris said. "Is it Dante? Life-threatening as usual?"

"Yes," he said, without elaborating.

Iris sounded unmoved. "How's five-thirty tonight? It's our only appointment."

He took it.

The day contained five hundred hours. Jonathan arrived at the vet's early, having showered twice, drunk six cups of coffee, and taken the dogs for four long walks. At 5:29 he demanded to know why they were running late. At 5:45 he was told it would be another twenty minutes. At 6:00, a young Australian named Dr. Mick Barnes stuck his head out and asked Jonathan to bring the dogs through.

Jonathan stared ahead stonily. "I'm waiting for Dr. Clare."

"Never mind, mate." Mick Barnes grinned, entirely undaunted. "Dr. Clare's off this week. Not back till Monday. But I've loads of experience with dogs . . . so why don't you just come on in?"

"You don't understand." He felt desperate now. "I need to see Dr. Clare. She's the only vet we've ever seen. Dante is highly phobic of vets. He becomes extremely agitated."

The Australian vet, Iris the receptionist,

315

and Jonathan all stared at Dante, who lay at Jonathan's feet. In the silence that followed, the sheepdog rolled over onto one side and began to snore softly. Sissy sighed, half closed her eyes, and wafted her tail gently from side to side.

"Come on, dogs," Jonathan said, making for the exit. "It's nothing personal, but there are huge issues at stake here."

They left.

He had to see her. But what would he say? Guess what? I dream about you with disturbing regularity, our dogs are actually friends, the woman who stole your boyfriend is my ex-girlfriend, which makes you single, so will you please please please go out with me?

It sounded creepy. Beyond creepy. Stalkerish and creepy. Desperate, stalkerish, and creepy. Desperate, stalkerish, creepy, and grandiose.

The same applied to waiting for her outside her place of work for when she arrived on Monday morning. Or setting up an ambush at lunchtime. All creepy.

And what if she wasn't single at all? What if she'd ditched poor Mark for another man and he'd gone for Julie on the rebound?

"Oh, please be single," he said out loud at the deli. "Please fall in love with me."

The young man making his coffee turned around, expressionless. "Dollar for extras."

What if she didn't like him? What if she refused to go out for a drink with him? What if, after all Dante's subtle machinations (he got it now, he got it!), she was the wrong woman? What if he didn't have the courage to tell her how he felt? What if he blurted it out all at once and she recoiled in horror?

This was one of the reasons he'd wanted to marry Julie, to get this horrible phase of life over with. Maybe (looking back) some people felt nostalgia for the good old days of trying to figure out if someone might actually be in love with you. Maybe if you were Johnny Depp or Frank Sinatra or Mick Jagger you didn't get paralytically nervous every time you considered asking a girl to sleep with you. Maybe some people considered the crippling anxiety part of the fun.

He tried texting Julie to say Dante was missing Wilma, could he have Wilma's phone number? But when he checked to see why she failed to respond, the text didn't record as delivered. She'd blocked him, the evil harpy.

He called to make an appointment with the vet.

"Well, I think you really hurt Dr. Barnes's feelings and we'll have to charge you for the skipped appointment. But I know you like to see Dr. Clare," Iris squeaked. "Can Dante wait till Monday?"

Did he have a choice?

In the interim he lay in bed thinking thoughts that kept him awake. He barely slept on Saturday or Sunday night and arrived at the vet's early on Monday looking ragged and tense.

"You should go out and get lunch," Iris suggested. "It's her first day back and she's very busy. Otherwise you'll just have to sit and read old magazines."

"That's fine," Jonathan said, running his hand through his hair and realizing he hadn't brushed it in recent memory. His clothes felt as if he'd slept in them, and he thought he might have developed a twitch. He wished someone had done scientific experiments to determine whether attraction could be completely one-sided. What if she felt nothing in his presence? Had anyone done definitive work on the subject? Was there time to google it?

She came out to tell him she was running late, but when he tried to smile his face contorted into something halfway between a grimace and a scowl. Did she look tanned and happy, as if she'd been to Greece with some new boyfriend? Not really, he thought, peering at her. She had faint purplish shadows under her eyes.

His hands shook so he sat on them. It was cool in the waiting room but he found he was sweating. He loved her just as much with purplish shadows under her eyes. Possibly more.

"Jonathan. You can come in now." Her smile seemed paler than usual.

He followed her in.

She looked at him and he noticed that the rims of her eyes were pinkish. "Is Dante still not eating?"

"No, no. No no. He's eating."

"Coughing?"

He shook his head.

"Limping?"

"No, nothing. He's fine, actually."

A silence fell. It seemed to last a long time. He struggled to speak. She waited.

"Dr. Clare, did you have a nice vacation?"

"Not particularly." Her voice had an edge to it. "I went to London. To see my parents."

"Parents," he said, nodding, thoughtful, as if unfamiliar with the concept. "Are they nice?"

"Nice?" She screwed up her face and shook her head slightly in confusion. "Jonathan, please. Why are you here?"

He inhaled deeply. "Dr. Vet," he said. "I've

discovered something."

"Excuse me?"

"I've discovered that your ex-boyfriend is Mark."

"My what?" She seemed genuinely confounded.

"I discovered that my ex-girlfriend left me for your ex-boyfriend. Mark. My ex-girlfriend is your ex-boyfriend's new girlfriend."

"Sorry?" Bewilderment followed by shock.

"No, *I'm* sorry. Very very very sorry. I didn't mean to. I didn't, in fact."

"Are we talking about Julie?"

"Julie. Yes."

"You're Julie's boyfriend?"

"Ex-boyfriend."

"How on earth did you stand her? She's appalling."

"You've met her?"

"Mr. Arsehole introduced us. Like we'd start a bloody book club together."

"You don't like him anymore?"

Her face emptied of what little color remained. "*Like* him? What do you think?"

"It's just that I've only heard about him from Julie, who made him sound like a cross between Nelson Mandela and Mahatma Gandhi. I thought you might want him back."

"You thought wrong."

"The thing is" — Jonathan searched her face for encouragement — "Julie said the dogs missed Wilma. I figured there couldn't be two dogs named Wilma in New York City. Or at the very least, it was exceedingly unlikely."

"So it was your dogs that caused the breakup."

"Not exactly." He felt a little desperate. "I don't think you can say they caused it. And anyway, by that logic, Wilma's not exactly blameless either. They're dogs. They had no idea they were messing up everyone's relationships by wanting to hang out together."

From the floor, Dante lifted his head, but Jonathan refused to meet his eyes.

"You were about to marry her."

"I didn't want to hurt her feelings."

She stared at him, dumbfounded. "That's why you were getting married?"

"I needed to change my life." The pitch was not going well. "Look, it's incredibly complicated, but . . ."

"If it was change you were after, why not jump in front of a train? It'd be just as effective. And quicker."

"I wasn't thinking straight. I often don't. It's not my best thing."

Dr. Clare covered her face with her hands

and then dropped them slowly. "If there are no actual medical problems, you'd better go. There are patients waiting."

"I've quit my job," he said.

"What?"

Jonathan sighed. "I worked for a third-wave marketing company called Comrade. It was hell."

"Why are you telling me all this? I haven't a clue what a third-wave marketing company is."

"No one does," he said. "It's a horrible job, but it paid the bills. I'm not sure what I'll do now. I, I just thought you should know. I guess I hoped, maybe . . . I hoped maybe telling you what a disaster my life is might make you feel a little bit better about yours. Your breakup, I mean." Oh Lord. "Dr. Clare?"

"Yes?"

"I wish I could make you feel better. Making you feel better would make me feel better."

She swiped a hand across her eyes. "I think you should go now." Was she crying?

"I hate the fact that I've been associated with your unhappiness. I want your life to be filled with joy."

She laughed, an incredulous laugh. "Filled with joy?"

"Joy and love and happiness. Exultation. I apologize on behalf of my dogs for spoiling that. And on behalf of my ex-girlfriend." He looked up and met her gaze. "You should be exultant. An amazing woman like you. You should be happy all the time." What could he say next? Could he prostrate himself at her feet? Offer references? Send the list of charitable donations from his tax return?

The silence deepened. He was done. There was nothing left to say.

"Please, Jonathan." Her tone was softer. "Please. Just go."

He'd been wrong. His dreams had misled him. She hadn't warmed to him. He was the enemy. He was that crazy guy with hypochondriac dogs or possibly a deep psychological problem projected onto two perfectly innocent animals. He was the moron who nearly married the harpy who broke up her perfectly happy relationship with the lawyer.

He stood up, gathered the leashes, and left with his dogs, hoping until the very last second that she'd call him back.

She didn't.

35

Jonathan took the dogs down to the East River and they sat for a long time, watching the boats go by in the soft light of a summer afternoon. Pulling out his phone, he stared at it and thought about texting Max. But Max would be at work, and later he'd be out having a fantastic time with his new gorgeous girlfriend. Probably the girl who'd taken Jonathan's job. The beautiful, employed one.

He slipped the phone back into his pocket and sat, thinking about Dr. Clare.

And sat, thinking about Julie.

And sat, thinking about the dwindling money in his bank account.

And sat, thinking about the shady characters who owned his apartment, wondering if they'd all been wiped out by a mob hit, or were just waiting for him to be so far in arrears that they felt justified in killing him.

Hour after hour he sat, thinking about his

life, until the light began to dim and shift and the setting sun cast shadows across the river.

All at once a wave of anxiety possessed him. His lungs twisted shut as he gasped for breath, his heart hurtled nowhere in frantic rhythm. Despite the cool evening, sweat ran down his face and neck. Sissy looked up at him and whimpered.

I'm having a heart attack, he thought, or something worse. I can't breathe, I'm going to suffocate in my own lungs.

He couldn't even scream for help. Pitching forward, he pressed his head to the ground, his breath coming in desperate heaves.

After five terrible minutes, his symptoms began to recede. His lungs unclenched, air flooded his chest. He wanted to sob with relief and misery. This was all just great. First a hysterical stroke, now a near-death panic attack. Whatever next?

He called Greeley.

"Hello," Greeley said. "How's it going?"

"Fabulous," said Jonathan. There was a long silence. "It's going shit, actually, Greeley. I don't know what to do."

"What do you *want* to do?"

"What kind of question is that? If I knew what I wanted to do, I wouldn't not know, would I?" Greeley the wise could be a real pain sometimes.

"How about coming up to the forest this weekend?"

Jonathan sighed. "I'll just ask." He looked at his dogs, who gazed back, expectant. "You don't want to go upstate, do you? Veer off the path? Stumble across a life-changing eddy? You don't want to have long walks in the woods, meet a moose, learn the meaning of life from Uncle Greeley with his Wisdom of the Ages? Or we could just stay here in a state of suicidal despair and wait for the Mafia to gun me down in cold blood."

Sissy wagged her tail faintly.

Jonathan turned back to the phone.

"Okay," he said. "We'd love to."

"Good. I'll pick you up at seven on Saturday morning. I have to be back Monday night, but time expands when you're up there."

"Okay."

"And pack light. My car's pretty small."

"Change of leash and a toothbrush," Jonathan said.

He could hear Greeley nod.

"We'll be ready," Jonathan said, and hung up. "Well," he said to the dogs. "We're going on a bear hunt. We're not scared."

Which was not strictly true.

Greeley arrived a few minutes before seven on Saturday morning and double-parked while Jonathan and the dogs came down.

"I hope the beds don't take up too much room," Jonathan said, placing them on the backseat, where they fit perfectly. Despite not being particularly conversant with cars, the dogs hopped up onto the seat, settled into their beds, and looked expectantly at Greeley.

"They're set," Jonathan said. "Let's go."

Jonathan's backpack contained dog food, a sweater, an extra T-shirt, clean socks and underwear, a toothbrush, iPad, phone charger, book. He dangled it on one finger and Greeley nodded approval. Three minutes later they were driving west, stopping two hours later for coffee and to stretch all twelve passenger legs.

The landscape grew wilder as they drove, the distance between signs of human habitation gradually increasing until there were mostly trees, punctuated by occasional sudden vistas opening briefly across a valley to mountains beyond. Jonathan thought about Dr. Clare and how he'd blown his chance, spinning in spirals of self-loathing until misery made him drowsy. Greeley didn't

327

seem to require conversation, so Jonathan allowed himself to doze off to the sound of the engine and the stream of music, all of which he liked but very little of which he recognized.

At the signpost for Finger Lakes National Forest, they pulled off the main road onto a narrow byway and from there onto a badly paved track that forked onto a dirt road, ending at last at a sand parking lot. Just beyond, a cluster of well-kept cabins perched along the edge of a lake. A square building sat at the end like a punctuation mark.

Greeley parked the car. They were greeted by a man in his thirties dressed in a plain green shirt and chinos, who leaned in the open window.

"Thought you'd be up yesterday," he said.

"Me too," Greeley said. "This is my friend Jonathan."

The man stuck his arm through the window and across Greeley. "Randall," he said, and Jonathan shook his hand. "Lunch is still on if you hurry."

Dante and Sissy shot out of the car and raced down to the water. Sissy waded in and began to swim, turning a smooth arc back toward shore when Jonathan called her name.

They dumped their stuff in Greeley's cabin and went for lunch, which was vegetarian or vegan: bean chili or pumpkin risotto with a green salad and walnut bread.

"Is this a cult?" Jonathan whispered to Greeley. "I only ask because, well, everything. The dirt road, the friendly people . . ."

Greeley chewed a mouthful of bread. "Scientists. They present culty."

Various stragglers chatted over coffee and tea; most came over and said a few words to Greeley. Everyone in the place seemed calm and busy; Jonathan wondered whether you had to have your blood pressure monitored in order to be considered for membership or whether something about the diet and the company caused your average twisted individuals with grudges on perpetual rerun to turn Zen. It was thrilling, like discovering the source of the Nile, but he couldn't imagine himself as one of these serene personages and guessed there must be a compost heap out back full of muttering rejects.

"They'd never let me live here," he said. "I'm the wrong psychological demographic."

Greeley smiled. "You're fine."

Jonathan wondered briefly whether he'd been invited here as part of a seduction.

Greeley was channeling field-station chic today in jeans, boots, and a baseball cap, his sole concession to individual style a pale blue cashmere sweater. Jonathan paused to check the air for vibes, felt none, and let the muscles of his jaw release. It felt unfamiliar but not unpleasant.

Greeley introduced him to every member of the team: Lucy, late twenties, serious expression, pale eyes; Elaine, fifties, slim, competent; Ben, tall, broad, and friendly; Macca, ginger hair, round glasses, slow smile; Kahlo, young face, short dress, muscular calves. Kahlo asked if he was planning to stay.

Was he planning to stay? Of course not. Maybe. Not much was stopping him except the fact that there was no reason on earth for him to be here and nothing for him to do. He could always give up his apartment, he thought, and the rush of relief he felt surprised him.

Greeley smiled his Mona Lisa smile. "Stop thinking so much."

They went to load a trailer with cut logs, working until Jonathan's arms and back ached. But the results were satisfying and he had to resist the urge to take a picture on his phone.

Greeley spent the remaining hour before

dinner entering data from his project into his laptop while Jonathan lounged on a somewhat dusty couch. The cabin had two small bedrooms, a living room, galley kitchen, and a tiny study. Basic but perfect.

"We're testing DNA from adjoining plant species to trace the evolution of ecosystems," Greeley told Jonathan, who tried to look interested.

At dusk they walked a long path through the woods as the light dropped. Kahlo joined them, striding ahead and conversing nonstop with the dogs.

"Is her real name Kahlo?" Jonathan whispered. "Like Frida? She looks more like a Beth."

Greeley shrugged. "Refugee from a bad family. I doubt she was born Kahlo."

Jonathan wondered if he'd be considered a refugee if he stayed here. Refugee from career humiliation, dangerous real estate, and the failure of what, for seventy-two hours, had felt like the real thing.

Late that night he lay in bed, trying to imagine living here for six months or a year, assisting one research team or another, or maybe working in the kitchen. He liked the feel of the place, the simplicity of life. He squinted, trying to imagine himself in L.L.Bean shirts, making hearty vegan stews and chopping wood, hanging out in a forest community of the spiritually pure with a lumberjack transvestite for a best friend (Greeley the Great, Greeley at one with Gaia).

He liked loam, of course he did. But he also loved people and crowds and noise. He loved New York in the rain, in a soft covering of snow, ankle deep in slush. He didn't mind the unbearable heat of summer because there was always somewhere cool to go, and anyway, you were supposed to complain all the time if you lived in New York. He liked the regular neighborhood crazies and the take-out restaurants where he and the waiters who barely spoke English greeted each other by name. He loved the blue skies and the pink sunsets glimpsed in slivered reflections on buildings. He liked knowing exactly how long it took to walk ten blocks and the outdoor markets and the Korean grocers and the fact that, in the age of Netflix, everyone still went to the movies. He even liked the acrid smell of New York streets on garbage day.

The woods were lovely, dark and deep, but was he finished with New York?

Greeley kept him busy most of Sunday with a mountain hike and a comprehensive tour of his DNA test sites, and when at last it was cocktail hour and they retired to the cabin for a beer, a faint buzz reminded him that his phone had been on silent since they arrived. It was nice not thinking about technology, even for a day or two. He picked it up and checked the display.

A new message from an unfamiliar number read: What is your best thing?

His heart pounded as he texted back: Dr. Clare?

You said thinking straight wasn't your best thing. What is yr best thing?

He trembled violently and tapped out, Making bad decisions, then getting out of them in the clumsiest possible way.

Wow, she wrote. That's quite impressive for a best thing. And yr worst thing?

Not till I've known you for a century at least, he texted. There was a long pause.

I'm sorry I was horrid the other day, she wrote. There was another pause. His phone indicated that she was still typing. It wasn't what I was expecting.

He took a deep breath. You couldn't be horrid if you tried.

An even longer pause.

And then, Thank you. And, Goodnight Jonathan.

Goodnight Dr. Vet.

A minute or two later, another text came

through. Zoe, it read.

Zoe, he thought. Zoe Clare. Zoe Zoe Zoe. Clare Clare Clare.

He read and reread the texts. After a few seconds, a nose nudged at him and he wrapped his hand around it gently.

"Good dogs," he said to his dogs. "You're such good dogs."

And they wagged their tails calmly because they knew this to be true.

36

On Monday morning Jonathan took the dogs for a long walk in the woods and down to the lake, where they all three swam and shivered and shook themselves dry, then had a huge breakfast of fresh-baked bread, local fruit, organic yogurt, and fair-trade coffee. Jonathan drew all the characters he'd met over the past twenty-four hours in his notebook, along with annotations and snatches of dialogue, and finally, having played it cool for as long as he was physically able, phoned her. It was not yet 7 a.m.

"My worst thing is getting into bad situations, like agreeing to marry someone I don't really get along with."

"You're not selling yourself," she said, yawning.

"Did I wake you?"

"No. Yes. But I have to get up anyway." He heard Wilma bark once in the background. "Coming, tyrant," she said to

Wilma, and to him: "I've got to go."

"Really?"

"Really."

"Okay, bye."

"Bye."

He didn't hang up. "Are you still there?" he asked, after a minute.

"No," she said, and laughed, and was gone.

He thought about her every minute of the day. He texted her at last at 4 p.m., his self-control having collapsed hours earlier.

HIM: I'm sorry my girlfriend broke up your relationship.

HER: I'm not.

HIM: Were you ever in love with Mark?

HER: Were you ever in love with Julie?

He stopped texting and called her. "To be honest," he said when she answered, "I was kind of relieved when it went wrong."

"I'm with a patient," she said.

"Oh," he said.

"But since you ask, I was outraged," she said. "When it went wrong."

"That's not quite the same as being devastated. Is it?"

"No."

Jonathan closed his eyes and thought of her expressive mouth and long nose and thatch of choppy dark hair. Then he took a deep breath.

"I wouldn't have left you for Julie," he said.

"Really?" she said, and then, "I have to go."

The practice closed at 7:00. At 7:02 he texted her again. Do you walk Wilma now that Mark doesn't?

She replied a minute later: Yes.

Would you like to meet for a dog walk sometime?

There was a pause before her answer came through. When were you thinking?

I'm in upstate New York, he wrote. Back late tonight.

After what seemed like eons, she answered. Sometime this week?

OK, he wrote. And then, Tomorrow?

Call me, she wrote.

He wanted to call her every minute of every day for the rest of his life.

"You seem more resolved," Greeley said, squinting slightly at him.

"I might have sorted out one thing," Jonathan said.

Greeley nodded.

"It's a start," Jonathan said. "Thank you."

"For what?"

"For being my spirit guide. You turned out to be right about things. Well, some

337

things anyway."

"Good," said Greeley.

As they packed up the cabin, Jonathan felt sad. He loved it here in the silent swishing woods, with owls and fish and loam made from composted pine needles and leaves and centuries of organic detritus. Before they left it rained, and he could smell it coming before it began, a cold sharp smell he'd never noticed in New York City, followed by a series of tiny rustles as each separate drop bounced through twigs and leaves. He imagined himself snuggled up under Hudson Bay blankets with Dr. Clare, the whole length of him pressed up against the whole long length of her.

He spent the drive back half dreaming, half waking, wishing her with him, excited and anxious all at once. What if what if what if, he thought, and then he stopped wondering and just thought about her in a thousand different ways, but mainly how it would feel to have permission to run his hands through her hair, to hold her face while he kissed her, to have a tall stern kind Dr. Vet person of his very own.

He didn't talk about her with Greeley because he couldn't bear to hear any warning Greeley might have, any wisdom that contraindicated what he hoped might be true, but for which he had no evidence and no experience to guide him.

They arrived home after midnight and he resisted the urge to call her, but only just.

37

It was a late summer evening like most late summer evenings in New York — full of heat and light and noise and bars and conversations with beginnings and endings and taxis and sidewalks and people and dogs walking out together, including people and dogs who had never walked together before.

"Why did you leave London?" Jonathan asked.

She thought for a moment. "I lived my entire life in West London; everyone I ever met lived there. It was like coming from a small village — Slackbottom upon Avon, it was that provincial. So where would you go? New York seemed more exciting than Leeds."

"Will you stay?"

"It's early days," she said. "But there's the buzz and the people and the food, obviously. And everyone forgot to tell me how beautiful New York is. It's crowded and noisy and expensive and the health care's appalling and all the homeless people . . ." She looked at him. "But also friendly and neighborhoody and glorious to look at. And thrilling. You feel as if anything could happen in New York."

Jonathan considered this for a minute. "It helps that you're English. Everyone in New York would rather be English."

She smiled. "Is that why people give me free drinks in bars? Though not so much with Mark."

"No one ever gave me free drinks with Julie."

Zoe raised a meaningful eyebrow. "Speaking of which, I was thinking I might do something different, just to get horrid Mark and simpering Julie out of my head." She glanced at Jonathan. "I shouldn't say 'simpering.' Though let's face it, she is."

"Simpering's fine."

"I thought I might climb a mountain."

"Mountains are good," he said. "Any one in particular?"

She shook her head. "A tall one maybe."

"What's your position on loam?"

"Loam?" Zoe frowned. "I'm not sure I know what it is. Should I have a position?"

"Never mind." They matched strides for a bit. "Do you know what today is?"

"No."

"It's the two-week anniversary of my non-wedding."

"You were getting married on a Tuesday?"

Jonathan shrugged. "That's when the film crew was free."

"The film crew?" She started to laugh, then put a hand over her mouth. "I'm sorry," she said. "It's obviously not funny."

He looked pained. "Not yet."

"How do you feel about it now?"

"About my wedding? Stupid."

"You had a lucky escape."

"I'm pretty sure I have post-traumatic stress, like people who've been through terrorist kidnappings." He stopped. "Zoe?"

"Yes?"

"Would it be okay to kiss you?"

She turned to face him and tilted her head, thinking it over.

"Yes," she said after a moment, adopting a serious expression. "Go on, then."

And so he kissed her, holding her face in his hands as he'd imagined, and wishing they might never stop.

When at last he stepped back, she smiled. "Well."

"Well, well," he said happily, looking at her as if he'd never really seen her before. She wore a white T-shirt and bright green jeans with green sneakers. She looked to him like a rare and wonderful type of woodland creature who might have enjoyed burrowing in loam. There were two spots of pink in her cheeks and when he met her eyes she didn't turn away.

He slipped his arm through hers and they walked a couple of blocks in silence. At the corner of Fifth Avenue, Dante stood on the curb, staring at the little red hand on the crossing signal. When it turned into a striding man, he stepped into the road. Zoe watched him.

"That is one intelligent dog. Even for a collie. We had a dog like him where I did my veterinary placement. Half-poodle, half-shepherd. His eyes looked completely human." Dante glanced back over his shoulder at her. "Like that." She paused. "Not that being human is such a great indicator of intelligence."

"He's way smarter than I am."

"Clearly."

"Your dog has webbed feet," he said. "I looked it up."

"Did you?" She half smiled, and this time it was she who kissed him.

"I've learned a lot about dogs in the past eight months," Jonathan said. "Hardly anything about humans. Look, why not go mountain climbing or whatever you want and leave Wilma with me? The dogs like each other, it would be fine. Then you don't have to worry about dog hotels."

"You'd do that?"

"Of course." He paused. "Dr. Vet?"

"Yes?"

Jonathan closed his eyes and took a deep breath. "I'd do anything for you. I thought about you all weekend. I thought about you before I went away. I've been dreaming about you for longer than I even knew I liked you."

"Your taste in women is definitely improving."

He stopped walking. "But what if my taste is improving . . . and due to, say, cross-cultural misunderstanding, the object of my taste just thinks it's a joke or a casual thing or something?" He turned slightly away from her and pretended to be interested in a mugging taking place across the street.

She followed his eyes.

"Jesus!" she said, diving across the road to the opposite side where two men were beating up a third. Jonathan followed shouting, *"Police!"* and all three dogs barked excitedly. The illusion of a mob comprising threatening dogs and angry officers of the law caused the perpetrators to drop their fists and flee.

The victim was young, drunk, and well dressed, his glasses smashed, his nose bleeding. Zoe and Jonathan each took one arm and pulled him to his feet, but he shook them off, insisting he could walk. A bus arrived; he staggered on board and was gone.

"Holy shit," Jonathan said, panting. "He didn't seem very grateful."

"He was drunk," Zoe said. "Embarrassed, probably. And in shock, by the look of it."

Jonathan patted Sissy, who trembled with excitement. Dante had regained his composure. "All in a night's work for the intrepid K9 patrol."

Zoe laughed. "Let's go find a place to sit outdoors, have a drink, and reminisce about our life in crime."

"Prevention."

"Crime *prevention.*"

"Yes," said Jonathan. "Or we could just sit around and say horrible things about our exes."

"Even better," she said.

"But . . . Dr. Vet? My question from before?"

She took his hand and kissed him again.

"Never mind," he said.

38

They shared a bottle of wine and then walked around the city, giddy with the feeling that they might be discovering something altogether earth-shattering in each other's company. They walked and walked and eventually ended up back at his building with three tired dogs, so they went upstairs and called for Chinese take-out because they both suddenly felt hungry, and when that arrived they ate it and watched a bad movie and laughed at all the same things and then they started kissing once more, and once more didn't want to stop. They managed at last to take the dogs around the block, and although Jonathan offered to walk Zoe home, he didn't insist, and having agreed that it was a very bad idea indeed, they kissed and kissed again, and against both their better judgments she stayed and so did Wilma.

The dogs were uncharacteristically quiet

all night and didn't scratch at the door or whine to go out, and in fact made themselves almost entirely and appropriately scarce.

When Jonathan crept out of bed to make coffee the next morning, he took all three dogs out and they didn't tangle their leashes or all squat at once or chase things in opposite directions, so it was no problem at all.

"Your apartment is nice," Zoe said about half an hour later, with a cup of coffee in one hand and *The New York Times* in the other and the lemony sun sparkling around the room.

"It is," Jonathan said glumly. "But I haven't paid any rent in seven weeks now."

She looked at him quizzically.

"No one's collecting it anymore. Everyone I know says just shut up, it's the deal of a lifetime and maybe it'll be free forever, but I think the guy who owns it is in jail. He could get out any minute and ice me."

"Ice you?" She giggled.

"Kill. Whack."

"I know what it means." She considered him critically, ticking off his assets on her fingers. "Job, no. Wife, no. Apartment, not really. Independently wealthy?"

He shook his head.

"Shame. Still. Young, ambitious, yes, and not desperately unattractive. You might still pull it out of the fire."

"You forgot beautiful Dr. Vet in my bed."

"That doesn't count as one of your assets."

"Does to me," he said, nuzzling her ear.

A little while later, gazing at the beautiful Dr. Vet in his bed, Jonathan wondered how it was possible that what he mostly felt was calm, as if he'd been waiting for her to appear all along so that things could return to a kind of normal they'd never actually been.

She stretched luxuriously, like a tabby. If she'd had a tail, he thought, she would swish it. "What shall we do now?"

"We could," Jonathan barely dared say what seemed absurdly obvious to him. "We could just stay like this."

"In bed?"

"Not necessarily in bed."

She waited.

"What I meant was." He paused. "We could stay happy."

"Hmm," she said.

"Hmm?"

"It's a good idea. Only, I have to go to work." She folded her arms up behind her head. "I work long hours."

"I don't mind you working any hours you want."

"And what about you?"

Jonathan's face fell. "I'll get another job."

"Any ideas?"

"Not really." Depression seeped through him like poison.

"Haven't you always wanted to be something?"

"Comics," he said. "I like comics. I've drawn Dante's *Inferno,* starring Dante the dog as Virgil."

"Really?"

"But you can't make a living drawing comics."

"You can't?"

"No."

She shrugged and swept the hair out of her eyes. "Okay. What else?"

"I don't know." Jonathan looked downcast. "You probably want a boyfriend who's rich and powerful and has a real job." He glanced at her sideways. "Like a lawyer."

"When did you get to be my boyfriend?"

"I'm speaking hypothetically."

She humphed. "Well then, hypothetically? No."

"But you probably want one who at least does something." He sighed. "To be honest, I don't know what to do next."

She sipped her coffee, shifted her long bare legs, and lay back on his pillows. His heart flipped over in his chest.

"Not advertising," she said.

He nodded. "Not advertising."

"Show me Dante's *Inferno*."

"Really?"

"Yes."

He crawled under the bed and dragged out a large box, from which he handed her a pile of notebooks with INFERNO written on the front.

She opened the first and began to read. "You don't mind?"

He shook his head.

And so she flipped slowly, page after page, mostly serious, but occasionally snorting with laughter.

He leaned over to see what she was laughing at. "The stuff about the wedding and Julie and Mark doesn't come till near the end."

"I can't wait," she said. "But right now, I have to go to work."

39

"You are not without talents," Dr. Vet said as they watched the dogs play in the park the following day.

"Flatterer."

"Talent's useless on its own, though."

"I know. I need a life."

"You don't just get one," she said. "As far as I understand the rules, you make a choice here and a choice there and one day you find yourself on a path."

"You sound like my spirit guide. He says stuff like that."

She frowned. "You have a spirit guide?"

"It's an unofficial relationship."

They were silent for a moment.

"The whole situation with the apartment is giving me panic attacks."

"Start there, then."

He nodded.

A little later when she'd gone to work, he called Comrade and asked for Greeley.

"Is today your last day?"

"Yes."

"Greeley?"

"Yes?"

"Were you serious about me coming to the forest with you?"

"Yes."

"Would it have to be as anything in particular?"

"We need someone to run the kitchen. And I sometimes need help with data."

"Could I do that?"

Greeley paused. "I don't know. Could you?"

"I could learn. Just till I figure out what to do next."

"The pay is terrible."

"Stop sugarcoating it. Can I think about it and call you back?"

"Yes."

"Have a good last day."

"Thank you, Jonathan."

Jonathan clicked off. He glanced around his apartment and looked at Sissy, who gazed back at him, expectant. He met Dante's alert, fathomless eyes. "What would you do, Dante?"

What advice could Dante possibly give him? Just when he managed to fall in love with a beautiful delicious vet, he no longer had a reason to stay in New York City. He supposed he could find another apartment and another job. Doing what? Something less soul-destroying than advertising and more lucrative than comics. Or maybe he should leave New York, find another place to live that wasn't so expensive. But what about Dr. Vet? All his life he'd been hoping to fall in love, really in love, and now? It occurred to him that falling in love could ruin your life as easily as fix it. It could stop you making important choices, tie you to a place that wasn't right or a timeline that didn't suit. Being with Zoe felt nothing like being with Julie, but in some ways it was worse. Love trapped you into orbit around the loved one. He wanted to spend every spare minute of his life with Zoe. He wanted to sleep every night with her, feel the soft rise and fall of her breath and the steady beat of her heart. But what about the days? He could stay in his free apartment if his nerve and his luck held out. And a free apartment would give him thinking time, time to sort out the rest of his existence, get a job, or at least figure out what job he wanted.

A free apartment in New York and true love: what sort of idiot would give that up?

Dante stared up at him and Jonathan knew what Dante would do.

He called Greeley back.

"That was fast."

"I've decided," Jonathan said.

"Good," said Greeley.

40

Jonathan packed the last box into his rented van. Max opened a beer and tossed one to his friend. They clinked cans.

"To change," Max said, and Jonathan nodded, stashing his can in the back.

"To change."

"When I'm running Comrade like Willy Wonka's Chocolate Factory," Max said, "you wanna come back and work for me?"

"Nah."

"Okay, pal. Find your own road. But don't come crawling to me when you're circling the drain with a fistful of food stamps."

He texted Zoe: Ten minutes?

And she texted back, Great.

He turned to Max. "Can you hang on here for one minute with the van?"

Max nodded, and Jonathan ran up the stairs to his apartment one last time, surveyed the empty space, hesitated for a second, then dropped the keys on the kitchen counter and clicked the door shut behind him. He turned and ran back down the stairs.

"Thanks for all the help, Max. Don't be a stranger."

"I won't," Max said, with a rare absence of sarcasm. "When you back?"

His friend shrugged.

"Well, don't be too long in the woods. You'll get termites."

Jonathan opened the passenger-side door and both dogs jumped in. He walked around and climbed up into the driver's seat, turned the key, and swung the van out onto 5th Street, waving out the window to Max and nearly hitting a woman, who shouted and gave him the finger. Max shot him two thumbs up.

He picked up Zoe and Wilma. Zoe handed him her backpack with a sleeping bag strapped to the base, which he tossed into the van with his things. Aside from his mattress and books, there was just one box of kitchen stuff, one of clothes, shoes, and one marked MISCELLANEOUS. He'd taken his drawing board apart and slid it on top. The 1950s kitchen table folded flat, but he'd left the two chairs.

Wilma jumped in next to Dante, and they greeted each other affectionately. Sissy squeezed in between them and Zoe clambered in last. Jonathan leaned over and kissed her.

"What an adventure," she said. "I can't wait to see the place."

"I really hope you like it," he said, and they set off.

Arriving midafternoon, they were met by Greeley, boyish today except for a touch of pink lip gloss. He showed Jonathan to a cabin not far from his own. With its square main room, out of which a small kitchen, bathroom, and bedroom were carved, it was not entirely unlike Jonathan's New York apartment except that most of the walls were windows and the views from most of the windows were trees.

Jonathan set up the bed and his drawing board and unpacked his clothes onto shelves in the closet and stacked his books against the walls. Within an hour it felt like home, and after a long walk and a swim in the river and dinner, he and Zoe went to bed, as did the dogs, and they lay under striped wool blankets smelling the trees and the fresh air and the rough pine smell of the cabin just as he'd imagined they would, the length of her body pressed against his, just as he'd imagined it would. He experienced a vague melancholy, already wishing she didn't have to leave.

"When are you setting off?" he asked her.

She pulled his arm over and around her waist. "Not quite yet."

"What if you get lost halfway up the mountain?"

"I won't," she said. "I have a map."

"I'll take good care of Wilma."

"I know you will."

"But that doesn't mean we won't miss you."

"I'll be back," she said drowsily.

And as she dropped off to sleep, Jonathan looked around him, noticing that many things he was sure had, in the past, existed mostly in two dimensions seemed to have gained a bit of substance, a slight curve here, a shadow there. Zoe wasn't at all the sort of two-dimensional being he'd grown accustomed to accepting as an object of love, and the dogs were more fully formed than most of the people he knew, complete with facets he was certain he hadn't begun to discover, while all around them the world seemed more nuanced, less hopeless and less flat.

Dante put his head down on his front paws and half closed his eyes. Wilma sighed contentedly, using the curve of her friend's back as a pillow. Sissy chased grouse in her dreams.

As Jonathan lay in bed, still awake, he began sketching out a new story in his head. In it, James renewed his contract in Dubai for another ten years so that the dogs lived with Jonathan forever, and after six months in the woods he returned to New York with a book about being young and single and confused and searching for work and meaning and love in New York City and the book did better than anyone expected and while it didn't exactly make him fabulously rich it gave him enough money to go on writing and drawing and not working in advertising ever again. As for Zoe, she and he stayed in love, and lived happily ever after. Or was it Greeley he lived happily ever after with?

At that particular moment, it didn't really matter how it turned out. It was his story, he thought. He could write what he liked.

ABOUT THE AUTHOR

Meg Rosoff grew up in Boston and worked in advertising for fifteen years before writing her first novel, *How I Live Now,* which has sold more than one million copies in thirty-six territories. It won the Guardian Children's Fiction Prize, the Printz Award, was short-listed for the Orange Prize and made into a film. Her subsequent five novels have been awarded or short-listed for, among others, the Carnegie Medal and the National Book Award. She lives in London with her husband, daughter, and two dogs.

The employees of Thorndike Press hope you have enjoyed this Large Print book. All our Thorndike, Wheeler, and Kennebec Large Print titles are designed for easy reading, and all our books are made to last. Other Thorndike Press Large Print books are available at your library, through selected bookstores, or directly from us.

For information about titles, please call:
  (800) 223-1244

or visit our Web site at:
  http://gale.cengage.com/thorndike

To share your comments, please write:
  Publisher
  Thorndike Press
  10 Water St., Suite 310
  Waterville, ME 04901